FRANK MAY

Killer Killer

LOST
RIDGE
PRESS

Library of Congress Control Number: 2021906257

First edition

ISBN: 978-1-7369150-0-4

This book was professionally typeset on Reedsy.
Find out more at reedsy.com

For Sam, the most creative person I know. I think you'd love this story, or at the very least, tell me it's awesome.

Contents

Preface

What started out as a simple idea, to write a thriller with orcas as the main subject, quickly grew into so much more. When I began writing, I thought I was familiar with their history in the wild and captivity. That lasted for approximately one day as I started my research. There was an extraordinary amount of information to learn. My journey to gather it carried me from Florida, to Tenerife, to South Africa and back home to Chicago. I've spent many nights reading articles, scientific research, and digging through Freedom of Information Act requests in hopes of presenting you with the most realistic portrait of these animals and their plight that I can. I sincerely hope you have as much fun reading it as I did writing it for you.

As you read and are introduced to the various orcas, you can find additional background information on them in the "Marineworld Orca Animal Profiles" section, located at the back of the book.

Happy reading!

Acknowledgement

Writing a book is so much harder than anyone ever tells you. You think it's a great idea until you're half-way through. I couldn't have made it to the finish line without my soon-to-be wife Ashley. She sacrificed her weekends by spending them in coffee shops with me, put up with late nights of editing, and was my constant companion on "research trips" to gather data. Without her encouragement and words of support, this book would have never been completed. She is the best example of a partner, and I love her more every day for putting up with me. Thank you.

To my family and friends: My mom and dad, who insist I've been a writer since I was little. Their support and encouragement provided the extra push of motivation that I needed. Thank you dad, for sharing stories of how you used to write in high school and thank you mom for letting me know weekly that you couldn't wait to read my book. To my brother Anthony, I'm glad this is going to be the fifth book you've ever read. For old time's sake, I can write a book report on it for you if you'd like. And finally, to my nephew (and upcoming niece!), sister-in-law, all my cousins, aunts, uncles, grandparents, you mean the world to me. To my friends who have shown interest from the beginning and tolerated me talking about orcas for the past five years, I hope the final product is worth it. I love you all.

To my early readers: Renee and Jess, thank you so much for giving my story a shot. It's terrifying to have anyone read something you wrote for the first time. Your feedback was priceless and helped me improve so much. Sorry you have to read through it all again, but it will be even better this time!

To my cover designer: Laurance, thank you for going above and beyond with the design. People say "don't judge a book by it's cover." This time they're wrong. Judge away, that thing is amazing.

To my editor: Eliza, thank you for all the time you took with my little story. You didn't pull any punches with comments or areas that needed improvement. It led to a book that is better than I could have hoped.

NIGHTTIME VOYAGE

G ravity grasped at Paul as the boat thrust towards the stars. His mind was seized with terror as the frigid water rushed up to greet him. Amplified by the force of a rogue wave, the choppy waters caused his feet to betray him. The rum from earlier in the night didn't help matters much either. At impact, he tried in vain to grab the railing of the boat, but there was a misfire between the neurons in his brain and the muscles in his arm. This failure resulted in a quick trip into the black waters of the Pacific. His body hit the water with a deafening crash. It cut through the silence that hugged the waters off the Coronado Islands. The icy water cleared Paul's head of whatever booze remained in his system; it pushed the air from his lungs and shocked him into sobriety. His clothes clung to his skin and tried to drag him to the dark depths. He kicked like a madman towards the surface. Water flung from his hair as he shook his head from side to side. He gasped for breath like it would be impossible to fill his lungs again.

Now wasn't the time to panic. He'd learned to swim before he could walk. Everything would be fine. It was a clumsy accident. A quick swim around to the back ladder would fix it. Then all there would be left to do was curl up inside the cabin to dry out. It would be easy, he reasoned, more of an annoyance. Maybe a trickle of rum was left for a nightcap. He tried his best to ignore it, but a thought scratched its

1

way to the front of his brain. Was it still in the water with him? No, it had probably continued to its destination. But what if it hadn't? Blood throbbed in his arteries. An eerie stillness settled in the air again; any sound would wake the ocean itself up from its sleep.

There was no need for a mooring light. The full moon illuminated the night sky and mirrored itself in the inky water. Paul swam towards the back of the Marlin Heritage sailboat. As his hands cut the water, he peeked to each side, checking for his visitor. Each thud against the surface echoed in his ears. Something wasn't right. He steadily increased his speed and came around the stern of the boat. The metallic ladder was a bright beacon in the darkness. He couldn't wait to cozy up next to the tiny electric heater. Warm blankets waited for him. Delicious rum beckoned. Paul grabbed the sides of the ladder and pulled himself up.

KHOOSH! It was a gunshot in a snowy forest. He panicked and slipped. The wooden cabin doors dropped out of sight. His kneecap rattled against the last rung on the ladder with a sharp crack. He screamed out in pain as he floated on his back. Paul's pulse quickened. Was it below him? He didn't have to wait long for an answer. The animal surfaced behind him. It was an enormous black submarine; the ocean foamed and frothed across the top of its body. It watched as Paul struggled to tread water. The pain in his knee reached an unbearable peak. Each motion earned him a fresh wave of agony, like the swing of a hammer.

Paul turned to face the animal, his back towards the boat. It continued to float silently. It dwarfed the sailboat. Outside a tank in San Diego, he had never seen a creature of such impressive size. A lightbulb flashed in Paul's brain. In an instant, he knew what this beast was. He laughed out loud to himself.

"Holy shit, buddy, you scared the hell out of me!" he said through the pain as he gingerly backstroked towards the boat. Paul's uneasiness lessened, but it didn't fade away. What a story this would be. It was a whale from the island; he could make out the tracking tag on its dorsal fin in the moonlight.

"Damn, you're a big boy. Like my boat, do you?" he stammered as he closed the distance between him and the boat. "Ocean's lovely tonight." Unfazed, the animal remained motionless. Well, the ocean was lovely from the boat; it wasn't so great from the water. Now a massive black monolith monitored his movements. The white patches around its eyes and on its stomach cast a dull glow in the moonlight, giving it an otherworldly appearance.

"You know, I should thank you for keeping the sharks away"—he forced a laugh—"that trick with the wave was something else." He couldn't explain why he talked to the whale. It had formed the rogue wave that had pushed him overboard. Paul had watched at the edge of the guardrail as the whale had rocketed towards the boat, then dived and flicked its tail flukes at the last second. It didn't matter now because the ladder was within inches of his outstretched fingers. Paul clutched for the rungs as he tried to focus on the orca. His fingers slipped on the stainless steel before they delivered a firm hold. The cold metal of the ladder was comforting under his fingers. Paul turned to push himself with his one good leg. This time he wouldn't be freighted off. A great rush of water lapped against the stern as the orca's teeth hovered near the steps. It covered the space between itself and the boat in a microsecond.

Paul froze in terror as he tightened his grip. He wasn't going back in the ocean, where his injured leg still dangled. Water dripped from his clothes as he peered at the animal over his shoulder.

"N-n-not gonna happen." His teeth chattered, more from fear than the cold. Paul could sense its presence, a massive sentient blob of oil. If he craned his neck, he could make out the wooden doors of the cabin. "See you later," he said as he motioned towards the ocean with one arm. Without effort, the creature turned and made a wide arc around the boat. It made the long route seem easy. Paul adjusted himself to get a better view of the spectacle.

"A showman!" Paul cheered as the animal lifted a massive pectoral fin into the air and slapped it hard against the water. No one would believe him. People would empty their wallets for the opportunity to swim with an orca.

Satisfied the danger had passed, he dragged himself up the ladder. The animal was a glorified water puppy. The boat's warm cabin beckoned. Paul pulled on his right leg. It wouldn't budge. Each try brought a fresh burst of pain straight to his knee. What the hell?

He was torn from the ladder with ease in one quick motion. His heart stopped as the orca delicately drew him backwards. Water jetted up his nose. Salt burned his eyes. He'd die here off the Coronados. He was being towed by a massive ocean liner with a cable attached to his leg. Just as it began, it ended. The orca let go. Paul was fifty feet from the boat. There was no trace of the animal. Blood pounded in his brain so hard it threatened to explode. It could be anywhere. Paul was helpless in an alien world. He could have been an Olympic swimmer, but it would be no use. The ocean wasn't his home. In a panic, he slashed through the water as fast as his injured knee allowed. What little adrenaline he had left drove him towards safety. His arms burned. Each breath came out in short, ragged gasps. He wouldn't be denied the security of the ladder. Paul had one goal. He realized how deep the fatigue had set in when his fingertips brushed the ladder again. Exhausted, he could sleep right there, but to end his nightmare, he needed to climb.

A searing pain tore through his flesh as the orca seized his heel. Saltwater singed the fresh wound. For a second time, it wrestled Paul from the ladder without a struggle. This time it was gentler, as if it understood it had used too much force. Paul's body stayed afloat at the surface, dragged back by the beast. No water rushed up his nose this time as the boat faded away into the night. He paddled towards the direction he thought the boat was, but it was useless. What little strength he had left paled compared to the orca's hold. It released its grip and retreated beneath the surface. He knew it hadn't left him alone. It was somewhere in the ink below, waiting for him to make his move.

Unthinkable. The orca was toying with him. Tears flowed down his cheeks to join the brine. It wouldn't let him leave the water. No rhythmic pace kept the cadence to his strokes this time. Paul clawed at handfuls of water without a strategy. He didn't remember the boat's direction. A man-sized dorsal fin broke the surface and glided towards him. Paul closed his eyes and sank beneath the waves. The massive animal torpedoed under the surface. He braced himself for the impact.

Paul's eyes snapped open. Sleep begged for control. His eyelids fell the same way his wet clothes tugged at him. He made a solemn promise to God and himself not to drink rum before bed. And the whale! What a nightmare. He tried to roll over in the cozy bed of the cabin, but an enormous pressure kept his arm from completing the motion. The weight of a collapsed building rested on it. He spun his shoulder and tried to release the pressure. A stabbing pain surged through his frame. He wasn't on the boat; he was still in the water. His brain spat back bits and pieces of the evening to him. He wondered how he stayed afloat. Fatigue had seeped through the fiber of his muscles. It prevented him from even treading water. Paul turned towards his pinned arm to learn the full extent of his horrors.

The orca imprisoned him. Its jaws interlocked through his shoulder; its mouth pressed against him. Teeth shredded his body, only separated by a thin section of muscle and sinew. They were the pins holding his rag-doll arm together. Once the initial pain subsided, a dull sensation pulsed through his limbs.

"P-p-please let me go...," he wheezed out as he closed his eyes to rest. His face was within a fingernail of the animal's rostrum. He didn't have the energy for fear. The two bobbed together for a moment. When it grew tired of its game, the orca obliged Paul's wish. With a sickening crunch, he split through what was left of his connective tissue and severed his arm. The orca vanished as a specter beneath the choppy waters. Paul was unconscious as blood poured from his axillary artery. He was dead by the time the sharks took their first nips and nibbles.

A CHANCE MEETING

I t was a postcard-perfect morning on South Coronado Island. Located sixteen miles south of San Diego Bay, the 450-acre island housed the Coronado Research Institute. Obscured by ocean spray and mist, it had been overlooked by locals before the evolution of the CRI. The institute itself was a marvel of international diplomacy. Mexico maintained ownership of the island, but San Diego–based Marineworld controlled CRI operations. The Coronados existed as part of Mexico's Pacific Islands Biosphere Reserve. A massive influx of capital had greased the wheels of the Mexican government and allowed the improvement of the island. The result was a sparkling state-of-the-art structure. But the island had seen its fair share of failed enterprises: a Depression-era casino, smugglers, rumrunners, and mining operations. Where they failed, the CRI flourished. Even with its rocky terrain, the island boasted an impressive variety of wildlife. Elephant seals, sea lions, brown pelicans, cormorants, oyster catchers, petrels, and the rare Xantus's murrelet called the island home. While diverse, these species were nothing compared to the true crown jewel of the CRI, the orcas.

Marineworld had fashioned their expansion around them from the beginning. Management billed it as the "World's First Marine Mammal Sanctuary." It was a misnomer, but the construction was a remarkable feat. The facility sprawled across the northern half of South Coronado

Island. Its sea pens extended westward to connect with the gravelly shores of Central Coronado Island. They encapsulated one square mile of ocean within their boundaries. Engineers had designed the pens to provide the orcas a more natural environment to live out their lives after years of service in the entertainment industry. Marineworld still maintained its complex in San Diego, but transitioned its orcas over to the CRI. And it wasn't only Marineworld; zoos and aquariums from around the world were lining up to retire their animals to the sanctuary. The ability to get a small slice of revenue from their exhibition provided enough incentive. People had come for circus shows with pitchforks and torches when they discovered how the animal performers were treated. They'd soured on watching elephants do handstands on chairs. With circuses functionally eradicated, the disheartened public had set their sights on orca shows. The industry had experienced several high-profile public relations disasters in recent years. Crowds for shows grew smaller and smaller each day. While savvy companies turned a profit selling ten-dollar pretzels to sunbaked tourists, the shrinking margins become too great to ignore when hundreds of people turned out instead of the usual thousands. This didn't go unnoticed by Marineworld, and they channeled an enormous sum of cash to the CRI. Sleek lines and modern art replaced the gaudy color schemes and cartoon characters of the past. The choice was simple—adapt or go extinct.

This high-tech complex was where Lee Ingram found himself employed as Head Cetacean Behaviorist. He wasn't sure he'd earned the title. On this perfect morning, he took the opportunity to reflect on how he'd gotten to this point. His career at Marineworld had started four years prior as an intern, through blind luck.

Lee had studied at San Diego State University, where he'd earned a bachelor's degree in biology with an emphasis on zoology. He'd picked his courses with little thought for how to apply them to a career.

His parents had been furious he didn't want to become a banker or a lawyer, something with "guaranteed money," but he'd known he wanted to work with animals. It had taken serious campaigning, but he'd convinced his parents his degree could transform into something bigger. A medical career was one path they waited for. He'd never considered another eight years in lecture halls and labs. He hadn't figured out his plan, but working with animals was a start. In the end, his calling had found him. He often wondered where he would have ended up if he spent the day lounging in the quad instead of attending class. Most likely stuck in a dingy lab, looking over endless jars of dirt as a soil scientist. Jars of dirt weren't in his future. Biology 527, Animal Behavior, was where the real seeds of his career were planted.

The class was jam-packed; the smell of unwashed students hung thick in the air. It was never this full. He hadn't bothered to check the syllabus. On a normal day, a spattering of twenty students dotted the class. Today, they filled the auditorium to the rafters. Regular students and people from around campus had shown up for a special event. A girl waited by the stairs to the hall. The soft white glow of her cell phone lit her tan face. Lee tried to get her attention.

"Hey, do you know what's going on?" She didn't bother to lift her head. She scrolled through whatever held her attention on the screen.

"Yeah, some guy from Marineworld's gonna talk about killer whales."

"Really?"

"It's not on the exam, so why bother staying?" She had a point. Lee peered into the lecture hall like a hawk surveying the landscape. Only one empty seat remained: in the front row, dead center. His alternative was to retreat to a shaded spot in the quad and relax for the hour.

"Could be interesting," he said.

"Nah." The girl finished scrolling, picked up her bag and made her way to the exit. Lee contemplated following her. He could strike up a conversation and see where it led. Instead, he stole a quick look into the packed auditorium. It had been years since he'd last watched a Marineworld orca show. The spectacle wasn't something easy to forget. The girl disappeared into the bright afternoon, and Lee forged his way through the masses. Questions swirled in his mind as he walked towards the head of the classroom. Weren't the animals forced performers? What made them tick? How intelligent were they?

An unfamiliar man with long white hair stood at the podium—a seasoned politician ready to give a reelection speech. An image of two orcas mid-aerial flip displayed on the projector screen behind him. Lee wedged himself into the last remaining seat and gave his full attention to the stage.

"Glad you could make it," the man said. "Make sure you thank these guys for saving you a seat." He adjusted the microphone pack tucked into his belt. "This thing is on, right?" He blew into the microphone before starting, "I get it. You're sick of listening to Dr. Marshal talk about chimps." He shot a sly glance at the professor. A few students acknowledged him with half-hearted claps and Bronx cheers. "Although their behavior is interesting, today you'll hear about something exciting."

"Opinions, opinions," Dr. Marshal interjected, which elicited laughter from most of the audience.

"For those of you who don't know me, my name is Mark Schmidt. I've been working with and studying orcas at Marineworld for over thirty years. Today, we'll be having a quick look at the behavior and psychology behind these animals. I say a quick look because we have fifty minutes here. It's tough to compress that research under an hour. Instead, we'll focus on the highlights." Dr. Schmidt pressed a button on the controller in his hand. A photo of an orca balanced on a stage burst across the screen behind him. Compared to the trainer next to him, the animal was a giant. Lee listened as the doctor described it as "a mere circus trick."

"However, these behaviors serve a purpose. The training serves as enrichment for the animals. Sometimes it's for veterinary reasons. Each trick requires the animal to learn or change behaviors through hand signals and gestures. They're quick too. It took the big boy, Akhlut here, a few hours to learn big splash equals big reward." Lee soaked up the words as Schmidt continued to describe their high level of intelligence.

"The processing power of orcas is much, much higher than other animals. Their brain-weight-to-body-weight ratio is close to Dr. Marshal's beloved chimpanzees. That being said, if you base their intelligence on brain-body ratio alone, you're underestimating their analytical capabilities. They have an incredible amount of cortical nerve tissue because of how their brain is folded and wrinkled. We call this folding of the cortex gyrification." Schmidt clicked his presentation forward. A cross-section of a killer whale's brain compared to a human's appeared. "In fact, orcas have the most gyrified brain of any animal on the planet. An astoundingly high cognitive capacity. Orcas are aware of what they're doing and why they're doing it. If we look here"—Schmidt circled a region of the orca's brain with a laser pointer—"we can see the orca's paralimbic system. It's related to spatial memory and navigation. Quite useful when moving through their world in three dimensions. Now, where things get interesting is with this region here. The amygdala, for emotional learning and long-term memories. We've had trainers leave the park and return years later, only to be recognized by orcas they've worked with. They can hold a grudge as well." He paused. "But the real kicker, the cherry on top, is this here, the insular cortex. We haven't figured out what it does. It's more complex than we see in humans. Our best guess? It handles emotions: compassion, self-awareness, empathy, but who knows? How do you measure their empathy? Compassion? If you're looking for the subject of your master's thesis, well…" He turned towards Dr.

Marshal and laughed. "There is so much to learn about their brain. We're only scratching the surface of what they're capable of." With a click, an image of an orca breaching high into the air appeared. "During shows, the primary reward is food. But we use a variety of incentives based on the orca. Things like ice chips—"

"You're saying these animals, with their 'cortex gyrification' and 'insular cortex,' are classically conditioned?" a student in the back interrupted.

"Ahh, there's the rub. Do these animals always respond to the cues our trainers give them? Hell no. Sometimes one 'has a bad day' or just isn't having it. You can see them 'thinking,' using that fantastic brain to figure out something else to do. They can be agitated, unwilling to follow commands. Sometimes they can't care less for the reward. So they aren't truly classically conditioned. An eighteen-thousand-pound apex predator does what it wants. It isn't a lack of intelligence. Let's have a look at this fascinating behavior."

A video played on the screen. An orca happily accepted a bucketful of fish from a trainer. The animal cruised around the perimeter before it circled to the center. Once in the middle of the pool, it regurgitated its snack and dove to the floor of the tank. The movement to the bottom was effortless. With one thrust of its tail flukes, the animal disappeared beneath the surface. Only a faint black shadow glided at the pool's bottom. An oily sheen, complete with chunks of undigested fish, floated at the top as the camera zoomed.

"Gross," someone chimed in from the third row. The camera focused on the sheen as gulls swooped from the upper rafters of the famous Marineworld stadium. They hovered above the vomit, picking up little fragments of fish and flying away. One landed on the surface. It pecked the chunks at its leisure. A fly-by assault didn't cross the bird's mind; it gorged itself instead.

Without warning, the bird vanished as the mammoth head of the orca retreated beneath the surface. The water around it erupted in a massive swell. Schmidt paused the video as the auditorium hushed.

"What did we just see here?"

"That seagull got wrecked," a student next to Lee belted out.

"Indeed, that seagull got 'wrecked.' Can anyone add to that?"

The girl who'd asked about the classical conditioning of the orcas waved her hand in the air. This time, she waited for the professor to motion toward her before answering, "Predation."

"Ah, but was it that simple? Are gulls a typical food source for orcas? What did we really see?"

Lee fidgeted in his seat. Another student in the auditorium raised his hand to answer. "It used its own puke as bait. It shows problem-solving abilities."

"Good, good. Isn't that interesting? Quite the ingenious way of capturing a bird. But what's happening here? Was there a problem? Why give up the fish to go after a gull?" The side conversations within the auditorium grew. Dr. Marshal's lectures weren't as interactive. The noise level was so loud, no one would notice if he chimed in.

"It was bored," Lee whispered. Schmidt's eyes widened and focused on him.

"Young man, why don't you repeat yourself for the class?" The noise in the hall simmered. The stage spotlights burned on Lee.

"I said, it was bored."

"Let's try to put it more forcefully, shall we? It was fucking bored! This isn't the typical behavior of an apex predator. Our friend here didn't attack this bird because it was hungry. I can assure you our animals are well fed. Not only are gulls not a normal food source for orcas, but they don't give up a known meal for a taste of something different. It was bored. What you witnessed is the killer whale equivalent of bouncing a tennis ball off the wall. Yes, we give our animals enrichment activities, but sometimes they still get bored.

They'll create their own games. They are thinkers first and foremost."

The rest of the lecture blurred in his memory. Lee was hooked. Dreams of observing the orcas at Marineworld floated through his head. As he exited the auditorium, a friendly voice greeted him.

"Young man"—Mark Schmidt approached him from across the walkway—"I trust you didn't find my lecture boring?"

"Not at all, sir," Lee said. He raised his hand up to block the sun.

"Much better than chimps flinging shit and using sticks, I take it?" Schmidt asked.

Lee didn't know how to answer the question without sounding like a deranged fan. Instead, he remained quiet. Schmidt continued, "You know I've shown that video hundreds of times. You're the first person to tell me the animal was bored."

"I doubt that. It was just a good guess," Lee said, trying to deflect the praise.

"Don't sell yourself short, son. It was more than a lucky guess. Tell you what, what are your plans for Saturday morning?"

Lee stood frozen. His only plans for the weekend included sleeping in, maybe catching up on studying.

"Not a lot, sir."

"Good. You can do 'not a lot' at Marineworld. Say eight a.m.?"

"I can manage that," Lee said.

"And cut that sir crap. Call me Mark."

THE VAULT

On his first Saturday, Lee arrived at the park an hour and a half earlier than Schmidt had told him to. Only a scattered few employees' cars were already there. The expensive visitors' lot was empty. He looked out of place wandering the empty parking lot in a dress shirt and slacks. The guard let out a heavy sigh as Lee approached the gatehouse.

"You know the doc don't arrive till seven, right?"

"Trying to make a good impression."

"Oh, you'll make an impression." The guard smiled. "Grab a seat in here with me. I can't let you in until he gets here." He made small talk, asking Lee about how he'd met Schmidt, what he studied in school, if he'd ever been to Marineworld before. Time seemed to stop as he waited for the doctor to show, but he finally drove up at exactly seven. He rolled down his window to speak to the guard.

"What time did he get here?"

"Six thirty." The dejected guard handed over a folded twenty-dollar bill.

"What did I tell you?"

"Don't you worry, I'll get that back. Take care of this kid today, he's one of the good ones." He pressed the button to raise the gate. After Schmidt parked, he came to collect Lee.

"What are you wearing? Where's your wetsuit?" he asked. Lee had

15

no clue how to respond. It had crossed his mind to text the doctor and ask what to wear after they'd exchanged details, but he'd thought it might seem like a dumb question. He figured he couldn't go wrong with dress clothes. "I'm messing with you, Lee. It's good to have you here. You ready to start?"

Lee did his best to keep up with the barrage of information that Schmidt assaulted him with, remembering introductions and catching pieces of conversations where he could. The doctor had decided to skip most of the regular tour and took Lee to a file room in the bowels of the park. With its rows of steel filing cabinets and storage racks, it looked like a Cold War bomb shelter.

"Don't worry, I'm not going to make you reorganize anything down here, but I'm sure you noticed things are a bit crazy around here today." It was hard to miss. Besides the guard at the gate, the small number of staff Lee had met seemed anxious. They were cordial to him, but not much more. "Now I'm not supposed to say anything, because we haven't made the announcement to the public yet, but we're planning on opening a new facility for the orcas on the Coronados." Lee was dumbfounded. Nothing like starting day one off with a bombshell. He didn't know what question to ask first. Schmidt saw him reeling and continued, "It's fine. But we just told staff this week and they're freaking out like it's going to be finished tomorrow. We haven't even broken ground yet. So, I've got to go deal with those fires."

"What do you want me to do, then?" Lee asked.

"We call this place the vault. It's where we keep our records. Find something to read." He pointed. "That whole wall is everything we have on orcas." Schmidt grabbed the door to leave. "I almost forgot. Technically, you're not supposed to see any of these without signing a nondisclosure agreement, so if anyone besides me comes back, hide behind a cabinet or something."

While huddled alone in the vault, Lee pored over the orca behavior logs and records, scrutinized them. Schmidt generated the reports on an ongoing basis; each one included information on a whale's activities for the day, including data provided based on firsthand interactions with trainers. Information on diet, medical history, and training records was noted in the smallest detail. Lee felt he knew the orcas from the files without ever meeting them. A tired Schmidt came to escort him out at the end of the day. He practically had to drag Lee out of the room.

"So I guess that means you'll be back next Saturday?" he asked.

Schmidt was far too preoccupied to babysit Lee during the rest of his weekend visits. Besides having to calm the nerves of his staff, he reported on and oversaw the trainers who interacted with orcas and dolphins. There were up to seven shows a day. That was on top of husbandry, exercise, play, and training sessions. The man couldn't find a minute away from the animals to catch his breath. When he finally did, he'd stop by to direct Lee towards a specific manual or file.

Lee read them all twice. There was input from others, but everything from the correct way to toss a fish to the standard procedure for orca training had Schmidt's signature at the bottom. They based training on operant conditioning. Positive reinforcement was used to change the animals' behavior. When things went well, rewards reinforced the desired behavior. They were typically food—capelin, herring, crushed ice, even Jell-O—but could include fin rubdowns or other stimuli the whales appeared to enjoy. The end goal was to increase the occurrence of wanted behaviors and decrease the unwanted behaviors. When an orca did something a trainer didn't want, they ignored it. This neutral response was a least reinforcing scenario or LRS. Trainers didn't have punishment in their repertoire. Nothing as barbaric as beatings occurred. It was beyond belief that they got the animals to do so much by plying them with food. The brightest orca calf could learn show routines in under a year with the right trainer.

One Saturday near the end of the summer, Schmidt returned to his office with a more defeated look on his face than usual. Lee didn't notice because his eyes remained on the files.

"You haven't quit yet?" Schmidt asked.

"No, sir... Mark," Lee tried to correct himself.

"Well, why the hell not?"

Lee was taken by surprise. He couldn't quit because the company hadn't hired him. He sat in shock at the thought of not being able to learn more, of never actually meeting the animals. Before his mind could wander further, Schmidt cut him off.

"Relax, kid. I'm just having a shitty day." The creases on his forehead softened. "You find anything good in those reports this time?" Lee didn't know where to start. He had separated a stack of documents half a foot tall to ask about.

"Kjetil and Kjell. They seem inseparable. Two orcas with one mind. Are they always paired together?"

Schmidt laughed. "They were brought in together, stick pretty close. But they don't always agree. Look for reports where Kjetil doesn't respond. Kjell will perform the behavior perfectly right in front of him. A little 'this is how you do it.' When he goes off script, she brings him in line."

"This one's good. Did Kassuq really bring someone's sunglasses back to them?"

"That one made me hold my breath. This guy was leaning over a partition next to the stage. These gas station sunglasses slipped right off his head, sank to the bottom. I thought he'd reach into the pool to grab them. Before he could, she comes flying out of the water. Got them in her teeth. A trainer came running over before he tried to take them from her. She gets Kassuq to let them go. He gets them back, undamaged, and the crowd goes absolutely wild."

"And Akhlut, he hates seagulls that much?"

"They used to land in the slide-out. He'd skid towards them with his mouth wide open. Usually, they'd get out of the way in time. He'd adjust his tactics. Try to move in slow. Maybe do a spin to bat them with his tail. I've seen him connect on a grand slam before. Feathers everywhere. Clogs up our filters like you wouldn't believe."

The descriptions of intelligence were staggering. Playing baseball with gulls was only the beginning. The daily reports showed unique behaviors. Each orca had its own personality. Schmidt cautioned Lee against using the term: "Personality implies they're a person. Don't anthropomorphize them. Now, if you want to tell me they show distinct character traits, I wouldn't argue with you." There was a balance to how Schmidt spoke about them. Firmly a behavioral scientist, he rarely let personal feelings break through. Still, they smoldered beneath the surface. He wanted his trainers to focus on behaviors, but he couldn't stop himself from describing orcas enjoying activities or becoming frustrated. The summer was coming to an end, but Schmidt made more frequent detours to chat with Lee. It didn't take him long to offer him a full-blown internship.

"Now I can't promise it'll be more fun than reading in this dungeon on Saturdays, but you'll get to see the animals you've read about." Lee couldn't refuse the offer.

FAST-TRACK

Lee didn't show up in dress clothes for his internship. Shorts and a T-shirt worked fine. It felt great to have an official Marineworld ID, even if it barely granted him access to employee bathrooms. Plus, he didn't have to hide from management behind filing cabinets. Instead, he shadowed Schmidt as he went through his daily routine. At least, he attempted to. Mark had unique ideas about what the internship should entail. He tried to abandon Lee whenever he had the chance. On his first full day, Schmidt dumped a nervous Lee in the "fish house." True to its name, the stench assaulted Lee's nostrils before he walked in the door. A crew buzzed throughout the warehouse, putting together the animals' daily meals.

"See that short guy over there?" Schmidt pointed towards the far side of the warehouse where a man worked. He wore the black-and-white wetsuit of a trainer. "That's Ed. Stick with him this morning."

Schmidt disappeared out a side door, and Lee stood alone at the entrance. He leaned against the wall to avoid the commotion in the warehouse. Workers and trainers at stations separated out fish, squid, and shelled mollusks. Some measured rations on scales while others eyeballed the food before it was tossed into buckets or bins. The warehouse moved and flowed. SWIT! With a loud whistle, the bustle ground to a halt. Across the warehouse, Ed pinched his fingers to his mouth. The man beckoned Lee with his hand.

"Amigo!"

Lee looked to his left and right, hoping he'd shouted at someone else. He hadn't. Ed pointed at him again and waved. A few workers chuckled as the buzz returned to the warehouse. Lee weaved through the space, dodging workers until he reached the table where Ed was.

"How long did you plan to stand over there?" he asked.

"I'm a little nervous."

"I couldn't tell. You're Mark's intern?" He divided the fish on the table. "The last girl, she was much prettier."

"Sorry?"

"No, no, no. No lo siento. Here, help me measure. He's testing you."

Without missing a beat, Ed continued his work. He explained the process to Lee. Each night the closing crew left frozen capelin and herring in buckets of water to thaw for the morning crew. It was their job to separate out the correct portion of each fish before taking them to the animals for feeding. Every orca required a specific base diet determined by their age, sex, and overall health. This base diet included herring, smelt, salmon, mackerel, and squid. The calculations were written on whiteboards behind the workspace. Ed grabbed handfuls of each fish, checked their weight on a scale and tossed them into labeled buckets. His movements were fluid. He was a machine who had performed this operation millions of times.

"Breakfast. It's the most important meal of the day."

"Don't they eat throughout the day?" Lee asked.

"Of course. You can't dump it all into the water at one time. But you'll see how they wait for these first buckets." Lee searched the board for Akhlut. He was listed as the largest in the reports. Two hundred and fifty pounds of fish a day. It was more than any other orca. As Ed worked, Lee noticed plastic bags filled with pills laid out across the table. They had labels that matched the names on the board.

"Is that medicine?"

"Mostly vitamins. To keep them big and strong." Ed flexed his arms in a body builder pose and continued to work. He grabbed a thawed salmon by the operculum. With his free hand, he carefully opened a freezer bag and slid the pills into the mouth. When the bag was empty, he forced them further into the fish. "Same trick you use for a dog." Ed laughed. In the corner, a member of the prep team took a large syringe and injected liquid into a fish before tossing it into the pails.

"What about that?" Lee asked as he pointed to the worker.

"*Agua*. Watch." Ed maintained the endless loop of grabbing, weighing, and tossing fish into buckets. After he filled an empty pail from the sink, the prep team member drew the syringe full of water and plunged it into a fish before injecting it.

"Why?"

"Ivar's dehydrated. It's not like he can drink the water in the tank. Their food gives them water. Sometimes we need to give them a little extra." The fish house hummed as Lee waited for instructions. They didn't come. He looked at the list of names for one that wasn't checked off.

"Can I help do the food for Shurik?"

"Ah, the big bull. Sure, sure."

Unfazed by the stares of dead fish, Lee jumped into the task. He didn't have the magic touch that Ed did. When he dropped food on the scale, the numbers climbed and fell without reason. Once they settled, they were far from the values outlined on the board. He'd clear the scale and start again. Cautiously, he'd add more. One fish at a time. He triple-checked his work.

Ed chuckled next to him. "We're getting their breakfast ready, not their dinner, no?" To keep up with Ed, he doubled his pace to fill up the steel buckets beside him. "Done?" Ed asked.

"Should be good," Lee responded.

"Did you check the name?"

Lee spun around the first pail he filled. Written in large black block letters was "Kassuq." Ed clicked his tongue and made a slashing gesture towards his throat. "FFFFFFT!" Lee was mortified. He'd failed his first test. When Ed saw the worried look on his face, he was quick to reassure him. "It's fine, my friend. As long as the weight is right. We'll make sure it gets to Shurik." Ed picked up the bucket and dumped it into an empty one labeled "Shurik."

Lee's face turned red with embarrassment. He was ready to move to the next task. "What now?"

"You take it to him," Ed said. His lips pulled into a mischievous grin. He motioned Lee towards a map of the park taped to the whiteboard. It wasn't a true blueprint but the colorful map visitors received. There was a hand-drawn line from behind the sea lion enclosure to the orca stadium. There wasn't a label for the fish house on it.

"That's the route. Right, left, right, left." Ed traced the path. It was simple, and Lee only had four buckets to carry. He picked up the first two pails, one in each arm. The weight made them sag to the ground. "Heavy? You sure you measured right?" Ed filled the last of the pots. Loaded with fish, each bucket weighed forty pounds. They were heavy now, but if he finished the trip, they'd tear his arms from the sockets. "If you can't handle it, I can get someone else to do it."

"No, I got this," Lee dismissed him. He stumbled out the door into the sunlight. They were the first unsure footsteps of his lengthy journey. By the time he made it to the back of the fish house, his arms ached. Lee made a right around the sea lion enclosure. The pain in his arms grew as a single gull cawed a warning to him. He was being watched. Lee grabbed the buckets and continued his quest. Before long, he came to an unfamiliar crossroad that wasn't on the map. A bicycle spoke of paths branched out before him.

Lee set the buckets on the pavement while he tried to orient himself. Lush landscaped areas crowded the path, but there was a single signpost with arrows labeled for different exhibits. An accomplice joined the gull following him. They took turns mocking him as they passed overhead. This time, there was more resistance in his arms from the renewed weight of the buckets. He picked the path with what he thought was a carving of an orca. The gulls disappeared overhead as he traveled along the path. Large ferns and fronds blotted out the sky. The park met its goal of mimicking a tropical jungle. When the vines and greenery threatened to overtake him, the path opened to a massive plaza with scattered shops and games. Since it was before the park opened, it sat empty. Only Lee and his two buckets of fish.

He sat on a bench and contemplated his next move. He'd made a wrong turn back at the wheel. A gang of gulls interrupted him. The bravest of the bunch plunged from the sky and scooped up a fish from the bucket. Others gave chase as it flew off and landed on the roof of a restaurant across the plaza. Lee spilled more fish before he ducked under the canopy of ferns. They chirped just outside his shelter. He was trapped.

"Need some help?"

A blond-haired woman in the standard employee uniform of khakis and a blue shirt stood outside the branches. Her tan skin hid the freckles on her face. For the first time that day, he didn't think of the orcas. He stared awkwardly for a moment before he settled on a response.

"Yeah, uh, can you point me in the direction of the orca stadium?" His voice cracked as he unsuccessfully fought off a lopsided smile. The woman couldn't help but laugh at first. It took her a second to compose herself. She'd seen lost sheep before, but never one hiding in the bushes.

"Well, you made it further than the last intern. She got to the sea lions before the gulls chased her off. Never saw her after that. First thing"—she pulled a hand towel from her back pocket and threw it over the pail—"we cover the tops of the buckets to stop the dive bombers. Now, you've got two options. One, you can walk straight across the plaza to the right. Do that and you'll get lost."

"My other option?" Lee asked.

"Your other option... is to walk back to the fish house and hope Ed hasn't finished loading the cart." She took the uncovered bucket from his hand and walked back the way he'd come.

"Guess we're going with option two," Lee said.

"Keep up." She disappeared down the path. When they arrived back, Ed was loading the cart with the last of buckets.

"I thought Shurik would starve," he said.

"Only lost a few to the gulls," Lee replied.

"It's tradition. No hard feelings?"

"No hard feelings."

"How far he get?" Ed put the buckets onto the cart and turned to the woman.

"Made it to the plaza," she said.

"Ah, the plaza. Pretty far. You're very determined or very stubborn," Ed chuckled. "Thanks for bringing him back to me." With a heave, Lee lifted the buckets Ed carried onto the rear of the cart.

"*De nada,*" she said.

"*Ah, su español es muy bueno.*" Ed entered the warehouse and Lee followed.

"Who was she?" Lee asked.

"Stacy? She works with the dolphins, started not too long ago. You ready to meet them now?"

Lee hopped in the front seat of the cart as Ed pulled away from the curb. The park came alive as it got closer to opening. As they sped through the park, there were surges of life. Workers rolled open the steel shutters to gift shops lined with sunglasses, sunscreen, and stuffed animals. Flamingos strolled across an impressive expanse of emerald-green lawn. Ed slowed the cart for animal and human alike to greet them by name with a wave.

"You've seen the park before?" he asked. The cart jostled along the bricks.

"Not like this."

It wasn't long before they reached the orca stadium. Ed squeezed the cart through a narrow alley hidden by a sculpted rock face. The backside of the stadium displayed none of the glamor or elaborate detail that were the hallmark of the tourist sections. It was utilitarian, meant only for the eyes of the workers. Ed parked the cart outside a heavy steel door painted with "Crew Members Only." He plucked a bucket from the cart and used his ID to open the door. Together they carried the food past changing rooms to a cramped storage room lined with metal racks. Each rack had labeled spaces with the names of the orcas. It was a demanding workout to lug buckets from the fish house. Even if it was from the cart to storage, it was one of the many reasons the trainers were in such good shape. After stocking the shelves, Ed turned to Lee.

"Now the fun part." He grabbed a bucket and led Lee to another heavy steel door, this time stenciled with "Main Pool." He stopped before throwing the door open. *"Eso!"*

From the darkness, Lee's eyes adjusted to the brightness. He stood in a cramped tunnel, but the glittering blue surface of the pool beckoned to him at the far end. Ed led the way. The compact space served as a funnel to amplify the noise. Lee paused and listened to the sound of the water that sloshed over the sides of the tank. From inside the stadium, it was calming white noise. Here it was roaring rapid. Carefully, he exited just as Ed had before him. Lee pressed himself up against the gray faux rock that acted as a backdrop for the stadium stage. The tank was extensive. Pools wrapped around each side of the stage forming a peninsula. He didn't dare venture towards Ed. The trainer kneeled on a shallow platform at the very edge of the forty-foot-deep tank. Lee clung to the plastered rock like a barnacle.

"You can come closer," he said as slapped at the water. Lee hesitated; he'd read the orca protocol. There was a sequence before you got within ten feet of one. Trainers spent years at the associate level while a mentor guided them. There were specific ways to walk around the pools, methods of moving across different surfaces, and ways to carry buckets. On the progress checklist to becoming a trainer, Lee ticked none of the boxes. He couldn't force himself to move from where he stood.

KHOOSH! A large black dorsal fin pierced the surface to Lee's right. He stared as the orca cruised through the water into the main pool. Lee knew his safety was guaranteed from his position on the stage, but his stomach betrayed him. It dropped to the ground. His mind went blank. A primeval response. Fight or flight. The urge to dart back into the tunnel grew, but he stuck to the wall, transfixed on where Ed kneeled. Where was the whale? Ed waited as he stared into the depths, tracking the animal. With a gush of water, the orca's bulbous head appeared. It was a mere foot from Ed's. Unfazed, he took a step back before blowing a whistle. It was a signal the orca had performed a desired behavior, a bridge before it received positive reinforcement. The orca opened its mouth wide to reveal a pink cavern lined with rows of conical teeth. Ed was in a vulnerable position. If it wished, the orca could seize him in its jaws. It received a handful of fish instead.

"No free meals!" Ed shouted as gave a signal for Shurik to swim a lap. The whale obliged and earned another helping of fish. This time, the vitamin-stuffed salmon was hidden among the rest. When the bucket was empty, Ed blew the whistle. A playful splash of water on the animal's head served as reinforcement. Shurik followed the splash backwards before twisting and diving.

"You want to feed him?" He didn't take his eyes off the whale.

"Not right now, I'm good," Lee said.

"You have to be confident if you're going to work with them. Do nothing halfway."

"Noted."

Lee helped Ed feed the other orcas by taking buckets of fish from storage and bringing them out. The animals were fed one at a time to ensure they received the right base diet and vitamins. With each set, he moved millimeters from the wall. He wanted to get closer, but the urge to sprint back to storage room lingered. Not once did he venture further than the dry portion of the stage.

Ed stooped on the shallow stage without an ounce of fear. If the work scared him, he did an impeccable job of hiding it behind false bravado.

"They're being good today." Ed explained how they needed to be under control before they could be fed. Orcas responded to a series of commands before earning their breakfast. But they never starved. If they didn't listen on the first attempt, the trainers took a break and tried again until the whale complied. After the morning feeding, they were given the rest of their food at random: a few smelt during a training session, another bucket of mackerel while they were resting, perhaps a squid during a show. It kept them stimulated. As Ed put it, they didn't want them "lining up like hungry baby birds" at regular times during the day.

It took months of the same routine before Lee got closer to observe. And when he did, the orcas were on the far side of the pool. When he eventually dared to dip a single toe in the water, a strange feeling welled up within him. It was a sensation, an itch to hurl himself in. A fleeting question—"What if I jump?"—and it disappeared as quickly as it had arisen. The idea of forty feet of water beneath him made his skin crawl. Add a few thousand pounds of orca and the anxiety caused his heart to palpitate. He researched it. The scientific term for it was "the call of the void." People experienced it when doing things with a high risk or danger. Commuters that wanted to jump in front of an arriving train, hikers that felt the sensation to jump from the mountaintop, a cabby's desire to yank the steering wheel into oncoming traffic, they all experienced the call. Out of the scenarios Lee read, the idea of being in a pool with an orca was the worst, but "the call" didn't stop. Researchers chalked it up to misinterpreted brain signals. A subconscious message to get back or move. When a person can't explain why they backed up, they assume they wanted to jump in first place.

There were procedures in place if it happened. If someone succumbed to the call. Both orcas and dolphins were desensitized to objects that fell into the pool. Following a plan laid out by Schmidt, they conditioned the animals to items in the water. It was a safety mechanism built into working with them. But an orca's innate curiosity was difficult to stymie. It wasn't a simple task to desensitize them. It took hours of training. They learned to disregard trainers unless they gave a specific signal for a learned behavior. They ignored trainers standing on the walkways, in the shallow slide-outs where there was less than a foot of water, or in the deep pool unless they were signaled. The process wasn't foolproof; not all orcas succeeded in this training.

From the first day with Ed, Lee spent his evenings at the top of the bleachers in the empty stadium. He volunteered to take the place of junior trainers assigned to the night shift. The stadium was identical to the pictures Schmidt had shown in the auditorium. He'd think how lucky he was. Lucky he'd decided not to skip class that day. Lucky Schmidt had taken a chance on him. The harsh halogen lighting mingled with the moonlight that flooded the back pools. He'd grin each time an orca surfaced to draw a breath. The familiar KHOOSH! echoed through the tourist-less stadium. With each breath, Lee logged the time in a notebook. He'd compare the data to baseline measurements for each orca. Too shallow or erratic, and he'd have to call the vet. They didn't sleep like humans. Half of their brain remained conscious, even while they "slept." If they were completely unconscious, they risked drowning. It never happened while he was on watch. The trainers were grateful he volunteered. Night watch was tedious. Assigned junior staff had trouble not dozing off themselves. For those completing their degrees, it was nothing more than an opportunity to catch up on their studies. Lee avoided the temptation. His time at the park was a retreat from his courses. A year and a half at the stadium slipped by and his time as an intern drew to a close. When it was over, Schmidt hired him without hesitation.

FRESH BLOOD

T hings changed for Lee once he became an official Marineworld employee, but his feelings towards the orcas didn't. For most workers, respect replaced awe. Respect for their power, their capabilities. For others, wonder morphed into affection. Only a rare few exhibited a balance between the two. Even then, the feeling of wonder dissipated. Not for him. His jaw still dropped each time one loomed up from the heart of the pool. He thanked the park designers for each pane of glass and every guardrail between him and the animals. From time to time his imagination ran wild, picturing what would happen if a slip put him at the mercy of the ocean's top predator.

Lee's day-to-day tasks grew. Management trusted him enough to let him occasionally fill in for Schmidt on various tasks. Schmidt was overwhelmed with preparations for the CRI and didn't mind. He knew it would be good for the rookie to experience as much as he could firsthand. While Lee could learn a lot from the vault, only so much found its way to the page. That was why, with only two months of wear on his shiny new ID, Lee stood poolside to receive a pep talk from Ed before observing an orca root canal. The two men waited for a second trainer to bring the antiseptic solution.

"You'll be fine. You stand off to the side and take notes," Ed reassured him.

"We don't have the vet do it?" Lee asked.

"They don't want to lose a finger. Just be glad it's me and your friend near the chompers. You going to talk to her today?" Ed pulled a variable-speed rotary drill out of a canvas bag. "Here. If you're not going to talk to me, plug this in over there. Don't get it wet."

"This is what we use? Did you bring this from your house?"

"No mames, güey."

By this point, it shouldn't have surprised Lee. It wasn't like they could use a human-sized dental drill. He had seen the teeth flushing before, not the drilling. That was a daily routine to prevent bacteria from entering the whale's bloodstream through the holes left by the procedure. The trainers flushed the openings in the teeth with povidone iodine using an oral irrigator that was a larger-scale version of the over-the-counter model. During shows, trainers made reference to whales receiving "first-class dental treatment." Somehow, Lee didn't believe that two trainers and a novice assistant performing a modified pulpotomy qualified. Biting concrete or a steel bar until your tooth cracked was bad enough. Having someone grind out the pulp with a drill before spraying it at high-pressure with antiseptic had to be excruciating.

"You boys ready?" Stacy entered the through the stadium's side door. She had been promoted from dolphins to orcas and wore the upgraded black to prove it. Lee fumbled with the drill but caught it before it splashed into the shallow water. She carried a plastic grocery bag.

"Hola, guapa! Qué es eso?"

"Animal Care said the shipment of one thousand milliliter bags was delayed. Someone went to the drugstore to get these bottles," she responded. Lee couldn't believe that they were about to perform a medical procedure with what amounted to household tools and products.

Ed volunteered to be the "holder" while Stacy played dentist. He signaled for Kassuq to surface near the edge of the slide-out. She dutifully rested her chin on the edge and opened her mouth. Rows of worn teeth shone in the sun. Ed rewarded her with a fish before he gently applied pressure to her rostrum and cupped the bottom of her lower jaw. He avoided pulling down on it. This encouraged her to keep her mouth open during the procedure without making her feel like he was prying it open, but Lee knew Ed couldn't stop her if she wanted to snap her jaws shut.

Stacy sprayed the drill bit with the antiseptic before she started grinding away at the damaged tooth area. Lee wondered how the animal remained so calm without anesthetic. Kassuq only occasionally twitched when Stacy returned to drilling after checking for any remaining exposed pulp. After a few rounds, she was satisfied she'd extracted it all.

"Can you hand me the Waterpik? I don't want to take my eyes off her." Lee exchanged the tools for her while keeping as much distance as possible between himself and the orca. "Thank you." She flushed out the exposed hole with antiseptic.

"You're welcome." Lee backed away and resumed his position, keeping a safe distance. In no time, Stacy had the rest of the orca's teeth flushed and the procedure was finished. Ed tossed Kassuq a handful of fish and dismissed her. The two trainers had made it look easy.

"If you don't mind cleaning up, I'm going to take a look at the others."

"No hay problema. Was it easier than the dolphins?"

"Muy fácil." Stacy headed off to the back pool. Lee helped Ed put the equipment away. He couldn't decide what made him more nervous—Stacy, the orcas, or Stacy working with the orcas.

"You survive medical work with her and you can only manage two words?"

"Don't start with me."

"Mr. de Nada," Ed teased.

33

* * *

The rift between management and Schmidt deepened as the deadline to switch facilities approached. With under a year before the ribbon-cutting, Schmidt was interviewed by an animal rights activist. He'd become accustomed to ambushes over the years, but this time his responses raised eyebrows. Interactions with media needed to go through the correct channels. If they didn't, they fell into the dreaded unsanctioned category. Enough of those strikes would catch up to any employee eventually. What made matters worse was that the interview reached the news. It wasn't relegated to a five-minute midday segment where it could stay relatively unseen. No, the footage of Schmidt holding an impromptu press conference in the parking lot went straight to prime time.

A man in a wrinkly button-up shirt had waited at the staff exit door. He recognized his target as soon as Schmidt left the building and moved to introduce himself. Rather than field questions on the run to his car, Schmidt offered a spot on the side of the building. It served as a better backdrop and didn't give the impression he was fleeing a crime scene. The man's line of questioning started innocently enough. He asked Schmidt about the progress of construction on the CRI, what animals would be moved, and what would become of the park on the mainland. The answers to these questions were well documented already. Construction of the main buildings was almost complete. More of the framework for the perimeter netting was erected each day. For the opening, only the orcas would be moved. Once they were settled in, other marine mammals, starting with the belugas, were slated to be transferred. These weren't the questions he had come to ask. His real questions didn't take long to make their appearance.

"What's your comment on those that say the tanks were never big enough for whales and dolphins? That it amounts to keeping them in a prison cell?" he asked. This was a softball Schmidt had heard thousands of times.

"I'd say they're absolutely correct," he responded without hesitation. "If staff are untrained and incompetent, if they aren't given the best veterinary care in the world. It's the same with all animals kept in captivity. Have you spoken to the keepers at San Diego Zoo as well?" Schmidt asked. His first mistake was referring to captivity. It was on a list of terms that management didn't want to hear from their employees. They preferred to call it "in human care."

"San Diego Zoo functions as a nonprofit. They don't make money off their animals." The interviewer was prepared. Schmidt was undeterred.

"True, but the money we make from ticket sales goes straight back into the care for our animals. I can't speak for the entire board, but we're not bloodsucking monsters. It's in our best interest, both financially and from a conservation standpoint, to keep our animals happy, healthy, and alive. If we have tanks full of dying orcas, the public won't visit. If we don't have guests, then we'll be out of business. The bottom line is, if it's bad for the animals, it's bad for the business. You're aware of our new facility being developed in the Coronados. You know the tanks here will be emptied?" he asked. Two more banned words in the span of five minutes. Tanks should be called enclosures or aquariums. And dying? Animals in the care of Marineworld didn't die. If visitors asked about a specific animal no longer on exhibit, the standard response was "I don't know."

"Yes. We can agree the sea pens under construction in the Coronados are a major step forward in housing these animals. But what do you say to those who argue they shouldn't be in captivity to begin with? That they are dying in captivity. That they should be released to their natural environment?"

"My team works very hard analyzing candidates for release. It isn't something we take lightly or rush. People have this misconception that it's as simple as dropping them back into the ocean. They've seen one too many movies. It doesn't work in real life. Real orcas, they die after a failed reintroduction. A return to the sea is best for animals from the sea. But some of our whales have been in captivity for decades. Even born in captivity. They've either forgotten or know nothing of life in the wild. They'd have to forget what they've learned while in captivity, or with our captive-born animals, and taught how to be 'wild.' When that goes wrong, we have a tragedy like Keiko. It's terribly unfair and downright cruel. Without proper research, we'd just be releasing them to die. Alone and starving is a dreadful way to go, don't you agree?" The young man's face scrunched. The openness of Schmidt caught him off guard. His use of restricted words grew.

"Look, what we're doing is moving the marine-park industry out of the dark ages. We've heard the concerns. People don't want to see shows to upbeat music anymore, they don't want to see dolphins jumping through hoops or orcas dancing with trainers. To carry on with those shows would be financial suicide. It's not sustainable, and in the long run the animals suffer. What they deserve is a 'retirement' where they can live out their lives free from as much stress as possible. It's not only going to do that; it's going to offer an astounding experience to our guests without the gimmicks that have become a hallmark of the industry." Schmidt closed out the interview by inviting the man for a tour of the Coronados when it was completed.

Management had turned a blind eye to Schmidt speaking his mind on issues for most of his career. He didn't speak down to the critics or dismiss their arguments. Sometimes he outright agreed with them. But he handled it in a way that made Marineworld come out the savior. They secretly loved his interviews with activists because he could beat them.

This one was different. Schmidt had been candid about the

company's purpose. It was making money, but the public didn't need to hear that. Shareholders required returns on investments, but that wasn't the image they wanted to project. Marineworld wanted "conservation and research" to be at the forefront of discussion. Schmidt's direct honesty was a tough pill for them to swallow. He didn't even try to spin his language positively. This talk of tanks and death was ludicrous. Their absolute faith in him was shaken. The interview sparked a downward trend in his standing, but the real dagger had dropped six months before the grand opening.

During his time as an intern, Lee had been rebuked for replying to an email request for information on the orcas. He hadn't sent information over, but the act of opening a dialogue was frowned upon. Sharing internal data on the animals was forbidden, part of the Marineworld rulebook. It wasn't a rule that Lee was willing to break. Schmidt didn't have that issue. He'd contacted the group that emailed, Orca Acoustics Research, back when Lee had failed to deliver, and he'd maintained a friendly relationship since. With the timer counting down to the transition, Schmidt wanted more data to determine if any whales were candidates for reintroduction.

In an unprecedented move, Schmidt brokered an exchange of countless hours of recorded orca calls. The group volunteered to compare Marineworld's files to their own audio logs recorded on the northwest coast. OAR sought to identify connections between the calls of the Marineworld orcas and the animals they observed. The goal was to prove a familial link between captive and wild animals so that reintroductions were less problematic. Schmidt's effort helped make the CRI release program a success. It didn't matter—the extension of an olive branch to a group of researchers in Washington was an unforgivable offense that led to Schmidt's firing.

Thomas Walsh, the man tagged to be the director of the CRI, saw red. It was the ultimate betrayal. Schmidt's logic was sound, but to hand over their audio collection had been a mistake. Walsh was handcuffed. He couldn't protect his colleague any longer. Schmidt should've selected specific files to send, then gotten his plan approved by the board. Tom could have justified it, gotten them to approve the idea and make them both look better. Instead, Schmidt had sent them the entire catalog of tapes.

There were bright recordings of euphoric clicks from positive training sessions, excited squeaks when a favorite toy was introduced, or chirps of joy when the gates between pens finally opened. The other side was sinister: wailing moans over separated families, eerie echoes of orcas left in isolation, and the mournful sobs over the deaths of comrades. Schmidt had sent the lot. The calls would find their way to YouTube, plastered with footage of orcas logging motionless near the surface.

They had only just recovered the public's trust when they announced the building of the CRI. Refreshing their memory of the evils of the past was a surefire way to have a less-than-stellar opening day. In any event, they'd planned to scale back the Head Cetacean Behaviorist's duties when the switch happened. Without shows or new tricks for the whales to learn, the position was obsolete. The veterinary staff and trainers they kept could manage day-to-day care for the animals. They supported the learned behaviors in place. Daily orca shows would be a thing of the past; trainers wouldn't need to get fully in the water. No more practicing rocket hops or lob tailing on cue. Tom had put up with Schmidt for decades. Enough was enough.

* * *

"They don't know what the fuck they're doing!" Schmidt's shouting was the first sign that something was wrong. Quick footsteps and the slamming of drawers that reverberated through their shared office wall followed. Lee tiptoed into the hall to poke his head into his mentor's office.

"Everything okay?" he asked. This set off a fresh tirade as Schmidt whipped files into a box on the floor.

"It's bullshit. I shouldn't have to listen to assholes who have their degree in business, not science." Schmidt's response was to himself. He whirred around his office, flipping through cabinets and scooping books from shelves. Lee noticed the hulking frame of a member of park security in the corridor.

"They didn't..."

"He did. Son of a bitch accused me of sharing company secrets in front of the board! Sometimes he's just fucking like him." Schmidt threw random trinkets from his office into the box. In seconds, he decided if awards, certificates, and mementos from years of work were worth keeping. His eyes lingered over handwritten journals packed on the shelves so tightly they threatened to explode. "Someone has to look out for their welfare. It sure as shit isn't that greedy bastard."

A security guard appeared in the doorway. "Mark. I'm sorry, you've gotta—"

"Can you give me one fucking second?" Schmidt asked. The guard pushed his hands out and stepped backwards. He gave a silent nod as he retreated into the corridor. Schmidt exhaled and lifted the box. Color returned to his face. He set it on his desk and smoothed back his long hair, pulling it into a neat ponytail. With another deep breath, he walked towards his awaiting escort.

"See you later." Park security ushered Schmidt off the property without the chance to say goodbye to another soul. A ruthless attack to rival any predator's.

They'd held the board meeting that morning without him. Tom had been the deciding vote on his termination. He'd sat before the board and argued his case for his replacement.

39

"Look, the kid can do whatever we throw at him."

"That's fine. But his lack of experience? Mark wrote the book on how we work with our animals. Lee's a bright kid, but he's hardly an expert in the field."

"His in-depth analysis of behaviors isn't on par with Mark's, no, but we won't need that at CRI." Tom flashed a smile at the board. "You remember when Mark started. None of us had a clue what we were doing. It was guesswork as to what worked and what didn't. He wrote the book on training, but we did the company a disservice to depend on him. Time after time, he put his ego above the good of the company."

"What about the trainers and their work with the reintroductions? Schmidt was the lead on that."

"We won't need trainers in the water." Tom twisted the truth to a definitive argument. There would be no more shows, but trainers still worked with orcas, especially those that were destined to be released. "The plan was always to reduce the Head Behaviorist role; you know that. We want the orcas to forget their tricks and move back to natural behaviors." An outright lie. The animals needed to undergo training to forget what they'd learned. Orcas wouldn't forget years of training and positive reinforcement because they found themselves back in the ocean. In all likelihood, the position of Head Behaviorist would expand in difficulty. But Lee was someone he could control. He couldn't persuade the board in one day, though. Not when the wounds of Schmidt's betrayal were fresh. "I know I can't convince you today. Tell you what, give me until next month's board meeting. You can think it over and we can put it to another vote."

At the next board meeting, Tom's motion to promote Lee passed unanimously. Tom fought for Lee, changed his pitch to suit each member of the board. He won them over one by one. He countered arguments against instating Lee with an excitement for the fresh blood. Schmidt had served his purpose during his time at Marineworld, but he was a man out of time. A relic from the era when they'd put top hats on dolphins for shows. Lee was the man of the future. The one to lead the CRI to sustained success. He wouldn't risk the financial well-being of the company to make inroads with an environmental group. Four years from intern to Head Cetacean Behaviorist. In any other industry it was infeasible. At Marineworld, anything was possible if you had the boss in your corner.

REINTRODUCTION

This year was the sixtieth anniversary of Marineworld. As part of the celebration, they'd opened the season with a ribbon-cutting ceremony on South Coronado Island. All parties agreed progress had been made. Animal rights activists, conservationists, trainers, and the public applauded the decision. The animals formerly housed in tiny tanks would be given the open space they needed. Other festivities surrounding the CRI had been scheduled throughout the year; special guest speakers, fundraiser galas at the on-site hotel, and fireworks shows filled the calendar.

Lee and Schmidt had debated the transition to the sea pens before his ousting. What were the benefits and risks of housing these animals in an open environment? In terms of equipment, there was no doubt it would work. Marineworld had spent months testing new netting, gates, and platforms that animals came into contact with. Failure from a containment perspective was unthinkable. Schmidt had worried the orcas would face psychological impacts. The two agreed on benefits—more space and no forced shows was easy, but how would the CRI sustain animal enrichment? Shows allowed for exercise, and certain orcas gave the impression they enjoyed performing. What would be the effects on their behavior of having the schedules and systems they'd known for decades removed? Would they lash out and become violent, or grow lethargic and depressed? And that didn't take into account their immune systems. During their stay in San Diego, the orcas had received a steady cocktail of antibiotics. How would they react to the pathogens from the ocean? Would they put wild orcas at risk with bacteria they'd been exposed to during captivity? There weren't simple answers to these questions, which had taken a toll on Schmidt. In the weeks before his dismissal, the lines on his face had deepened and sagged. Daily verbal sparring with Tom ground him down. Their superior didn't share the trepidations of Lee and Schmidt. Putting them in the sea pens wasn't the problem. He fixated on the selection of orcas for reintroduction to the wild. Progress plowed forward no matter the cost.

After endless meetings with Tom and the board of directors, they decided only one of Marineworld's seven orcas would be a perfect fit for reintroduction to the wild. The whales had been judged as potential candidates based on their behavior files, length of time in captivity, and the region they had been removed from. Officially, the Navy created a checklist outlining the standards that needed to be achieved before a cetacean was put back into the ocean. Their checklist had been developed with warfare purposes in mind. That had dreams of reconnaissance and espionage without the need for human involvement. To determine if it was even possible, they on experimented with captive orcas and dolphins taken by dropping them back into the ocean for extended periods of time. They proved it was possible to call them back to a ship using underwater tones. These studies ultimately provided the basis for any reintroduction of a cetacean back into the ocean. Based on the guidelines, in order to be released, an orca was required to be physically fit, free from disease, and able to hunt on its own, avoid human interaction, and integrate into the native population of its species. For orcas held in captivity for extended periods of time, satisfying the last few criteria was tricky. They needed to unlearn what they had been trained to do. Wiping their memory was no slight task. Some orcas were driven to perform. Rewards came secondary to the mental stimulation they received from interaction with humans. Humans as an easy source of amusement or reward were not easily forgotten. More often than not, infatuation with them proved fatal for released animals.

While clearing an orca's memory was a daunting task, integrating an orca back into its native population was overwhelming. There was a large variance between the animals. They mingled in their tanks, but socially and physiologically, they might as well be different species. Orcas swam in oceans around the globe. Like humans, each region had spectacularly diverse animals. Southern residents, found in the Pacific Northwest, traveled in large pods. Their diet consisted primarily of salmon and other fish. Transient orcas moved in smaller groups, often just three whales. As their name suggested, they didn't occupy a particular home water but lived a nomadic life in the coastal and offshore waters of the Pacific. These animals preyed on other marine mammals: seals, sea lions, and other whales were fair game. When reintroducing a transient orca, it could be impossible to track their original pod. Research on their movements was sparse. They were more fluid in their pod dynamics compared to the southern residents. There was always the possibility that members of the original transient group had died. Then there were the offshore killer whales. Smaller than the other types, they were rarely observed because they voyaged far beyond the coastlines. When found, their teeth were worn from extensive feeding on sharks. There were two separate types of eastern North Atlantic orcas. And that was only considering killer whales found in the Northern Hemisphere. The Southern Hemisphere was home to at least five distinct ecotypes. Marineworld's collection contained transients, southern residents, eastern North Atlantic killer whales, and a pack ice orca from the Southern Hemisphere. To facilitate the release of any one was a significant feat.

Both Schmidt and Lee wholeheartedly agreed that the release of Nayak was the correct choice. She had been brought to the park in the 1990s as part of a rescue operation on the coast of Northern California. She'd separated from her pod during their regular migration and had ended up beaching herself. Marineworld had stepped in and saved the whale from an untimely death by mobilizing a team to the site of the incident. After she was freed of her predicament, staff decided she needed added care and observation. They documented the reasons for holding her as health issues with the beaching and stress from the separation. Nayak's skin lesions, caused by thrashing on the rocks and sand, healed under the watchful eyes of veterinary staff. The logic behind continued care for stress from being separated was absurd. Schmidt argued it made the most sense to shoot for a quick return. Tom pushed for added observation. The problem was, the additional care continued indefinitely. Marineworld failed to carry out her reintroduction promptly.

Animal rights activists criticized them for not releasing her after rehabilitation. The public outcry drew the attention of government groups, specifically the USDA's Animal and Plant Health Inspection Service and the Marine Mammal Commission. However, after a brief investigation, both agencies deemed that the park had acted in the animal's best interest by not forcing a reintroduction. APHIS stated that the continued care Nayak received at Marineworld was necessary. They'd review the progress in a year's time. Each subsequent year, Marineworld made the case for her captivity. Backed by an army of lawyers and legal experts, they secured her prolonged residence at the park.

From the day Marineworld had intervened on the beach, Schmidt had championed for her release. Keeping her on display was a greater tragedy than a failed release. At the time, Tom disregarded him because a mismanaged release would be disastrous for the company.

Nayak lived in a gray zone of legislative boundaries. Her pod was in decline. Since 2005, the southern resident population had been on the Endangered Species list. It was granted endangered status after it failed to recover from captures conducted by marine parks. Tom argued that keeping her in captivity could benefit the conservation of the species. He convinced the board that breeding her offered a step forward in the southern residents' conservation. His plan never came to fruition. Even if it had, her offspring would never know the joy of splashing in the ocean. Lee suspected the failure was because of Schmidt's interference, but Schmidt never openly admitted it.

From San Diego, it was easy to locate Nayak's pod. It was the most well studied and monitored group of orcas in the entire world. Researchers and amateur whale watchers photographed them, then cataloged members of the population by their identifying marks and dorsal fins. For most of the year, the pods traveled around the waters of Washington and British Columbia. They were often spotted near Puget Sound or the Strait of Juan de Fuca. After holding on to her for so long, Tom now made the exact opposite case. She needed to be returned.

Marineworld showed penance for their wrongdoing by organizing her release. The history of reintroduction after captivity was short and unfortunate, but Lee held high hopes for Nayak. Along with the team at the CRI, he worked tirelessly to develop a successful plan. He leaned on the advice of Schmidt, who didn't hold a grudge against his former protégé. It wasn't Lee who'd pushed him out. Schmidt authored the original document for Nayak's release, which was a vital resource in the plan's evolution. The document acted as a template to be customized for future releases. If Marineworld was determined to put orcas back in the wild, he wanted to ensure their survival.

"Now what you have to remember when dealing with the trainers, not all of them know the psychology behind the training. They get attached. Hell, I've been guilty of it myself." Schmidt sighed. "Their heart is in the right place, but they won't understand the science behind it. It's hard for the animals to forget what we've taught them, but if you want them to make it, they have to."

A select group of trainers could get away with being overly attached to the orcas. Ed Morales was the best. His knowledge of animal behavior was hard earned over years of experience at the park. The orcas responded in kind, following his lead with curiosity. Lee held his breath whenever Ed flipped into the pool for an impromptu fin rub. No other trainer was foolish enough to attempt such a feat unless they wanted trouble.

"They'll fight you on the process. Accuse you of pressing the animal too hard," Schmidt said. "They'll see her as a friend, a family member that they know what's best for." He paused, realizing how harsh he sounded. "Look, it's not that they're not talented trainers—they are. It's just, they can take away from the goal of release. The ocean sure as shit won't take it easy on them." Schmidt gave instructions to Lee on what points should not be conceded before the plan's submission for approval to APHIS and the MMC. "Don't let them take out data-specific goals. Stick to those the best you can. Tom will want to make them vague to say they've been met. To speed up the timetable." The thought of debating the minutiae of the plan without Schmidt's help made Lee nervous. Deep down, he knew the board believed he hadn't made his bones yet. They'd default to someone who'd been around longer, even if Lee's work was exceptional.

This time, Schmidt wasn't in the room to fall back on. It was only Tom. The list of people who'd butted heads with him and won was short. In the end, even Schmidt had been unsuccessful. So it was a major accomplishment when Lee came out the victor. The board agreed on the need to stick to the data-driven plans. That it couldn't be rushed. Tom bowed out of urging for cuts to it. He knew Schmidt's ideas when he saw them. There were board members who still exalted him; to make them his enemies was counterintuitive.

Once the plan was approved, Nayak's progress happened swiftly. It surprised the senior staff. What helped immensely was the fact that she hadn't been used in performances to the same extent as others. Her learned behaviors consisted of husbandry practices associated with medical monitoring and breeding. Since she wasn't a show animal, there was less training for her to forget. The team turned their focus to other criteria outlined for release.

Prior to their move to the CRI, they'd weaned the orcas off their traditional diet of medicine-laden herring and capelin. Animals marked to spend the rest of their days at the CRI were still supplemented with the drugged fish. Those identified for potential release had them removed from their diet entirely. Instead of the thawed fish they'd grown accustomed to, orcas received live fish fed directly to their pen. Lee had devised this alternative method of feeding. As part of a release, an emphasis was put on captive orcas being able to hunt live fish before being set free. In a perfect world, each ecotype could hunt their preferred prey, but Lee didn't press the issue. Besides the economic challenges of such a program, tourists didn't want to see big-eyed loveable seals mauled daily. It was the same reason zoos didn't release live deer to feed wolves. People were comfortable with a butchered slab of beef being eaten, but casting a fawn into their den to be devoured was inhumane. The fish-feeding system had an enormous advantage: it decreased the orcas' dependence on human interaction. He was proud of his design. The engineers had done an amazing job of bringing it to life.

Stocked daily with the desired fish, they released the food at random intervals throughout the day. Not conforming to a set feeding schedule kept the orcas thinking. When Ed had first explained the random intervals to Lee, he hadn't been entirely honest. Trainers tried their best, but it was easy to fall into a routine. The truly random feeding schedule created by the electronic system was a fantastic means of enrichment and kept them engaged during feeding. Waiting at the surface with their mouths open like birds actually became a thing of the past. Each feeder box could give a low-level electric shock to the fish before sending it into the pens. The stunned fish made for easier hunting. As the orcas adapted, they decreased the voltage. More aware fish made for a more challenging hunt. Nayak transitioned from eating buckets of dead fish to pursuing live ones through the pens around the island. In her years of captivity, she'd never forgotten how to hunt. Only the luckiest mackerel slipped out of the perimeter netting and into the ocean.

The release team was given weekly updates on Nayak's pod from researchers in the northwest. It was a rare instance of Tom allowing collaboration. Moving her up the coast would have been a chore, so when they got an unexpected call from a whale watching group in Monterey Bay that her pod had come much further south than usual, it made sense to jump on the opportunity. The team was skeptical at first. The week before, they had received news that her pod was near the Oregon-California border, but Monterey Bay? After a brief conversation, emails with cell phone pictures were exchanged. Lee used the photographic records on file to confirm they were southern residents. There were salmon fisheries in that region. Orcas hunted their catch before the prey escaped upriver. The timing could not have been more perfect. No one was comfortable opening the gates and letting Nayak swim off alone. Transporting her to the Pacific Northwest would be a formidable undertaking. They prepared for months; it was an exceedingly rare opportunity.

As part of her release plan, Nayak was trained to follow a specially designated boat. Christened the *Shepherd*, it had the sole purpose of being used for reintroduction. The team conditioned Nayak to follow only the *Shepherd*. This safeguarded against the development of an unhealthy fascination with watercraft. Other orcas selected for release underwent similar conditioning. They received daily contact from humans for much of their lives, learned that humans equaled a chance to get fed. An orca that chased trawlers or jet skis in search of a meal wouldn't last long. The easiest way for an orca to end up dead after being released was to get run over. Starvation was also a genuine possibility. Nayak learned to ignore boats except the *Shepherd*, which she dutifully shadowed. Once they were within range of her pod, the engines were cut and Nayak had to make the ultimate journey home. It was up to her to leave the guide boat and rejoin her pod.

On the day of her release, Nayak warily circled the *Shepherd* as the boat stopped a few hundred yards south of Monterey Bay. Lee crouched in the pilothouse next to other members of the team. Before they led her to Monterey, Lee instructed the crew to remain hidden from Nayak. They needed to avoid giving her unintended signals or interest.

"Peek out the window. Is she still circling?" Lee whispered to the trainer closest to the window. He carefully tilted his head. Nayak was logging right off the bow. The trainer ducked his head back below like a soldier in a trench.

"She's stopped," he returned in a whisper. Lee's legs ached from crouching. Lactic acid built up in his muscles. Slowly, he leaned against the wall. He signaled to the young crewman across from him, pointing to a headset resting on the console. The headset connected to a hydrophone that dangled beneath the boat. The crewman picked up the headset and mimed as if to throw it to Lee. He suppressed a laugh, maintained a stern face and shook his head no. Satisfied, the crewman shuffled closer and handed him the headset. The ocean was quiet except for scattered background noise.

"Is it on?" he whispered. The crewman nodded. A single confused chirp ran through the silence, followed by a series of clicks that crescendoed and transformed into a high-pitched squeak. The crew remained quiet. Lee waited. "What's she doing now?" he asked. The crewman cautiously checked. No Nayak. Only a whitecap where the animal had dived. With a puzzled look, he hunkered back and shrugged his arms. EEKK! Lee ripped the headset from his ears. It was an explosion of sound. He stood causing the surrounding crew to follow suit. Nayak powered along the surface towards the wild orcas. Booming squawks reverberated through the headset resting on his neck.

"Are you getting this?" he asked the wide-eyed crewman who had given him the headset. Like a bobblehead, the boy nodded. This time, the cabin erupted triumphantly, breaking their peace. Cheers and high fives flowed freely.

He worried she wouldn't make it, but he knew she had a first-rate shot. She hadn't been dropped into the ocean without warning. The team had had an opening and had executed the plan flawlessly. Besides, there was her tracking data. If something looked out of sorts with respect to her adjustment to life with her pod, the terms of her release bound Marineworld to step in and help. When the team returned to the CRI, Tom was ecstatic. He didn't bother to congratulate them; instead, he asked a question. "Are you ready for the next one?"

THE LIGHTHOUSE VISITOR

C had Kelly relaxed in the empty restaurant of the CRI. Soon it would be overrun by throngs of tourists. Not yet, though. In the hours before the island opened, it was peaceful. He was serenaded by the sounds of the kitchen preparing for the first service of the day. Servers periodically emerged to straighten the marble-topped tables with fresh silverware and fan-folded napkins. They offered no consideration to the man nestled away in the white leather corner booth. He was a piece of scenery. Chad scrolled through his phone. Images of boats glided by with each swipe. When he'd arrived on the first ferry, a police boat had been escorting a Marlin Heritage sailboat to the mainland. The vessel was beautiful. It stood out from the futuristic yachts that plagued the bay. The simple silhouette and mahogany-trimmed craft had left him inspired. He was so engrossed in his imaginary shopping spree, he didn't notice the trainer that snuck across the dining room. She leaned over the back of the booth until she saw the images on the screen.

"Whatcha doin'?" she asked. Chad scrambled to exit out of the browser window and dropped his phone.

"Shopping," he replied.

"Boats? I didn't know interns made that much. Especially tech guys never at their desk."

"For a trainer, you spend a lot of time away from the animals."

"Got me there. Have you seen your best friend this morning?" she asked. Chad froze.

"Best friend?" he repeated. It was an honest question. He couldn't tell from her tone who she meant to tease him about. He wanted to escape the booth.

"Lee," she said, satisfied with making him adequately uncomfortable.

"Oh, Lee! Yeah, he should be—" Chad stopped himself from spoiling a secret he'd promised to keep.

"Should be where?" she asked.

"I, uh, saw him earlier. Don't know where he is now." He picked up his phone and renewed his search. The trainer waited for him to crack. He fidgeted in the booth to cover the radio next to him, pretended she wasn't there.

"It's like you two dug a secret bunker to hide from work. Tom needs him. If you see him, let him know," she said.

"Secret bunker? The lighthouse?" He couldn't help himself from the slip.

"Why couldn't you just say he was out there?" she asked.

"Because he's not," Chad said.

"If you haven't seen him, how do you know? I'll go check. You could always radio him," she said.

* * *

The southern tip of South Coronado Island was Lee's getaway from tourists that filled up the CRI. The past six months without Schmidt had been difficult. Marineworld hadn't funded the construction to do what was best for the animals; they shuttled tourists from San Diego to the island. At approximately 10:00 a.m. daily, brightly clothed visitors disembarked from the second ferry of the day. The animals enjoyed their new accommodations while the company made a nice profit off the sightseers ready to view the animals in their "natural environment." Lee didn't see a problem with this. It was a win-win. The animals were retired from shows but still received the required care. The tourists viewed the orcas in an educational setting and didn't have to feel guilty about watching them do tricks.

But the small size of the island increased the difficulty of finding a quiet space to work. If he spent time in his office, there never failed to be a special guest who needed a tour, a board member that demanded a signature, or a coworker who wanted advice. When he tried to get actual work done, there would be a knock at his door. The northern half of the island was constantly crawling with people. They emptied from the hotel or museum and occupied their time by watching the sea pens from the outdoor viewing decks or basked in the sun. The southern tip was deserted. Its development wasn't scheduled yet. The lighthouse sat a mile from the main CRI buildings across the unimproved rocky outcrops. On the north side, they cut into them for the constructions of the CRI. Here, they were desolate and toothed, which created a natural barrier against unwanted guests. If that didn't dissuade them, the bull gate with "Under Development" and "Hazardous Terrain" warnings did.

Automated for years, the lighthouse was a blank canvas waiting to be painted. Lee had created his second office there. He'd labored to furnish it with items secretly borrowed from the on-site hotel. No one batted an eye if a single desk or couch turned up missing during the last phase of construction. Orders from the mainland often arrived with broken or missing items. That came with the territory of construction on an island. And they never suspected him as the culprit. Besides, he wasn't taking Marineworld property off the island, just recommissioning it. Hauling the furniture across the knife-edge outcrops to the lighthouse wasn't a simple task, so he enlisted Chad's help. It took little to pry the IT intern away from his work. From what

Lee could tell, Chad finished early most days. This left him ample time to look up surf conditions or new parts for his Jeep. Lee liked him from the start.

When the tourists were tucked away for the night, their work began. Lee and Chad set out from the hotel and lugged the furniture across the stony landscape. An impressive amount of swearing followed. The challenge of the endeavor was the reason the lighthouse hideaway remained minimalist in its interior design. Through their partnership, they acquired a love seat, coffee table, writing desk, and two chairs. In exchange for his discretion, Lee allowed Chad to use the lighthouse to dodge work, as long as he wasn't using it at the time. Lee used the hideaway to get work done, not escape from it. This agreement worked out for both of them. Lee had a secluded space to work. If someone came to his office, they assumed he was off running another errand. He was a busy man. Persistent pursuers chirped him on his radio. Once called, Lee made it to the main building in fifteen minutes.

Chad used the lighthouse for less productive purposes. He finished his work in the first hours of his shift, which gave him ample free time. There were bugs to fix, but with the money dumped into the CRI, few major issues existed in their systems. The most strenuous part of his day was when he explained to helpless administrators they needed to "try shutting it off and turning it back on again." If Chad's cubicle was empty, Lee knew he was sleeping on the couch in the lighthouse. He couldn't care less what Chad was up to. The intern didn't report to him for official Marineworld business, and it wasn't Lee's job to keep track of the interns or what they did during the day. Plus, Chad had helped him build his sanctuary. It was a fair trade.

Lee currently found himself at the writing desk, his bloodshot eyes exhausted from reading over a massive stack of behavior files on Akhlut. He took a break from tracing his finger across the engraved Marineworld logo on the desk to stare towards the sea. He disagreed with Tom's decision. It weighed heavy on his brain. He absently scanned the breakers for signs of a dorsal fin. Nayak's release was a dream, the ideal situation aligned perfectly. When they had put Akhlut back into the ocean, it wasn't as clear-cut. The colossal bull had been the defining mascot of the park for years. Tom had advocated for his release. He'd explained how the company's image would improve if they successfully reintroduced the centerpiece of their empire. If the public saw their crown jewel breaching free, it'd hammer home that corporate priorities had changed. Share prices would crack the stratosphere. Lee pictured Tom's smug smile and hand gestures towards the board of directors. He'd sat through enough of his sales pitches to memorize his arguments.

Lee ran his hand over the well-worn manilla folder that bowed outwards with papers. He regretted filing the log that rested on top of the pile. Outside the lighthouse, white-capped waves crashed. Lee gritted his teeth. He thought of the day when they'd used his own report against him. The sharp crackle of his handheld radio snapped Lee from his reflection. Outside of the main buildings, cell service was terrible in the lighthouse. The easiest way to get ahold of someone was over the company radios. He listened intently for a voice through the speaker.

"Hey, Lee, there's a lady looking for you. She's headed out to the lighthouse now. I wanted to give you a heads-up." Chad's familiar voice beamed through the radio. Lee waited for the transmission to end and pressed a button to respond.

"Wait, who's coming out here? Why are you telling people I'm out here?"

"Stephanie or Sarah, some trainer lady," Chad said. "Look I'm sorry, but she said the boss man sent her to find you." Stephanie or Sarah? Lee went through the trainers in his head. There wasn't a Stephanie or Sarah who worked at the orca stadium. Was it someone who performed with the dolphins? Either way, he wasn't keen on the discovery of his secret office. He gathered the documents spread across the writing desk and stuffed them into a large accordion folder. With it tucked under his arm, he rushed down the spiral staircase towards the exit. Halfway to the door, it dawned on him. He stopped and chirped Chad on the radio.

"Chad. Chad, it wasn't Stacy, was it?" He waited impatiently for the response.

"Yeah, man, it's totally Stacy. Thought I'd surprise you," he chimed back.

She was an orca trainer now but still possessed the remarkable ability to make Lee's brain cease to function. He didn't want to be caught hiding out by her. She'd never let him live it down. He continued his race towards the door. She'd catch him outside. Lots of employees walked the island to take a break. He'd explain he was out for a quick walk. But what had Chad told her? Lee paused at the door and pressed the call button.

"Did you tell her I was 'in the lighthouse' or 'out by the lighthouse?'" Seconds ticked by as he waited for a response.

"Out by, duh. I'm not giving away the hideout," Chad said.

"Thanks," Lee said. He clipped his radio back on his belt and threw the door open. The intensity of the sunlight temporarily blinded him. It was much darker inside. He squinted as his eyes adjusted to the change. When they finally focused, a figure climbed across the rocks towards him. Seeing her in khaki shorts and a blue Marineworld shirt instead of a wetsuit was strange. It was like he'd traveled back in time to the days of his internship. Khakis or a wetsuit, she looked gorgeous. The trainer waved back and forth wildly.

"Hey, Lee!" she called out. Even from the distance, her smile lit up the island. Lee's palms sweated as he contemplated making conversation on the walk back.

"Hi, Stacy!" he fired back as he plopped down on a boulder. She was getting closer. He kept his glances towards her short as he tried to gauge how close she was. She approached the bull gate and headed right for him. Before she arrived, Lee radioed Chad.

"Have I ever told you how much I hate you?" he asked.

"First time today," Chad's voice cracked back over the line. "Tell you girlfriend I said—" Lee hurried to turn the volume lower until it clicked. He lifted his head, right in time to catch Stacy's blue eyes.

"Who do you hate? Me? You don't even look at me while I walk over here?" She brushed his shoulder.

"Just radioing my favorite intern." Lee waved the device in the air. She laughed.

"Chad? He told me you were out here. Tom's looking for a file." No doubt he'd popped his head out his office and told the first person he saw to go find Lee Ingram. He could have sent a worse person to hunt for him.

"Yeah, I was just going for a quick walk around the island." Lee held up the folder.

"Huh, do you always go for walks with your files?" She crunched her brow and stared directly at him. He found the freckles on her cheeks adorable.

"Uh, no." Lee hesitated. At no time could he lie to her.

"You going to give me the tour?" She walked towards the lighthouse.

"Tour of what?" He stood aside as she pulled open the heavy metal door.

"Your clubhouse." She walked in.

Lee weighed his choices. He could bolt to the main building and leave her to explore the lighthouse alone. It was less of a choice and more of a childish outlet. The only real choice was to follow her and share more uncomfortable banter. He made the most of an opportunity.

"Oh my God, what is that?" She stopped as Lee stood in the doorway behind her. A framed photo of Chad with the words "#1 Intern" written across the top in permanent marker hung above the couch.

"Yeah, the, uh, number one intern did the decorating," Lee said as he tugged at his hair.

"I knew you two loved each other, but I had no idea you'd made your own little love nest," she said. Stacy glided up the spiral staircase towards Lee's clandestine office. He followed diligently. She stopped at the top of the stairs, across from the writing desk.

"What a view," she said.

"Yeah, it's much better than my office," Lee noted. "Fewer people to bother me out here." The pair stopped to watch a pair of birds dive towards the crystal-blue Pacific beneath them.

"So, you guys throw parties out here?" Stacy joked as she walked to the exit. Chad had come out for drinks with the trainers before. Lee had yet to attend the festivities.

"Yeah, if you count Chad taking naps and me finishing reports," Lee said.

"You go to all that trouble to build your fort and don't even use it for anything fun?" she asked.

Lee couldn't keep the pace. He tried to think of snappy comebacks, but his mind drew blanks. One day he'd work up the courage to ask her out. Not today, though. It was nice enough to spend a few minutes together. She opened the door and Lee walked behind her. He half-dreaded the walk back. They stood together in the sunshine. Stacy moved towards him.

"I'll make you a deal," she said. "I won't tell anyone about your love nest, but you'll have to do something for me."

Lee blushed; he reverted to being fourteen around her. "What's the deal?" His heart raced.

"I keep my mouth shut, but you have to go back to San Diego tonight," she said, setting the terms.

"Why not? I was planning on going back anyway," he admitted.

"Good, then it's settled," she said.

"What's settled?" Lee said nervously.

"I'm taking you to dinner tonight."

ACCIDENT IN THE PARK

The Pacific Ocean extinguished the last rays of sun as Lee and Stacy relaxed on the patio of the Coastal Basket Bar in San Diego. A golden glow hung in the air as light from the tiki torches on the deck flickered in the sea breeze. An empty bucket of beer sat on the table between them.

"Seriously, you never wonder how they name them?" Stacy asked. "They throw darts at a foreign dictionary."

"I always thought it was a contest. I remember voting for one as a kid," Lee said.

"And where do you think they get those names to begin with? Someone just looks up names from the region of the world based on if they sound good or not. Did you know that Kjetil and Kjell are both men's names?"

"No shit?"

"I didn't know until I was helping a guest from Sweden find a seat in the stadium. He asked me why the girl whale was named after him, then flashed me his passport. His birthday was after hers. I told him his parents probably saw a show and named him after her. We both had a good laugh."

"Okay. Here's one I know you get a million times. But what's it like to swim with them?" Lee asked.

"What, you've never slipped in poolside?" Stacy lifted her drink.

"God no, I'd have a heart attack and die if I didn't drown first," he said.

"Drown?" She leaned across the table.

"Yeah, I've always thought I'd make a good pirate," Lee said. Stacy scrunched her brow.

"What's that mean? You're after the booty?" she asked. Lee laughed uncomfortably.

"It means I don't know how to swim," he said as he picked at the label on his beer.

"Are you serious? You're surrounded by water every day and can't swim?"

"More of a controlled sink, you know?" Lee paused. "Seriously, what's it like?"

Stacy leaned back. "Terrifying. But you can't show fear. With them, it's different from the dolphins or sea lions. More of a thrill, something addicting," she said.

Lee couldn't imagine what part was addicting. He could conceive the terror. Floating in the pool, that wasn't your environment, it was theirs. You were at their mercy. His pitiful doggy paddle wouldn't work if he fell in. Any mistake was a chance for catastrophe. Observing from a distance or reading it in a report was one thing. To be in the pool when it happened was another magnitude entirely. Lee waited for her to continue.

"It sounds corny, but there's a partnership to it. It's weird. They work with you because they want to. We can't make them do anything. You know that. They perform because they want to. It could be for the challenge, something to do. It's like a dance. Only our partners weigh thousands of pounds and can easily kill you. So, it's not ballroom dancing."

"You never look scared," he said.

"It's healthy fear. The day you aren't afraid is the day something will happen." Light from the torches danced in Stacy's eyes. When she'd first saved him from the seagulls, he couldn't fathom how difficult it was to become a trainer, let alone work your way up to performing with the orcas. From the audience's perspective, the only prerequisites were being young, beautiful, and athletic. But it was a constant competition to be at the top. Her interview was a gauntlet compared to his internship. He'd never seen the hiring before the switch to the CRI. Stacy described it as the "Miss San Diego Beauty Pageant she had no business being in." It was the closest she ever came to admitting that she belonged in the real Miss San Diego Beauty Pageant.

She'd finished her studies at UC Santa Barbara, and the thought of returning to landlocked Nebraska hadn't appealed to her. She'd wanted to get away from the Midwest her whole life. Returning there to work as a farm vet was a last resort. One of her roommates heard Marineworld was hiring and let Stacy know. She submitted her application and found herself in a lineup of models keen to get the job. The ones without a biology background or experience with animals were immediately cut. Since she had both, she made it to the next round. For the "talent" portion of the contest, they swam laps underwater for as long as they could before surfacing to breathe. When they finished with that, they dove to the bottom of the main pool and picked up training tools. Then they repeated it. No pageant was complete without the on-stage question, so to cap it off they were given a microphone and asked to describe their favorite animal in the park. She thought she was done for after all the swimming. Somehow, she managed to spend two minutes talking about the differences between dolphins and porpoises. She nailed it and was rewarded with a job at the dolphin stadium. It saved her from the long drive back to Red Cloud.

"What want me to grab another bucket? Maybe some food?" Lee asked.

"Why not? It's Friday," she said. Lee got up to bring the empty bucket to the bar. She stopped him.

"Hey"—her eyes darted towards him from the beach—"you were working when it happened, right?"

Lee's stomach dropped. He hadn't planned to talk about what happened. No one at the park spoke of it. He regretted bringing up the line of questioning at once. The night had gone so well.

"Yeah, I was over the stadium," he responded.

"You ever talk about it?" she asked.

Besides what he had written in the official report, he hadn't said a word. It couldn't hurt to talk. To get things off his chest. She could offer more insight than the counselors Marineworld provided.

"I tell you what, let me get this round, then we'll talk," he said.

Lee returned with a fresh bucket of beer. She looked as perfect in a flowery sundress as her blue work polo and khakis.

"You really want to know?" Lee opened a bottle and slid it across the table to Stacy.

"Only if you want to talk." She took a sip from the beer. "You know Amanda should've worked that night. Ed was covering for her."

"I didn't know." He sat his bottle on the table. Waves softly crashed along the shore. "It was like I wasn't even there. Like I watched it happen to someone else, not Ed."

Lee had had the finest spot in the entire stadium. It was one of the first shows he ran on his own without Schmidt. From his perch, high in the catwalks, he could monitor orcas in each of the separate pools. Visitors clad in a kaleidoscope of colors were filing in through both entrances. Soon they packed the stainless-steel bleachers. Each of them waited the entire day for the main event. While the daytime shows attracted their fair share of crowds, the night shows were a Marineworld trademark. They were a special souvenir to remember forever. The tanks were lit from below. It transformed the pools into milky turquoise gemstones against the blackened night sky. The temperature dropped along with the sun. A refreshing breeze blew through the stadium. Lee surveyed the pools. Kjetil and Kjell floated near the surface in the back pools while Ollju swam in front of the gate that separated them from the stage. The motions reminded Lee of a race car driver keeping his tires warm. There was a whale the trainers could count on for a crowd-pleasing show. He scanned the pools for the others. Finding them was more difficult than normal. The water was cloudy lemonade instead of its usual crystal blue. In the far pool, he finally spotted Kassuq and Akhlut. Kassuq gently bumped the gate as Akhlut swam the boundary. Circling and bumping the gates wasn't a good sign. He reached for his radio.

"Are you guys seeing this in the booth?" He waited for his answer as two trainers streaked out to the far pool. They gave signals to Kassuq and Akhlut to bring them under control.

"Yeah, we're seeing it, Lee. Not sure what's got them so worked up," the radio crackled back.

"What behaviors are those two doing during the show tonight?" he asked.

"Standard show. Flips, breaches, and slide-outs. Kassuq's lined up to do waterwork, including a rocket hop," the voice said.

"Which trainer is paired with him?" Lee asked.

"Looks like Ed." The trainers at the back pool brought Akhlut under control. His pectoral fins dropped, and he received buckets full of ice. Kassuq kept her distance on the opposite end of the pool. A feeling of uneasiness crept over Lee. Something had them riled. Lee switched the radio to the trainer's radio frequency.

"Ed, wave if you can hear me."

The trainer who sloped the buckets of ice into Akhlut's mouth turned and waved to the audience. He pressed the button for his radio, which was dangling from his ear.

"Lucky you caught me. I was just putting my radio away. *Qué pedo?*" Ed asked.

"Our friends are worked up. Are we all right to proceed?" Lee asked.

"Yeah, we got things under control down here. Tell the booth I'll switch the waterwork part to Akhlut. He seems calmer," he said.

"You got it. What's got them so excited?" Lee asked.

"Think it's the water. One of the pumps isn't working. Maintenance knows," Ed said.

"*Aguas!*" Lee tried his best Spanish.

"*Tu español es mierda*," the trainer responded.

He switched to the primary channel as Ed waved to him.

"Booth, just talked to Ed. He's switching the waterwork to Akhlut. I'm fine with it. He has the big boy under control," Lee said.

"Copy that. We'll keep an extra eye on it," the booth said.

Lee settled into his post on the catwalk as the show began. The floodlights dimmed as the massive screen above the main pool played the introduction video. Images of orcas swimming through kelp forests, ice floes, and crashing waves towered over the audience as Marineworld's message of conservation thundered over the loudspeakers. This season's show was titled "Open Ocean." The absurdity of the title wasn't lost on Lee.

"Here at Marineworld, we're committed to sustained conservation efforts. Top scientific studies conducted right here have greatly increased our knowledge of orcas in the wild. This has allowed us to—" Lee repeated the video word for word as he monitored the activity. Trainers unlatched the back gate to let Akhlut and Kassuq into the pool with the others.

The main screen folded away as water cascaded from a faux waterfall. Speakers pumped in thundering splashes and gull noises. A ding of a buoy pierced the air as the host skipped across the stage.

"This is the open ocean!" She waved her hands towards the back pool previously covered by the screen. On cue, Kjetil and Kjell slid through the waterfall into the main pool while Akhlut and Kassuq entered from opposite directions. They darted along the exterior wall, churning up a massive wave that spilled over into the walkway. The audience roared with applause. Trainers poured out from backstage to pair with their designated orca. They glued bright smiles on their faces and threw their hands in the air towards the audience. Lee counted five trainers, but only four whales.

"Booth, Ollju doesn't want to come out and play," he radioed.

"Should be okay, at least she won't tip the kayak. We'll see if we can get someone back there to entice her out," they responded.

Kjetil and Kjell were spraying mouthfuls of water on guests in the front row as the others moved back to the rear pools. Their targets screamed with laughter as the whales alternated above the water like pistons. Each pump brought a fresh jet of water. They earned a few fish as a reward before being waved off for the next part of the show. The stadium lowered as images flashed on the divided screen.

"The coastal waters of Washington are known for their abundant wildlife, including orcas. Some of the most widely studied pods are from this region." A foggy coastline materialized on the screen. A kayaker in a bright orange life vest navigated through rocky outcrops. Whales elegantly cut through the water beneath him. This was Lee's favorite part of the show. As the kayaker reached the corner of the screen, a kayak with a trainer appeared from behind in perfect synchronization with the image. Movie magic. The trainer paddled towards the center of the pool as Kassuq torpedoed out in pursuit. Lee held his breath as the animal approached the kayak. Kassuq erupted from beneath the surface and breached over the kayak as the trainer stared up in astonishment. She executed the behavior perfectly. Audience members whooped and hollered their approval.

During the early rehearsals, it wasn't that easy. To make sure the shows ran smoothly, they tried to train most show orcas on each behavior. That way, if an animal didn't feel up to performing, another could replace it. Ollju was the first whale trained on this behavior because she performed show-stopping breaches on cue. First an empty kayak was used to get the animals acclimated to a foreign object in the water. Desensitization at its finest. Ollju performed the breach perfectly each time the kayak was empty. With a trainer placed inside, it was a different story. At practices, Ollju refused to breach. Instead, she'd speed towards the kayak, then dive with a flick of her tail. The resulting swell had enough force to flip the kayak. Ollju circled the trainer, waiting for another cue before coming under control. Lee asked Schmidt about the behavior.

"Hunting behavior. Plain and simple. Ollju's from southern waters." It was commonplace for orcas in the Antarctic to choose this tactic. They used the technique to knock seals off ice floes. "They aren't leaving that in the show?" he asked.

"Yeah, they are. She doesn't bother the trainer once they're in the water," Lee said.

Mark's voice was exasperated. "Does management even think when things like this happen? I know you don't have much pull, Lee, but try to get them to cut that shit."

"It's not that bad. We get a nice breach or she'll push the trainer to the stage. Crowd goes nuts either way."

"They're asking for trouble."

Lee shook the conversation with Schmidt from his brain as he watched the show. It was time for the grand finale. Ed and the other trainer treaded water on opposite sides. The black outlines of orcas zipped beneath them. They dove the forty feet to the belly of the pool while the trainers floated above. Lee waited for the spectacle. The trainers were set to do a rocket hop with their partners. The orcas propelled themselves from the bottom of the tank to throw the trainers into the air with their rostrum. Trainers capped off the display by performing a front flip or swan dive back into the water. Because the trick was so physically demanding, only the most seasoned trainers were asked to do it. They had to position their feet precisely to receive the push. It required significant trust between the animal and performer. The whale needed to travel at a specific speed and trajectory. Ed slapped the surface while waiting for the push. The slap on the water was a sign; it meant "stop what you're doing and come to the surface." It was the trainer equivalent of whistling to call a dog back. Something was wrong.

As he treaded water in the cloudy pool, Ed peered to the bottom to locate Akhlut. He needed to know where the orca came from. If he mistimed the hop, it guaranteed him an injury. Fractured ribs would put him out for weeks. He picked out the shape of Akhlut's back under him and prepared himself. Akhlut stared back at him. The orca waited for the signal with his mouth agape. His white teeth shined clearly in the murkiness. Ed's heart thudded in his chest. He slapped the water sharply and looked for support from his fellow trainers. He could try to swim to the slide-out, but there was no way he could make it before Akhlut. It'd be best to get him under control. He slapped again. At the floor of the pool, Akhlut snapped his jaw closed. With a nod he pushed himself upwards. Ed adjusted his feet. He expected a rush as he catapulted gracefully through the air. Akhlut split his legs apart as he broke the surface.

Instead of gently sailing, Ed cartwheeled through the air. His arms flailed as he careened towards the other trainers on the stage. Lee turned away at the last moment, but he couldn't close his ears to the sound. His body hitting the slide-out echoed through the arena like a bag of wet meat dropped from a balcony. There was an abrupt snap as his arm folded underneath him and his head ricocheted off the ground. The crowd gasped in horror. Ed's crumpled body lay in the shallow water. Violent tremors coursed through his frame. Each spasm elicited fresh shrieks from the crowd. Blood dribbled from his head as trainers waded towards him. Cheery music blared as ushers herded the guests towards the exits. Akhlut made a lap around the outside of the pool after the failed trick. He swam towards Ed. A trainer grabbed him underneath the arms and dragged him backwards off the stage. Akhlut pursued the pair through the shallow water until they were out of reach. Lee's radio crackled with emergency messages from the booth and stage. Frantic shouts drowned out by joyful melodies. He was helpless on his perch. The trainers pulled Ed backstage and out of sight. Ushers cleared the audience from the stadium. The wails of an ambulance competed with the music from a distance. Waves churned by Akhlut's motions mixed Ed's blood with the cloudy water. In a matter of moments, the water returned to its original hue. Cloudy, but turquoise. Not a trace of blood.

Lee finished his last swig of beer as he met Stacy's gaze from across the table. "It was like nothing had ever happened. Trainer error, right?"

ROUTINE MAINTENANCE

The sun beamed brightly on the Coronados the next day as Mike Fischer closed out his shift. Part of a team of certified divers employed at the island, Mike's job was to keep the underwater sea pens in perfect shape. Nets needed to be adjusted, patched, or re-anchored. Gates and moorings required welding or repairs. It was demanding, but for what the company paid he didn't complain. He'd come a long way from cleaning barnacles off pleasure crafts in the bay. Mike unzipped his wetsuit as he slid into his computer terminal. He entered the repairs he'd conducted that day. A red-flagged email labeled "Sector A6 Central Island–Potential Repair" sat in his inbox. The clock showed half past four; surely it could wait until the morning? He ignored the email and continued with the Marineworld Maintenance program. Furiously typing, he was startled when his radio went off.

"Mike, do you check your emails?"

He sighed as he returned the transmission. "Yeah, Rick, what's up? Something about A6?"

"Did you read it?"

Lying, saying he had, and waiting till morning crossed his mind. Mike's finger rested on the call button while he calculated his response.

"I know you didn't, I asked for a read receipt when you opened it. Do me a favor and look at it," Rick said.

He begrudgingly opened the email. It was an urgent message showing pen A6 needed to be inspected ASAP for damage.

"Reading it now. You want me to check on A6? It's almost five."

"Yeah, I was out there earlier. The gate shifted. Have a peek at it. You won't even need to get wet."

"Can do."

Mike zipped his wetsuit and headed out. No matter what Rick said, he'd need to dive to confirm there was damage. It was a quick walk from the floating piers to the A6 workshop, ten minutes to get his gear checked, and another fifteen to check the gate. Add in the extra time to write up the report and he could still make it off the island on the 7:00 p.m. ferry. A few hours of overtime wouldn't hurt his paycheck. He scurried across the piers. The water conditions were great, unlimited visibility.

"Where you headed in such a hurry?" Mike's dive partner Terry called to him as tried to sneak past on the walkway.

"A6. Rick wants me to check something out," he said.

"I'll come with you. Can't go jumping in alone."

"It's fine. I won't even get wet."

"If you're sure. I'm trying to catch the five thirty off this rock."

"Get out of here," Mike said.

Terry gave a mock salute as Mike brushed past him. The workshop hut sat on piers above the water ahead. He decided the best course of action was to walk the perimeter of the pen and check the gate first. Mike understood his partner's concern. The gate for A6 was the only direct connection to the ocean. They only placed animals in A6 before reintroduction. Neither of them would have a job much longer if one found their way out. But it wasn't an issue because none were scheduled for release. The last one had been set loose months ago. He approached the gate from the catwalk. Right away, he noticed the floating markers sat offset. They weren't close to being in position.

"Son of a bitch." He slung his head low as he trudged to the workshop to pick up his dive gear. So much for not getting wet. Terry's voice burst from his radio while he pulled an air tank from the equipment rack.

"All good out there? You still dry?" he asked.

"Yeah, still dry. See you in the a.m.," Mike said.

He loaded a cart to wheel out to the gate. It was stupid to enter the pen from the workshop portal, then swim out. As he was exiting the dive shack, his radio sprang to life once again. This time it was Rick's voice.

"You got eyes on it yet?"

"Just from topside, it looks way off. Going to see if there's damage. We might have to send a team out here in the morning to close it. Make sure management knows to keep the animals out until then."

"Will do. Terry with you?" Rick asked.

"Of course," he said.

"You boys be careful. We'll send a full team out tomorrow."

"Don't worry, I won't fix it myself." Mike stood on the pier above the gate and put on his gear. He tightened his connections and checked his dump valves were working. His BC held air and his tank was secured. He double-checked the air was on. Mike inspected his gauges for pressure and frowned. Only enough air for twenty minutes. He considered walking back to get a different cylinder, but it would take too long. Both his primary regulator and octopus were fine. He buckled in and prepared to dive.

"Well, Terry, double-check, am I ready?" He turned to the empty pier before sliding off into the blue-green water. Visibility was clear to the seafloor. Calm. Gently kicking his fins, he approached the gate and started his inspection. It sat roughly thirty feet below the surface in the middle of netting. Anchored to the bottom, it didn't appear damaged. The posts and netting that surrounded it were intact. He let off a stream of bubbles as he moved towards the hinges. It was completely out of the upper hinge, leaving it ajar to the ocean. He paddled through to have a better look and checked for signs of damage. There didn't appear to be any. The gigantic bolts that held it in place were missing. It was odd. There hadn't been a storm in weeks. Someone should have noticed it earlier.

A crack rolled through the water. The sound thudded dully in Mike's chest. He kicked to get away. A few hundred pounds of steel would crush him if it fell off the hinges entirely. As he floated with distance between him and the gate, the surrounding silence became deafening. It was quiet as the moon. His own breath echoed in his eardrums. He wheeled around to his imaginary dive partner.

"Scared by a gate! Glad you didn't see that!"

An extra ten-minute dive, off the island by seven, and a few hours overtime couldn't be beat. Waves gently rocked above him as he ascended. His goggles were right beneath the waterline when he felt a tug on his leg. He spat out his regulator and screamed a stream of bubbles.

The orca held his dive fin with a vise grip. His heartbeat quickened until it felt like it would break through his ribs. He writhed in the animal's gaping maw. An immobile statue, the animal remained locked in place. It didn't register the movements of the human in its massive frame. Mike stretched. His goggles pierced the water to give him a view of the walkway. He felt the wind on his forehead before he was yanked below like a chew toy. Five feet down, ten feet down. It hauled him to the bottom. Fifteen feet, twenty feet. He struggled to jam his regulator back in his mouth. Twenty-five feet down, thirty feet down. He closed his eyes and kicked at the beast with his free leg.

It released its grasp without warning. The dive fin that tethered them snapped. Mike recoiled away. The orca bobbed its massive head as it tracked him. He paddled hard and rose. This was his chance. Twenty feet down, fifteen feet down. The black of the orca loomed beneath him. It took two powerful strokes of its tail to catch him. This time, the hold was on his right dive flipper. He was drawn to the bottom again. This was a cruel game of tug-of-war for the creature. A game it would win. When the pair reached depth, this dive fin held strong. Mike tried to remain calm. He took a breath from his regulator and checked his gauge. Seven minutes of air left. Whatever he was going to do, he had to do it fast. His wouldn't survive another trip back to the depths. Adrenaline coursed through his veins. He had his dive knife. His hands were free to grab it. A few jabs would teach it that he wasn't prey. Or it could enrage it. He crunched his body forward, bringing it closer to the animal's eye, closer to its teeth. One quick thrust and then a race to the surface. He reached for the handle of his knife. There was nothing. The sheath was empty. It must have fallen during the struggle somehow. His backup plan was less violent.

Mark leaned in and caressed the tip of its snout. He remembered trainers used the same motion. On cue, it let out a few happy clicks. With its mouth open, Mike was free once again. Rows of teeth sinisterly smiled at him. Against his instinct, he didn't kick towards the surface like his life depended on it.

This time, the orca broke first. Its white underbelly flew past the top of his head. It swam figure eights silhouetted by the sun. Cautiously, Mike swam towards the dislodged gate. He kept his eyes on the orca above him. There was a booming slap as it breached. If he made it through, he could put a barrier between them. He easily slipped past the opening and steadily climbed. The orca finished his lap above him and renewed its pursuit. He needed to reach the platform, to taste the fresh air. A terrifyingly familiar feeling seized his leg as he surfaced and coughed.

A single breath of air was all he was allowed before it wrenched him under. His freedom faded. Waves rocked further above his head. He struggled, but it was futile. This was his last dive, and he was powerless to stop it.

SECOND TRY

With the success of Nayak's release, Tom's lobbying had convinced the board that Akhlut could be their next achievement. Not even Schmidt had considered releasing the animal during the original assessments. And after what had happened to Ed in the show in San Diego, Lee didn't want to set him loose either. But he was inexperienced, and Schmidt didn't work there anymore. As far as the board was concerned, Tom had the only opinion that mattered. He argued for a reconsideration and got it.

Like Nayak, the company had rescued Akhlut, but they'd held him since the 1980s. Whereas Nayak was a southern resident orca, Akhlut was a transient. Lee had used the differences in diet and pod structure to sway the company away from releasing Akhlut. Schmidt had tried the exact argument before him. For Akhlut's entire life at Marineworld, he had known nothing but eating fish. Before his rescue, he'd feasted on a variety of seafaring mammals. Because he was a transient, Marineworld couldn't locate his original pod. No orca in captivity had ever integrated into a new pod. The likelihood of it happening was infinitesimal. Lee pleaded with the company higher-ups to keep Akhlut at the sanctuary. While it wasn't ideal, at least he wouldn't die by himself out in the ocean. He tried to appeal to the PR of it. Forget Nayak—what if the company released its star, only to have his rotted carcass wash up on a beach months later? Tom effortlessly swatted away Lee's concerns. Lee didn't have Schmidt's voice in the room. There were precautions put in place, tracking devices, they could step and rescue him if things really went south. Before Akhlut's release plan had been finalized, Tom set up one last meeting with Lee to go over the details. One key behavior log was the only ammo Tom had needed to convince the board that reintroduction was viable and he wanted to discuss it with the new Head of Cetacean Behavior.

It had been scheduled weeks in advance, but Lee dreaded the interaction. Meetings with Tom were strikingly similar no matter who attended. If you were a trainer or a janitor, they ended the same. Once you entered Tom's office, you presented your side, there was a brief discussion, then he went ahead with doing what he'd originally planned. Historically, there was zero probability of changing his mind.

Lee had entered the office that day with a printed outline of topics in his hands.

"Lee! How's it going today? Have a seat." Tom motioned to the black leather chair across from his. A plastered-on smile and enthusiasm disarmed the best-prepared employees. If Tom brought you into his office to fire you, you thanked him after he itemized your transgressions.

"It's going good," Lee said. He had slid uncomfortably into the chair. The bleached jaws of a great white shark hung on the wall directly behind Tom's desk. This toothy decoration served as the office's sole embellishment. Tom glanced at his watch as he sat.

"Good! So, are you ready to discuss the reintroduction of our orcas?" His voice boomed through the room.

"As ready as I'll ever be," Lee said.

"All right, let's dive in!" Lee rolled his eyes before he froze. He hoped his boss didn't catch it. The insincerity in his voice was palpable. "As we've gone over before, looking out for the welfare of our animals comes first. We need to keep sending a sound message that we're not the Marineworld of the 1970s."

Lee did his best to focus. He heard that exact line dozens of times. "We are not the Marineworld of the 1970s" had become Tom's unofficial mantra to the staff. It made matters worse that the air-conditioning in the office wasn't working properly. For all the money they dumped into the CRI, some things weren't running perfectly yet. Not a single drop of sweat beaded on Tom's forehead. Lee adjusted his tie and held the outline.

"We know Nayak was an ideal candidate for reintroduction, but we have serious concerns about Akhlut."

"She's doing wonderful out there. We can't thank you enough for the work you put in. I think we can say it's a done deal with her." Tom stared at his watch. "I'm more than happy to hear your concerns. What are you thinking?"

Lee straightened up in his seat and leaned forward. "Well, uh, we've taken into consideration every piece of data at our disposal," he read from the paper in front of him. Tom stared blankly at Lee. "In theory it could work, but it would be a lot of work. Akhlut's healthy, but his wild diet doesn't match what we've been feeding him for years. There have been no attempts to retrain transients on hunting behavior." Lee was running full speed through his points now. "Not to mention that he's had aggressive and fatal encounters with humans in the past. We also take into consideration that they travel in—"

"Let me stop you," Tom interjected. "We fully support the conclusions your team has reached on every other whale." He waved his hand around like the conductor of an invisible orchestra. "The capital required to move them would be astronomical. I hear your concerns for Akhlut, I really do. But I've been looking over this recent behavior log." There was a manila folder positioned on the middle of the desk. Lee had been so caught up in his script he hadn't noticed the file. It was instantly recognizable; the edges were beginning to wear from constant opening. He'd memorized it. "Lee, this log details the hunting behavior you're concerned with, does it not?"

Lee ran his fingers through his hair nervously before he spoke. "Yes. It details... behavior I observed earlier this year."

"I've read the report." Once more he flashed a smile that mirrored the jaws on the wall behind him. "A few times, actually. Would you be able to give me a rundown, firsthand?"

"Uh, yeah, sure. But this was a onetime event. We've seen nothing like it since," Lee said.

"Sure, sure, sure, that's definitely under consideration. Please go on," Tom said.

"That morning I was observing Akhlut in the pen located to the west of the island. He was spy-hopping and investigating where the anchors attach to the central island. Something caught his eye."

"And?" Tom asked.

"There was a group of sea lions splashing around the pen. They were careful to stay on the northern side of the island, outside of the enclosure. They saw Akhlut, but they weren't concerned. Maybe they knew the netting contained him. Hell, they might have taunted him by speeding along the fence. Sea lions are smart, maybe they made a game out of provoking him," Lee said. Tom impatiently waited for him to continue. "One on the rocks. It lost its balance and fell into the pen. Akhlut"—Lee paused—"he went after it."

"Did he go after the sea lion or attack it?" Tom asked. He had Lee right where he wanted him.

The strike came as a shock. He'd observed the orcas in captivity. He wasn't particularly clear on what their natural behaviors were. Sure, he researched them. He'd spent long hours in discussion with Schmidt, but he hadn't seen them for himself. Lee was familiar with minor aggressive behaviors towards trainers. It was alarming at first, but it became routine. Hardly a week passed without an animal that motioned towards a trainer with its mouth wide, or kept one from exiting a pool. Minor incidents made his heart skip a beat. He couldn't fathom how they shook it off and continued their work. To them it was part of the job. A few shouldered the blame for aggressions on themselves. It was their fault for frustrating the whale. Marineworld leaned into this line of thinking. With the precautions, the manuals, the training, these minor aggressions were accepted. There was Ed's accident, but that was dismissed as "trainer error." The attack on the sea lion wasn't a minor aggression.

The speed and brutality were awe-inspiring. As soon as the sea lion broke the surface, Akhlut dashed beneath the waves. It resurfaced and nosily barked at its accomplices safely above. Lee remembered thinking the worst-case scenario was sending a team to free the animal from the pen. It was impossible to scale the sheer rock face.

Without warning, there was a great geyser of water from Akhlut's tail flukes as they thrashed violently skyward. His entire body was horizontal, presenting the white underside of his belly. The sea lion hurtled thirty feet into the air. It flipped and twirled over itself like a gymnast. A refrain of barks came from the sea lions huddled on the island. Their necks were pointed towards the heavens as they focused on their helpless colleague. With a crack, it bounced off the rock face and plummeted to the sea. Lee grimaced as the body went limp and collided with the waves. The earsplitting barks from the rocks grew shrill. Their ill-fated friend floated lifelessly. Akhlut resurfaced, barely disturbing the water. He tenderly grasped a back flipper in his jaws. It twitched to life and flayed, spraying a fine mist onto the rocks. It was too late. The orca dragged its writhing meal underwater to finish the kill.

A steely chill ran down Lee's spine. How did trainers volunteer to get in the pool with them? He watched every show. They were a game of Russian roulette. It was far easier to push the idea out of his mind than answer it. It was a miracle Ed's was the only major accident that involved an orca.

"You still with me?" Tom stared at him across the desk.

"Yeah, yeah. I must've lost my train of thought for a second," Lee said.

"You were just describing how Akhlut attacked a sea lion, his natural prey. You don't think this behavior is something he'd continue regularly?"

"I'm, uh, not sure. Like I said, I think it was a onetime event." Lee wasn't concerned with Akhlut being able to hunt. He knew he could do it. Instead, his mind lingered on what happened to Edgar Morales.

"We'll take your opinion into consideration, Lee. Remember, we're not deciding today," Tom said. He snapped him a last grin. That flash of white told Lee what he needed to know. Tom had already decided.

Akhlut had been reintroduced during the sixtieth-anniversary celebration, and there was nothing Lee could have done to change Tom's mind.

OPEN INVESTIGATION

"Can you please explain to me how this could happen?" Tom fumed but held his calm demeanor. He grilled Terry McAndrew and Rick Parker. Mike's body had been discovered in pen A6 when the maintenance team had been dispatched to repair the gate in the morning.

"Tom, we followed procedure. It was just a horrible accident," Rick said from across the table.

"Our procedure is very strict. No one gets in the water alone. That's a breach of protocol right there," Tom said.

"Mike told me he was with Terry and they were prepping to check the gate before they ended for the day. I didn't think he'd lie to me," Rick said.

"And, Terry, where were you while he was diving?" Tom asked.

"I was on the ferry back to the mainland," Terry said. He sat four feet from Tom but was a million miles away. The sensitive bastard was probably thinking of Mike's wife and kids. Tom had only considered how he'd have to pay them.

"So, he broke procedure and did a solo dive to investigate the damage, correct?" Tom's voice grew louder than he intended. It shook Terry from his thoughts.

"That's what it looks like," Terry said. Intrusive thoughts pried their way into his mind. *He* should have stuck around for the dive. His partner would still be alive. To run out of air was a miserable way to go. Your last gasps begged for a breath of fresh air, only to be betrayed by mouthfuls of salty brine.

Tom inhaled deeply before he spoke again.

"Look, this is tough. I completely understand if either of you need to take some time."

Terry nodded softly.

"Have you both completed your written statements?" Tom asked.

"I'll make sure they're in by the end of the day," Rick said.

By now, the San Diego County Coroner was on his way. Tom needed to make the call to OSHA. Mike was a skilled worker, but his accident put the park in a precarious position. Two deaths within a year. If they didn't crucify the company, the media would. Thank God there was no animal involved this time. It had taken everything in Marineworld's power to stay solvent after Ed Morales. The only thing that kept them satiated after the incident was the construction of the CRI and the scheduled orca release program.

He ran through the details of Mike's accident before he picked up the phone. It was cut and dried. He had gone in without a dive partner, which was against procedure, lied to his boss, and drowned. What had happened in between was worrisome. When the maintenance crew had fished the body out of A6, Mike's tank had been empty. Dive equipment was well maintained and checked regularly. At least, it was supposed to be. If his equipment was faulty on a routine dive, even during a solo dive, it would blow back on the company. Tom's only concern was how to pin the blame on the diver. He lifted the receiver. It was a quick, all business. With workplace fatalities, there was an eight-hour window in which they needed to be reported. Then there was the on-site inspection, and an incident report was typed up based on the information gathered. Unfortunately, Tom was familiar with the procedure. OSHA informed him a representative was on the way out at once. That was new. Something unexpected. He'd handle it regardless. With the ferry schedule, the inspector wouldn't arrive until later that afternoon. He undid his tie and stuffed it in the top drawer of his desk. There was plenty of time to meet the coroner at A6 before the inspector arrived.

Tom began his deliberate march to the pen. After two successful releases, to have the facility shuttered by OSHA would be a nightmare. Closing for one day meant a monumental loss of revenue. All because an idiot diver hadn't followed company protocol. He smiled at the groups of tourists he passed. The man's family was fortunate. They'd receive a massive payout. Cutting a check was the quickest way to avoid long-term ramifications. In his time, Tom had dished out hefty settlements. Unfortunate accidents led to others being more fortunate. Since this moron had drowned himself, Tom didn't intend to dole out payment in the realm of what they'd given Ed's family..

A single security guard acted as the sentry outside the A6 workshop.

"Good morning, Mr. Walsh," the guard said. He maintained his stiff posture as he spoke.

"No one's been in there since earlier?" Tom asked.

"No one, sir," he said.

Tom forged ahead without another word. He didn't need to ask permission or give a reason for being there. The slatted bamboo shades swayed behind him as he shut the door. Per his orders, maintenance had placed the body inside the workshop. At his feet lay the outline of a man wrapped in a thick blue tarp. It looked like a child hiding under a blanket, only Tom knew Mike wouldn't leap up to surprise him. Stupid bastard. His gear was stacked in a neat pile next to him. Tom doubted Marineworld hired the best of the best. They hadn't listened when he'd told them not to touch his equipment after they hauled him out of the pen.

It made things easier to investigate, though. He needed to be quick. If the coroner caught him alone with the body, it would raise suspicion.

Tom reached into a stall and pulled out a pair of neoprene dive gloves. He donned them to inspect the pile of gear while he kept a safe distance from the actual body. It was out of an abundance of caution. A crime scene investigation unit wasn't coming to dust the workshop, but a single fingerprint was too much to leave. You could never be too careful. He started his search with the dive tank. His maintenance crew weren't liars—it was empty. He spun it in place and checked the regulator and gauges. They appeared in decent working order. Odd. There was only one dive fin. What the hell had happened? No signs of damage on the other equipment. It didn't add up. Tom looked over his shoulder towards the door. He was running out of time.

He ripped the tarp back. Grotesque images of a distended face, deep lacerations, and gashes poured through his mind. Who knew what had taken a bite of his bloated corpse as it floated in the pen overnight. Tom slowly opened his eyes. His imagination betrayed him. There was nothing outlandish about the body. He could be sleeping peacefully. Tom paused before he removed the cover completely. There had to be nothing. Nothing on the body that refuted a drowning. He carefully examined the body and was more relieved with each passing moment. No fresh wounds, no trauma. His wetsuit wasn't torn. It was astounding he'd spent the evening in the ocean and remained intact. Satisfied with his investigation, Tom covered the body. He scanned the workshop before he peeled off the dive gloves and tossed them into a locker. It was a clean case. With fully functioning gear, this moron had drowned. A new thought occurred to him. Maybe he had been drunk? That would be perfect.

Tom exited the workshop and stood next to the guard.

"It's a shame. Poor guy had two kids." Tom hung his head. He clasped his hand across his mouth and yawned. The salty air smelled infinitely more pleasant than the damp body. "You want to grab a quick break while we wait for the coroner?" he asked.

"Yeah, I've been holding it in for a while. Thanks." The guard shuffled off to the maintenance building. Tom trusted him to return before the coroner arrived. It looked better if he was present. Tom teetered on the catwalk as he approached the gate. He wanted to assess the damage before the crew returned for repairs. Tom stopped in his tracks. Something familiar churned his stomach. A small black box that sported a plastic antenna was trapped against the underside of the walkway. The pit of despair in his gut widened further. Anyone else would dismiss it as a floating piece of trash. Tom knew better. Each wave threatened to jar the device loose from its unstable position. He couldn't let that happen. He calmly moved across the catwalk and thrust his arm into the water. He searched around until he felt the tracking device lodged against the decking. With a peek over his shoulder, he retrieved it.

Bits of flesh clung to the surgical titanium pins. There was a yearning inside him. He tried to convince himself it belonged to an orca from the pens. He imagined the device with only two pins. Orcas destined for a lifetime of retirement were tracked with two pinned tags. No matter how many times he counted, there were three. He was well aware which animal it belonged to. But Tom was certain Mike had drowned. There was no doubt it was a pure accident. He brought his arm back and prepared to cast the tag into the sea. Instead, he dropped his hand. If the tag was still transmitting, that could be an issue. It sent a signal until the battery ran out. Wild allegations would follow if the wrong person discovered it and asked questions about the data. Marineworld's share price would take a nosedive.

Something needed to be done. He retreated to the seclusion of the workshop. He was in a race against time again. Tom paid no attention to the body as he went straight to the rack of dive gear. The noise he was about to make was a calculated risk. He removed a dive tank, raised it above his head, and swung it downward, smashing the tag. Undamaged, it glared at him. Tom attacked with a violent fury. Someone could catch him at any moment. Each blow had more force than the last until the sharp snap of the plastic housing rang out. He searched the floor for pieces of the device that might have flown off. Satisfied the only damage was a great crack in the housing, he returned the dive tank to its place on the rack. That would do the trick. Tom wiped the sweat from his brow and cautiously exited with the remains of the tag.

There was no sign of the security guard or coroner. Without wavering, he tossed the tag over the railing. Saltwater flowed into the housing. The electronics inside were destroyed as it sank to the seabed. A thin trail of bubbles rose as it descended. Tom concentrated on the stream. He waited for the last bubble to burst.

"Sorry, I"—the guard advanced down the catwalk—"I took so long." He tried to catch his breath from the hustle over. Tom's eyes locked on the spot where the tracking tag landed. He willed it to vanish before he greeted the guard.

"That's fine! Any word on the coroner?" Tom should have taken a radio with him. They'd probably tried to reach him in his office.

"Yes, sir, he's on his way. We're escorting him out here now," the guard said.

"Perfect," Tom responded.

* * *

Lee quietly typed at his desk. He hardly registered that a meeting had occurred in Tom's office. It was an easy Saturday. He'd slogged away at his computer for hours, grinning through the tedium as he pecked at the keys. The night with Stacy had gone as well as he could have hoped. Not exactly the conversation he'd planned, but it had been a relief to talk about the accident. His phone next to his keyboard beckoned. Should he text her? Was it too soon? Maybe he should play it cool. There was a tap at his door.

"Co—" Before he finished, Chad let himself in and closed the door behind him. Lee couldn't say hi before he started talking.

"Dude, did you hear what's going on?"

Lee looked up from his phone and shook his head. "Why do you just barge in here?"

"Why not?"

"Maybe I'm doing important work."

"Yeah, and maybe you're texting the sexy trainer."

"Shut up," Lee dismissed him. "What's up?"

"A maintenance guy drowned in one of the pens. A6, I think."

"What? When?"

"Don't know, coroner from the mainland came in on the ferry."

"That's horrible. Who was it?"

"Don't know that either. I'll let you know when I hear more." Chad ducked his head out before reemerging. "Should I text Stacy for you before I leave?" he asked.

"Get out." Lee pointed towards the door.

Chad slipped out of Lee's office as fast as he'd come. For an intern, he had a remarkable talent for collecting morsels of gossip. Lee wasn't close with the members of the maintenance crew. He greeted them with a quick hello or wave as he made his way to conduct observations. They weren't around when orcas were in the pens. Two deaths in a year. Unbelievable. The high-pitched whine of the air-conditioning compressor abruptly stopped. The temperature in the office rose. He had no desire to sit there waiting for the compressor to cycle back. Lee hurried to read a new message from Stacy on his phone. In the empty office, no one saw him smile as he got up to leave. He added a stop at the medical pool to his schedule before making his rounds.

* * *

"Washington, huh?" Amanda suppressed a laugh as she unpacked the supplies in front of her. After the veterinarian left the lab, she was free to express her disbelief openly.

"Yes, Washington." Stacy nodded. She'd worked with Amanda long enough to know she wouldn't believe it until she had one foot out the door.

"I just don't see it, Stace. You, holed up in a tiny shack, stuck in the pouring rain, listening to orca sounds." She moved her fingers above Stacy's head to mime rain.

"What's so hard to believe?" Stacy asked.

"You, huddled in a sleeping bag, surrounded by filthy grad students?"

"My thesis is on orca vocalizations!" Exasperated, Stacy finally cracked. The two laughed before an uncomfortable silence engulfed the lab. As it settled, the door to the lab swung open.

"Are we ready to"—the vet hesitated, having the unsettling feeling that the girls were gossiping—"start with the bloodwork?"

"First kit is good and ready to go." Amanda handed him the cooler of prepared supplies. "We'll be out to help in a second." The tech exited towards the pool. It was the only thing he could do to distance himself from the discomfort. She waited for the door to click closed before she continued, "Have you put in your notice yet?"

"No, not yet."

Stacy planned to submit it soon. She was committed to leaving Marineworld. A draft of her notice waited in her outgoing messages folder. Stacy had memorized it. She read it each morning right after the other emails she received from OAR, the same group that Schmidt had sent the audio recordings to. Their initial skepticism had dwindled when they'd received his letter of recommendation. It was a glowing endorsement. Before his correspondence, they'd believed they were admitting a flighty entertainer into their ranks. Her degree didn't matter; to them she was part of the problem. Another ditzy blonde who had grown up with colorful dolphin posters on her wall. Whatever Schmidt had written squashed that idea. The follow-up email had been warm and inviting. Ellen Hayes, the lead researcher, had outlined potential arrival dates that worked for the group. Teams of researchers rotated biweekly as their schedules allowed, but the main nucleus of OAR remained to ensure that the overall vision of the group stayed on track. Stacy wanted to integrate into the project during a transition to avoid disrupting the ongoing studies. While the position wasn't paid, OAR got a slice of funding from the National Science Foundation. Her savings from Marineworld needed to last until she got accepted into a funded fellowship program. She meticulously budgeted for conceivable expenses and then some.

"Well? What are you waiting for?" Amanda asked. "I'll survive without you."

"The right time," Stacy said.

"That's bullshit and you know it," Amanda laughed.

"I'm serious," she said.

Amanda stared at her, not blinking.

"What? Why wouldn't I leave? I can't dive into tanks forever. I've seen enough broken ribs and wrecked sinuses to know it isn't a long-term career. How many fifty-five-year-old trainers do we have?" Stacy asked.

There was a part of Stacy that didn't want to leave. Even if she wouldn't admit it. It was the same reason Amanda never left. Most trainers felt the same. Someone had to be there for the animals. Not a single one of them didn't become attached to a particular orca.

It began as a working relationship. The dangers of interacting with them were underscored emphatically. Management made it clear; Schmidt made it clear, drilled it into their heads. You were trespassing in the lair of a beast, a monster capable of turning on you at any moment. But danger had a strange way of fading over the weeks and months together. Days without incident caused the primal dread to erode. Not truly gone, it lingered in the grooves of your brain until there was an accident. With a flash, the sinking feeling of swimming with the ocean's top predator returned. Then, something peculiar happened. Days passed with no incidents. They'd turn into weeks. The erosion of fear, it was a cycle. Love for the orcas kept you going. You rationalized it. "If only I had done this different, he wouldn't have snapped," or "she's just had a long day, you'd be cranky floating in a tank for hours too."

"You know, they'll be okay without you," Amanda reassured Stacy.

"I know they'll be fine without me." She wasn't worried about the orcas.

* * *

As Lee trekked through the building, he passed through the stainless-steel doors of the staff offices to the entrance hall. Colorfully dressed visitors and the sounds of interactive displays hummed around him. Marineworld had devoted a huge chunk of funds to the development of the CRI's main hall and museum. It was the showpiece guests first experienced after disembarking on the island. The upper atrium was lined with pale-blue skylights that filtered the sunlight. Designed by a famous architect from Stockholm, they simulated the light that trickled through the epipelagic zone. The effect was breathtaking and made more impressive by the colossal whale skeletons strategically hung from cables in the ceiling. Tom had seen a southern right whale displayed similarly during a trip to Gansbaai, and it left an impression on him. He'd insisted to the board that they needed an equally striking presentation. Tom wasn't content with a single skeleton, the atrium of the CRI boasted nine different cetaceans, articulated to give the sense they swam in a large pod. Coupled with the dramatic lighting, they created an unforgettable display. The support pillars for the atrium, light beige columns of fossiliferous limestone that contained millions of shell fragments that had been quarried and brought in from Missouri, echoed the oceanic theme. Lee had passed beneath them hundreds of times but still appreciated the spectacle. He hurried from the atrium as the CRI introduction video played on the screens that dotted the main entrance.

"Here at the Coronado Research Institute, we're deeply concerned with the preservation and conservation of our oceans and their rich biodiversity. With your support, we've been able…" He wondered if the tourists waiting in line or heading to the museum ever got sick of the video. How the receptionists at the main desk dealt with it was beyond him. He pushed past people and touched his badge to the digital lock marked "Staff Only." Stacy had texted him to meet her at the medical pool to "teach him how to swim." He prayed she was joking. No road led to him swimming in the medical pool. Not if it was empty. Not if she was with him. Nope. He shook his head. The medical pool was contained in a large warehouse. One wall was entirely windows that dropped to the waterline. It was open to the first of the sea pens and surrounded on the exterior by a breakwater to curtail flooding. In the event of a storm, a large watertight door could extend from above to seal the complex from the ocean. On regular days, this opening was used to bring animals in for routine tests and exams. The veterinary laboratory attached to the medical pool housed the newest technology available. Besides the typical pharmacy, surgical, medical, and necropsy supplies, there was specially designed X-ray machines, an MRI big enough for the orcas, and a fully stocked dentistry practice. A hoist from the pool could lift the animals directly to the operating room. It substantially cut the risks of traditional procedures. Lab staff conducted tissue, blood, urine, and fecal analysis from this building. It was also where extra vitamins and drugs were dispensed to the animals, either directly or in prepared food.

Stacy was standing poolside with a vet who carefully labeled and bagged vials of blood. A plastic cooler of equipment balanced neatly on the dry ledge outside the water. Stacy walked into the shallows.

"Slacks and a dress shirt? That's hardly a swimsuit." She stood in the ankle-deep water and waited for the equipment. Lee moved toward the trio of people gathered at the ledge.

"You weren't serious, were you?" he asked.

"You've got two choices—you can either ask Amanda to borrow her wetsuit, or you can roll up your pants," she said.

"Hi, Lee." Amanda dug through the cooler.

"You're serious?" He stared wide-eyed at Stacy. She crossed her arms.

"I'd just roll up my pants. I like you, but you won't fit into my wetsuit." Amanda continued her search. Stacy impatiently tapped her foot on the water.

"Fine, but I'm only standing there. No swimming." Lee rolled his pants up to his knees and shook off his shoes. He pulled off his socks and laid them on top of his shoes.

"No swimming," Stacy echoed. She held out her hand to pull him over the barrier and onto the ledge. The chilly water lapped at his feet. Amanda pulled a large syringe and sample kit from the cooler. He realized what was happening.

"Shit. It's bloodwork day, isn't it?" Lee groaned as both the vet and Amanda gave him a side-eyed look. These sessions were baked into his schedule. It was important to see how the orcas behaved during medical procedures. With the morning's events, it must have slipped his mind.

"Did you actually think you were getting a swimming lesson?" Stacy walked out to where the ledge dropped off to deeper waters. Maybe the text she'd sent was only a reminder of his professional duties.

"So, whose turn is it?" Lee asked.

"You'll see. Just make sure you stay back a bit." She waved him off. They didn't need to tell him twice. He usually observed behavior on bloodwork days without getting his feet wet. He held tight to the barrier, ready to scramble over it at the first sign of trouble.

A black outline glided in under the windows from the neighboring A1 sea pen. As it torpedoed closer, he recognized her ragged dorsal fin. It was Ollju. Lee's heels pressed against the wall as she skidded onto the ledge and divided the group.

"Good girl!" Stacy said. She gave the orca a pat on her rostrum. "Do you want to come say hi?"

"Nah, I'm fine where I'm at. Wouldn't want to get in your way," he said from his position of relative safety. She gave him an icy gaze.

Stacy pushed gently on the animal's beak. Ollju gently lay upside-down in the pool and presented her tail flukes.

"Perfect." Stacy sat on the drop-off with her legs hanging over the deeper water and guided the large tail flukes onto her lap. Lee cringed as he considered the powerful slap they could deliver. The vet kneeled next to Stacy with his sample kit. He ran his fingers along the main blood vessel until he found a proper spot to draw from before he rubbed an alcohol swab around the skin. Stacy spoke to the whale in soft tones.

"Wonderful, girl. You're doing great."

The vet expertly punched the needle into the vein. Ollju didn't flinch as they drew the blood. Once it filled, the vet withdrew the syringe and cleaned the area with another alcohol swab. He handed the sample to Amanda and backed away. Stacy tapped twice on the tip of Ollju's fluke to let her know they'd finished the procedure. The animal slid past her and swam around the pool.

"Lee, could you bring me that bucket of fish?" she asked as the vet and Amanda exited to the lab.

He grabbed the metal bucket and cautiously tiptoed to the edge of the platform. A low wave brushed halfway up his calf. Ollju surfaced nearby, mouth open and chirping. Startled, Lee dropped the bucket and backed away. Stacy blew the whistle around her neck and scooped the reward back into the bucket.

"Oh, you did great, girl!" She tossed the fish down the orca's gullet. Ollju happily received the prize and nodded for more.

"That's it. Sorry, girl." Stacy made a fish face at the orca before she disappeared.

"You always make it look easy," Lee said. Ollju bobbed to the surface like a cork, spraying a mouthful of water at him. It drenched him from head to toe. He brushed the water from his hair.

"That was because I didn't say hi, wasn't it?"

"Of course it was. You hurt her feelings. Will you come back before the end of my shift? I'm gonna analyze the samples before we're done here," she said.

"I think I can manage it. I'll go dry off for the next few hours." Lee pressed the water out of his shirt and khakis.

"Thanks for your help!" She joined Amanda in the lab. Lee watched through the window as the trio started their work. The vet cataloged the samples for a different examination while the trainers prepared a package of equipment for the next animal.

There was a crackling chirp as Ollju resurfaced and floated lazily to where her blood had been drawn. Her eye remained transfixed on Lee as he slipped his socks and shoes on.

"Hi, girl." Lee threw a half-hearted wave. Satisfied, she dove towards the gate to the sea pens. He crossed another restricted access doorway and followed her out. It was uneasy standing on the walkways interlocking the pens. Although they were anchored to the seafloor, they shifted with the movement of the ocean beneath them. Solidly engineered, they hadn't tossed an employee over the railings yet. He didn't want to be the first. Stepping into the medical pool was enough excitement for the day. The palm-thatched roof of the maintenance building stood out against the other modern buildings at the CRI. The labor-intensive work of the dive staff made the old-school thatch strangely fitting. As a courtesy, Lee knocked as he swung the door open. To his surprise, Rick sat at the main desk, adjusting a radio.

"What can I do for you, Lee? If you're looking for Tom, you just missed him." His tone was gruff. He didn't look up from his task.

"I was on my way out to see the orcas, but I wasn't sure where they've been moved to," Lee said.

"We're doing the repairs on A6 now. The animals should be in the pens closer to the med pool. I think they're doing blood testing today." Rick stopped and the lines of his face deepened. "Don't they tell you anything?"

"I didn't know if they'd shuffled them around," Lee said.

"Sorry. There's a lot of shit going on. Why are you wet?" He paused. "Forget it. I got a team out at A6 right now—want to help me supervise for a minute?" The offer was his way of apologizing. Lee didn't hesitate to take him up on it.

"Why not? The whales can wait."

Rick barked orders into his radio as Lee tried to keep up along the walkways. He got a rough idea of what had happened from the one-way conversation. The gate to A6 was damaged. A dive team was ready to go, but Rick didn't want anyone to enter the water without his direct oversight. They'd waited on standby since Mike's body had been removed from the pen earlier in the morning. Tensions ran high. They wanted to complete the repairs.

"No one dives until I get there, do you understand?!" Rick said over the radio before turning to Lee. "Sometimes I wonder if they even think."

The maintenance crew was gathered on the walkway. Two men in wetsuits sat with their legs in the water while another member of the crew was helping a third diver don his tank. The damage to the pen was significant, judging by the hydraulic winch setup.

"What happened?" Lee asked.

"You'll see." Rick discussed the strategy for repairs with his team. Lee moved to the edge. The markers for the gate were out of alignment.

"What damaged it?" He looked back towards the dive team. They started their descent. The fourth team member operated the winch while Rick supervised.

"Strangest damn thing. No damage to the gate, bolts got knocked out of place. It's hanging by a thread there." Rick waited for a response from the divers. One resurfaced to report he'd secured the winch around the gate. They were ready to begin repairs.

"Pull it up," he said. The winch engaged with a mechanical shudder, and the cable wound tight with a whir. "Easy! Easy! You don't want to rip the net!" The operator dialed back the throttle and secured the gate in an upright position. From the catwalk, the floating markers appeared aligned in their correct place. "That's good, that's good," Rick repeated himself and held his hand out in a stop motion. He turned to Lee.

"After they replace the bolts, it should be perfect. I'll have them weld the bastards in this time."

"Why weren't they to begin with?" he asked. Tom had assured him they'd welded the bolts in place.

"All the interior gate bolts are welded. This gate opens to the ocean. They weren't welded in case we needed to remove it during a release," Rick said. Lee frowned.

This damage was recognizable. When they'd built equipment for the CRI, they'd tested it at Marineworld San Diego. Everything from observation windows to netting had been trialed in the pools. It was stupid to test a batch of unproven and potentially dangerous equipment with the animals for the first time at the unveiling. The company wouldn't risk it. It was the right decision to guarantee their welfare in an unfamiliar environment, but it came at an exorbitant price.

They'd tested each piece in one-week intervals. Lee's observations of the orcas' interactions with them had been vital in determining if the gear would be approved for installation. When they'd placed a section of netting and prototype gate across the main pool, there had been a minor hiccup. Kassuq had tried to breach the top to reach the rear pool. Lee had cautioned the team not to hastily redesign it. When the net was checked while attached to a sample catwalk, there wasn't an issue. Something about the walkway made her reconsider going over the top.

Gates were another matter entirely. Shurik found the hinges on the gates particularly interesting. He'd mouth and bite at them. It had taken him a day to discover he could mouth the head of the bolt. From there, he'd figured out how to move it up in its setting and drop it with a satisfying thud. He worked the top hinges of the gate because the bottom of the pool prevented him from gripping the lower ones. Delighted chirps were elicited each time he dropped the bolt. It was a fun game.

"Can you guys distract him? Make sure he stays back from the gate," Lee said to the trainers poolside.

"Yeah, of course," one responded. Lee waited as the trainer grabbed a target pole. It was one of Shurik's favorite training aids. He slapped the water with the target, then held it up for the orca to touch with his rostrum. When he hit the target, the trainer blew his whistle and reinforced the behavior with a tasty fish. The trainer repeated this behavior as he settled in to distract the orca. Lee jogged up the stadium steps to the Show Operations Manager room overlooking the main pool.

"Uh, Tom…" Lee's voice trailed off as he noticed that the man behind the desk was on the phone. Tom held up his hand and finished his call before he spoke.

"Sorry about that, what do you need?" He forced the apology through gritted teeth.

"We have to get that gate out."

"What's the problem?"

"Shurik keeps playing with the bolts. Is there a crew available to take it out?"

"Just have him moved to another pool. The gate comes out in a few days. No need to panic."

"What about at the CRI?" Lee asked.

"We'll have them welded in place. Problem solved." Tom's answer was quick. "Did you need something else?" He paused. "Are the others interested in them?"

"Not really. None of the others seem to care. I'll have him moved, then." Lee was an idiot for not thinking of the simple solution. Tom thanked him for coming to him, but it was only a reflex. He'd wasted his time. Shouting exploded from poolside as Lee began to leave the room. Trainers and workers frantically darted around the stadium. In unison, the two men raced to the balcony.

"Somebody call the vet!" The trainer reached towards the gate with the target pole. But he wasn't trying to signal the animal; he used it for leverage to lift the gate. It was a futile attempt. The pole snapped before it budged. Shurik was pinned at the bottom. The gate had crashed into him like a guillotine. He thrashed and sprayed water madly into the air. The crystal-clear pool darkened crimson as blood poured into the water. Even if they freed him, a vet was useless. The damage was done. The remaining orcas dove and resurfaced repeatedly. They loudly called and bumped their companion, tried their best to free him from the trap. They were in danger. If the gate toppled, they'd have bigger issues. Tom screamed from the balcony; it silenced the human voices.

"Get him separated! We don't want the others injured! Roll the net out!" He waved his arms and directed the members of staff.

Across from the doomed whale, trainers slapped the water, sounded whistles, and did whatever it took to bring the animals to their side. As the other orcas responded to the calls, Nayak stayed at the gate. Her jaw scraped on the rough bottom as she strained to pry the gate off. A thick rope of blood drifted from a fresh cut on her chin.

"For Christ's sake, get her out of there!"

It was madness as a staff member prodded at her with a target pole. She burrowed at the gate and ignored the minor annoyance.

"The eye!"

The man with the target pole stopped to understand what Tom screamed. He repeated himself with fire.

"The eye!"

He obliged the boss's command and jabbed the foam ball into Nayak's eye. She snapped at it and pursued her attacker. Once she was far enough from her fallen comrade, they deployed a safety net to cordon Shurik off from the rest. Led by Nayak, the orcas patrolled the perimeter, exasperated they couldn't reach him. The orca's thrashing stopped. Blood from his wound obscured his body. Lee dropped his face in his hands. He was powerless. Shurik was dead. Trainers poolside dropped to their knees, in tears. Their sobs joined the funeral choir of the orcas. Of the two men on the balcony, Tom spoke first. He leaned in to whisper in Lee's ear.

"Probably should have moved him before coming up here." He patted him on the shoulder and withdrew back into his office.

101

TRACKING DATA

"Uh, do you have a minute?" Chad ambushed Lee as he returned to the offices. Lee's mind wandered. Hiding in the lighthouse was a better option than coming back to his office. More room to think. Fewer people. Chad's tone was different. A serious note intruded on his usual joyful demeanor. "It's Akhlut's satellite data. I know it's nothing, but can you have a look?" Chad motioned towards his cubicle.

Lee pulled up a chair and studied the white lines displayed across the map on the screen. They fitted each animal with a specialized tracking tag designed by a company called Wildlife Systems. Tags for the orcas were bolted on through holes made near the base of the dorsal fin. Each tag had an antenna that transmitted to the Argos satellite network, an indicator light, and wet/dry sensors to check when the animal breached. When it did, this triggered the dry sensor, and the tag sent its position to the computer database. If there was a breakdown of enclosures, escapees could be tracked and recaptured. Reintroduced orcas' tags were designed with an extended battery life. The goal was to watch them for a period after they reintegrated into their pod to make sure they remained healthy.

"What are we looking at here? I was gonna look at these later tonight," Lee said.

"I was going through the data when I noticed something strange," Chad said.

Lee studied the lines while Chad adjusted parameters on the settings. The data showed Akhlut had stuck to the Coronados. His movement was a bowl of spaghetti surrounding the islands, but it showed frequent trips near San Diego Bay, with a few out west to the open ocean. Marineworld accounted for this. Transient orcas only passed the Coronados for a brief period during the winter and summer months as part of their migration. They hoped after a few months he'd meet up with a pod when they paid one of their semiannual visits to the region. Transient groups were more prone to accept an outsider.

"There's nothing strange. It's what we expected," Lee said.

Chad hit the Enter key on the computer, eliminating data except for the selected time frame. It reduced the bowl of spaghetti to a few strands tangled around the Coronados.

"What about now?" Chad asked.

It took Lee a split second to comprehend. "A6." He tapped the location of the pen. It was surrounded by a white line.

"That's gotta be a coincidence, right?" the intern asked.

"Yeah, I'm sure it's nothing. Weird, but probably nothing." Lee wasn't so positive, even as the words came out of his mouth.

"Do you think I should bring it up to Tom?"

"I'll do it. I'll tell him I noticed it when I checked the nightly data log."

"Thanks, man, I'd appreciate it. Don't want to get in trouble for looking at things I'm not supposed to."

"Is this what you always do when you finish your work?"

"Not always, just sometimes."

Lee followed the long hallway to the executive offices. Tom was practical. He'd tell him he was a tinfoil-hat-wearing nutjob. There was no basis to believe the two events were remotely related. Tracking data showed Akhlut had been near A6. What did that have to do with Mike's death? Absolutely nothing. Unrelated events happened in the same place. Life was inherently random. Despite his best attempts to convince himself the incidents weren't correlated, he couldn't shake the feeling that they were. He stopped short of knocking on Tom's door. Instead, he sat in the small waiting area like a defeated student outside the principal's office.

* * *

The director's stern voice was dialed back. A familiar face sat across from him in his office. Bradley Pirri was the Occupational Safety and Health Administration representative who had investigated Ed's death. OSHA had had them under a magnifying glass since the accident. The scrutiny was intense, but it could have been much worse. They benefited from the plan to take trainers out of the water at the CRI. The board had focused on that during the hearings. As atrocious as Ed's death was, Marineworld reasoned it couldn't happen again because no one would be in the water with the orcas. Rumors flew that pressure from OSHA had forced them to make that decision. That wasn't the case, but it had eliminated the strain on the company. If worthless employees could keep themselves alive, that would be even better.

"Please continue with your statement." The OSHA representative thumbed over his notes.

"Mike entered the water alone. His partner, Rick, had already left the island for the evening when he began his inspection. He should have put it off until the morning. It violated protocol. You need a partner on dives," Tom said.

Mr. Pirri scribbled on his notepad. "Is there a reason Mr. Fischer felt pressure to carry out the inspection without his partner?" he asked.

"Not that I'm aware of. We train our teams to be safety-oriented." Tom paused. "There isn't a job they're sent on that's safer, or easier, as a solo dive."

"Do you believe his gear was faulty? What's your policy for maintenance?" Pirri continued his series of questions.

"It wasn't his equipment. That's checked daily by both a diving and a nondiving member of maintenance staff. We keep meticulous logs of conditions and make replacements as necessary. I can provide you with our records for dive equipment if you'd like."

"That would be perfect, Mr. Walsh. I'll look at those before I collect initial statements from the dive crew."

"I'll have my secretary run the copies for you. Do you want to go out there now? I can walk you out."

"No need for that. I'll have security take me over." It wasn't the response he'd hoped for, but Tom figured it was worth a shot. The dive crew would've chosen their words more carefully if he hovered over them. They had no reason to lie, but they didn't need to add anything extra either. "When I'm finished, I'll be in touch." He stopped writing in his notebook and placed it neatly inside his briefcase. As he reached for the door handle, he addressed the director. "I've been doing this a long time. Don't beat yourself up too much. Accidents happen. Just be glad it wasn't a repeat of that Morales kid."

* * *

Lee checked his phone as he contemplated how to approach Tom. It seemed like he had waited for hours already. Just when he thought he couldn't wait a minute longer, the door to Tom's office swung open and the OSHA inspector stepped out. Lee couldn't forget his face. It reminded him of all the questions he'd asked investigating Ed's death. It was clear he didn't make the same impact. He recognized Lee, but his eyes were blank as he searched for his name. "Popular guy, huh?" he asked.

"Comes with the title," Lee said. The inspector's eyes lit up as the voice helped him register who he was talking to..

"You were the spotter when—" He stopped. "I'm sorry—"

"Lee Ingram." He reached out and shook his hand. They'd never seen each other under pleasant circumstances.

"Right. Can you point me toward Schmidt's office? I'd love to catch up with him."

"Schmidt's"—Lee contemplated his choice of words—"retired."

"That's a shame, but I understand why. Who's looking over the whales now?"

"You're looking at him. Head Cetacean Behaviorist."

"Congratulations." Pirri didn't look convinced.

"I still call him as an outside consultant."

Pirri's furrowed brow relaxed. "Smart. I would too. The way he talked about the orcas, he was invested in getting it right. Glad to hear it. Well, I won't keep you from your meeting any longer. Will you be in the office later for a chat?"

It was a polite way to say he'd be stopping by for the interview phase.

"I'm always around here somewhere." Lee waited long enough for Pirri to disappear before he snuck back to his office. Tom would have said it was nothing. He'd shoot down the notion with a veneer of cheerfulness. If it was something, now Lee had an alternative. But he wasn't ready to put it on the line for a hunch.

* * *

Tom basked alone in his office before he slumped over, utterly exhausted. He didn't know if his meeting with the coroner or the one with the OSHA rep had drained him of more energy. It could be worse. He could be stuffed in an empty walk-in freezer like Mike. To be fair, it wasn't his idea, but it was brilliant. The coroner suggested it. Why traumatize the tourists by hauling out a body in the middle of the day? Since there was only one landing dock, it'd be difficult to sneak him out. They could've radioed in a helicopter, but why not save some money? The café attached to the hotel wasn't fully operational yet. It was located off a wing that was still receiving its final touches before opening. There weren't any workers. They hadn't even stocked it with food. It was the perfect place to leave the body until it could be carried out under the cover of nightfall. Tom was jealous he hadn't thought of it first. The coroner had reached the same conclusion Tom had. Nothing remarkable. He'd complete the full autopsy on the mainland. They needed to determine if Mike had had any health issues prior to drowning. If it wasn't faulty equipment, he'd probably had a heart attack mid-dive.

Tom's eyelids drooped, but he found the energy to raise his head and open the computer. He launched Wildlife Systems' Tracking Data Portal. There was one thing he still needed to do. Lee was clinical. He checked it every evening before he caught the ferry to the mainland. There wasn't an issue. That asshole had drowned, and nothing was out of the ordinary. Tom repeated it over and over. There was no reason for anyone to be skeptical. The coroner had called it a drowning. Hell, the OSHA rep had said it was an open-and-shut case. If there was a chance, albeit microscopic, that it wasn't an accident, that information had to be buried. No one could entertain the fantasy of another reality. Lee could be a problem. He might have seen where Akhlut was already.

Tom couldn't gamble that Lee would keep his mouth shut. He reminded him of Mark when they'd first started together. Quiet and sincere. Too much of his mentor had rubbed off on him. His opinion on tracking data was exactly the type of thing he'd share with OSHA, but they wouldn't go so far as to track missing data down. Lee wasn't as dangerous as Mark. If he hadn't seen it already, he'd breathe a sigh of relief that nothing was there and get back to work. If he had seen it, he wouldn't risk his career to go public with no definite proof once it was gone. Lee wouldn't rock the boat; he was grateful to have a job he wasn't qualified for. A second-rate replacement wouldn't be his downfall. Not after he'd worked so hard. Still, there was a slight risk Lee could decide to grow a pair.

To take that risk was a waste. Why should the shmucks he cut settlement checks to get the benefits? The time for him to cash in his stocks and enjoy an exorbitant retirement package was so close. It was his turn to get a slice of the pie. Forget the legacy of the company. They'd be judged, not him. When he was gone, the board could run the CRI into the ground. He'd be drinking daiquiris in a tax haven far, far away.

He clicked through the tabs on the Tracking Data Portal until he reached the screen with information on the orcas. Tom had administrator privileges on the CRI's account. He could save, copy, and delete data as he desired. He selected Akhlut's tracking data from the interface. With a click, he highlighted the information from the previous day. His finger momentarily hovered over the Delete key. Was he just being overly paranoid? No, he had to do it. The trail led back to A6. To that dumbass diver. He struck the button. A gray pop-up box flashed before him. "Are you sure you want to remove this data point? GPS data collected for the time selected will be removed." Again, he paused briefly before he clicked "Yes." Content, he scanned updated logs. It wasn't enough to remove the day's data. That wouldn't do. If it was the only day that went missing, it'd be suspicious. He highlighted data from Akhlut at one-week intervals since his release and made a mental note of the dates he removed. There was no longer a hint of hesitation as he struck the key. He went back through the program and selected the next orca on the list, Ivar, highlighted the same dates, and deleted them. A thin smile crept across his face. He moved through the list of orcas and deleted the same information for each animal. Obviously, there was an issue with Wildlife Systems data management.

THE ORIGINAL BEHAVIORIST

Nothing was wrong with the tracking tags. They were functioning as intended. Ideally, it was nothing to worry about. A squiggle in the data was to be expected. Lee needed reassurance, though—a second opinion to calm his fears. He found himself outside a bungalow in the Normal Heights neighborhood of San Diego. He'd made a call to Schmidt. The man had forgotten more about the orcas than Lee had ever learned. Schmidt had been there when they'd arrived at Marineworld. He had written their original files. They had grown up under his watch. If it was more than a string of coincidences, the doctor would set him on the right track. He deliberated how to broach the subject with his former mentor. "Hi, Mark, I think Akhlut might be killing people again" wouldn't be the best way to start the conversation, but Schmidt would appreciate the direct approach.

"The hell are you doin'?" There was a sharp rap on his window followed by Schmidt's familiar face. Lee cranked the window down to respond.

"Just pulled up, was getting ready to come in."

"Just pulled up, huh? From the porch I counted fifteen minutes of you talking to yourself."

"Ten tops." He switched off the ignition and stepped out of the car to shake hands with Mark. He morphed the handshake into a hug and gave him a massive pat on the back.

"You didn't say much on the phone."

"Work stuff." Lee delivered the biggest understatement of the century.

"Well, we can deal with work stuff. C'mon round back, kid, we'll get you a drink." Schmidt led him through the stained oak gate of his front yard, across the stone pavers that lined the house, and into the backyard of his bungalow. He gestured to a set of folding chairs set up around a glass-topped table before he stepped inside the house. Most yards in the neighborhood came equipped with a tiny patch of grass. Schmidt had covered the entire backyard with river rock instead. A cast-iron firepit and stainless-steel cooler lurked within arm's reach.

"Bottle opener." Schmidt waved the tool in his hands and sauntered out towards the table. He took two bottles out of the cooler, popped the cap on the first and handed it to Lee. "Do you like the garden?" he asked.

"It's a step up from the trailer in De Anza," Lee said.

"Hey, I'd still have that trailer if the city wasn't turning it into a damn park. Figured I needed something more respectable. Less to mow this way."

"It's a nice place. I just didn't figure you settle in a neighborhood full of hipsters," Lee said.

"Why? Because I'm old?" Schmidt took a sip of his beer. "Nah, the food's good around here. You didn't come to chat about the new place or food, though. What's up? Tom still making your life miserable?"

"A maintenance diver drowned yesterday." Lee's tone changed.

"Geez, sorry to hear that. Who was it?"

"Mike Fischer. He was looking at a gate that opens to the ocean. It was damaged."

"I didn't know Mike. How the hell did that happen? Don't they work in teams?"

"Dive partner had gone home for the day. They said there might have been a problem with his equipment. His dive tank was empty when they found him. Tom thinks he had a heart attack."

"Jesus Christ, that's terrible. Regular heart attack is bad enough. Two deaths in how many months? OSHA'll have a field day."

"Inspector was out at the CRI today. Spent the entire day there, even after the coroner left."

"How's Tom handling it?" Schmidt asked. Lee shrugged. He didn't have an answer. It seemed like it was just another thing he had to deal with. Tom handled things his own way.

"You know how he operates better than me."

"He's saying the right things. Calm and collected while he figures out how to come out squeaky clean."

"Sounds about right," Lee said. Schmidt got up and turned on a propane tank next to the firepit. With the flick of a match, flames crackled to life.

"That all there is to it?" Schmidt asked. He settled into his chair and readied his second beer.

"Not really. We've got tracking data. I'm sure it's nothing, but it seems off. Kinda hoped you'd tell me I'm crazy," Lee said.

"From which orca?" Schmidt asked.

"Akhlut." As Lee said the name, Schmidt's eyes grew wide, then narrowed.

"He was around the pen when this diver drowned?"

"Roughly. You know the data's only so accurate. It shows him near the pen yesterday. It's nothing, right? We expected him to stick close to the CRI. Why would he have anything to do with a maintenance diver drowning? That's just me jumping to conclusions. It's stupid." Schmidt grew quiet while Lee rambled. There was plenty he didn't know, especially about animals like Akhlut.

"Mark, you with me? I'm crazy, right?" Lee begged for reassurance.

"No, you're not crazy. You've read his file. You've written logs for him."

"After Ed. It was so deliberate. Calculated. He didn't just snap. He'd thought about that for years."

"They're wild animals. Always have been and always will be. Hell, a dog will bite its owner if he pushes it too far. I tried to tell them. Rob wouldn't listen then and Tom won't listen now. You'd think it'd be different at the CRI, but nothing's changed," Schmidt said.

"You think there's something to this?" Lee asked.

"It's possible. But you'll need more than tracking data and a feeling." Schmidt's demeanor changed.

"What should I do? Take it to Tom? OSHA?" Lee asked.

"No. Don't bring up your little theory to Tom. He'll sweep it under the rug. OSHA will find the tracking data while they investigate. You know they ask plenty of questions, so you might as well mention it. But you said he drowned. No way to tie that to Akhlut even though he was in the neighborhood. Going to the media might be your best bet." Lee's shocked face didn't surprise his mentor. He was too busy with his line of thought to pay attention to it. "The problem is, you signed an NDA when you started. We all did. If you break it without proof on something like this, they'll sue you into oblivion. Best not to do that on a guess. You'll need more before they'll listen." Schmidt dumped out his full beer and switched off the firepit.

"What are you doing?" Lee asked.

"More evidence. We're going to get it for you." He walked through the back door of the house into his office. It was a neat replica of his old office in San Diego. Rows of biology textbooks on one wall and a Marineworld 25th Anniversary poster on the other. It looked like a team photo of all the staff, trainers, and board members. They looked out of place posing in their suits in front of the pool at the stadium. Lee crouched in the front row.

"You looked different with short hair."

"Should I regrow the 'stache?"

"I'm surprised you and Tom aren't on opposite sides."

"Believe it or not, he wasn't always the biggest asshole at Marineworld."

"Who had the honor of that title?"

"That was our boss, Rob. He's the fat bastard in the top right." Schmidt dug through the drawer of his desk and tossed a small key to Lee. "Start searching through Akhlut's logs from the early nineties. Look for files with red in the name. Incidents of aggressive behavior." Schmidt got up to make space. Under the poster was a set of filling cabinets filled with orca research. They were organized by year, location, and research group. Tucked away in their own section were the files from his years at Marineworld.

"You took the behavior logs with you when you left?"

"I did. What if I needed copies for my research?"

"Where are you going?"

"To make a pot of coffee. We've got a lot to talk about." Schmidt left Lee to look through the files as he made his way to the galley kitchen. The number listed as red was surprising. He thought he'd seen them all when he'd taken over, but these were different. The sheer size of them dwarfed those he was familiar with. Marineworld didn't label incidents of aggressive behavior as red. That was a product of Schmidt's own filing system. Most didn't trigger Lee's memory. He'd never seen them. In the '90s, Akhlut had been a very bad boy. He bit at trainers, rammed them, and stopped them from exiting pools. Events had occurred on a near-weekly basis.

"Did you find it yet?" Schmidt asked from the other room. Coffee mugs clanked against each other as he took them out of the cabinet.

"Find what? There are a billion files here," Lee responded.

"July seventeenth, 1990."

Lee exited out of the folder, found the date Schmidt had suggested, and read the report. After he'd completed his set of behaviors, Akhlut had refused to let his trainer exit the pool. While she'd attempted to escape from a side platform, he'd repeatedly swum in front of her, ignoring signals from other trainers to come under control. This blocking behavior had continued for two to three minutes while she'd tried to leave.

Lee shuddered. He'd stood in a pool with Ollju for a minute this afternoon, and it had been a lifetime.

When the trainer had tried to paddle to another platform to leave, Akhlut had become "extremely agitated." He'd pursued her. She'd reached the platform, but he'd mouthed the bootie of her wetsuit and dragged her back. The report noted the trainer hadn't been injured from this, and Akhlut had been "quite gentle" in his manner. After towing her to the front of the pool, Akhlut had "dunked her under the water repeatedly" and held her under for "a few seconds at a time." The standard report writing made it sound good-natured. Dunked. It sounded playful, not vicious. When orcas swam over the top of trainers, they hammered their bodies onto them. The only way to counter this was to push themselves off the animal at the moment of impact. If they didn't time their counter right, Tom wrote the compensation checks.

"Mark, why haven't I seen these before?" Lee asked as Schmidt entered the room carrying the two mugs of coffee. "This trainer's arm was fractured before the others could bring him under control."

"You haven't seen that before because after I wrote it, Tom marked it to be read by senior trainers only. They tried to move her back to the dolphin stadium after that. She never got back in the water."

"Why? That doesn't make sense. The people in charge of studying their behavior should have access to this."

"They should, but the higher-ups think differently. Tom's argument was, since the trainers were the ones in contact with them, they're the only ones that need to know."

"Still doesn't make sense."

"You're twenty-six and the Head Cetacean Behaviorist. Go ahead, tell me what makes sense," Schmidt said. "Do me a favor, pull up Akhlut's acquisition file."

Lee searched through another folder with acquisition data on the orcas. He could find information on the other whales, but nothing for Akhlut.

"There's nothing's here."

"There wouldn't be. I stood next to Tom while our old boss redacted it. That's what he called it when he tore the damn thing up. They've done that with plenty of files. Redacted them. Sanitized the language. Don't you ever wonder why the incidents in the animal profiles have gaps that last years?"

"What are you saying?" He looked up from the screen at Schmidt.

"Tom always says, 'This isn't the Marineworld of the seventies.' You know why he does?"

Lee knew. Orcas' history with man was tumultuous. They'd served as target practice for the Navy in World War II. And it wasn't in the international waters of the far-off Pacific. When San Francisco had been blockaded after the bombing of Pearl Harbor, blimps had guarded the offshore waters from Japanese subs. The bored crews had dropped their depth charges on unsuspecting orcas while they'd waited for an enemy that had never come. After the war had ended, things hadn't improved. In the 1950s and early 1960s, they'd been marked as vicious killers that threatened the fishing trade by stealing the fishermen's catches and destroying their fishing nets by getting stuck in them. The Icelandic government asked for the United States' help to preserve their economy. The US jumped on the chance to test new ordnance and answered the call with machine guns and rockets. They exterminated hundreds of orcas off the coast of Iceland.

Things changed in the 1970s. Orcas became golden tickets for the entertainment industry. Before then, dolphins and belugas had belonged to an exclusive club. The game changed when man discovered orcas could not only survive in captivity but perform spectacular shows for giant profits. It was a biological gold rush. Profit was a powerful motivator. It caused rational men to do things they wouldn't normally consider. Without regulation, it was a matter of time before someone pushed the boundaries too far.

Orcas were rounded up by the handful. Their captors were men with dollar signs in their eyes. Each one sold for thousands of dollars. A massive sum at the time, but nothing compared to their current million-dollar price tag. Capture methods were deceptively simple. Despite their ability to rip most nets to pieces, orcas showed them an unusual respect. In fact, laying a safety net across a pool was a last line of defense against a dangerous orca who couldn't be brought under control. A captor only had to surround the orca. Even though the whale could break through the net with ease, it didn't. It acted as a magical barrier that prevented escape.

Their captors used two fundamental techniques. The most basic method involved herding the animals into a narrow inlet of water. After they entered the channel, a net was strung across to stop them from backing out. Orcas were chosen based on health and size and sold to the highest bidder. The alternate tactic involved using a purse seine. A seine net hung vertical with its bottom edge weighted and its top edge buoyed by floats. Along the bottom were several rings. A purse line passed through the rings and, when pulled shut, prevented the animals from diving to escape. They were netted like goldfish at a pet store. With either method, orcas were chosen based on health and size and sold to the highest bidder.

Marineworld didn't fund the expedition off Puget Sound in 1970, but there were ramifications for the entire industry. They planned to purchase animals from the expedition too but were beaten in the bidding war. The men tasked with the capture behaved more like Wild West bandits than professionals concerned with animal welfare. Boats buzzed by at breakneck speed as crews on board hurled explosives lit with acetylene torches. Each explosion created underwater shock waves that ripped through the pod. Their goal was to herd the whales inside a cove. Men shouted instructions from boat to boat as the terrified animals scrambled to escape the madness. Orcas surfaced to check which members of their family had been captured. They cried out to each other as they were corralled into the inlet. Nearly a hundred were trapped together at one point. It was far more than the crews could handle. The captors separated calves from the rest of the pod. They prodded adults outside the main net. Infants screamed to their mothers in deafening tones and high-pitched cries. Prior hunts were clandestine. This great roundup occurred during the peak of tourist season. It wasn't only the Whidbey Island locals left with an unwelcome memory. The breaking point occurred during the night. An unnamed activist couldn't bear the screams any longer. He slipped into the cove and slashed the nets to reunite the families. It only added to the tragedy.

The hunters kept a watchful eye on the nets even in the darkness. Before long, they noticed them floating towards the surface. With the chance their paycheck could swim away, they had no choice but to investigate. Armed with spotlights, they dove into the shadowy depths. The water vibrated with the beating of unseen whales outside the beam of their lights. Before long, they arrived at a gruesome scene. As the orcas had struggled to rejoin each other, they'd become entangled in the freshly cut net. The more they struggled, the more the cords wrapped around them, burrowing deeply into their flesh. To their credit, the men hacked and slashed to free the calves, but the macabre tapestry had been woven. Four calves and one adult hung lifeless in the netting. By the unearthly glow of their lights, the divers cut them free and repaired the damage.

But the dreadful event wasn't finished. The leader of the expedition had to dispose of the remains. In prior years, they'd offered the bodies to the government for research or a local rendering works for fertilizer. Neither group wanted a hand in the debacle. Instead, he ordered his men to cut the bellies open and fill them with stones. They wrapped chains and anchors to their tail flukes and sank them in an unceremonial burial. With their bodies tucked away on the seafloor, the ringleader slept soundly.

But there were no secrets that time didn't reveal. Later that year, a fishing trawler dredged the bodies of the drowned calves. The captain displayed the corpses on a beach for a newspaper reporter from Seattle. The sounds of the tortured pod still played in the minds of the townspeople. It wasn't long before the story followed the seasonal visitors of Whidbey Island back to their homes around the globe. Shortly thereafter, the US passed the Marine Mammal Protection Act. From then on, no more orcas were taken for display from Washington State or any other US waters. If Marineworld had purchased animals from the incident, they would've been skewered in the court of public opinion. When Tom repeated his mantra, it wasn't because he was ashamed of the former tactics—it was to remind himself and others how important public support for the company was.

"Do you know what his job title was before he was director, before he was Show Operations Manager?" Schmidt asked.

"No idea." Lee continued to browse the files. There was so much information he'd never known existed. It was the first day of his internship all over again. He'd emptied his coffee cup an hour ago.

"Corporate Director of Collecting."

"That sounds made up."

"He was in charge of finding new assets. The one who charted the boats, filed for collection permits. His job was to make sure animals made it safely to the park."

"And?"

"I was on the crew."

Lee thought hard before he asked his next question. There were phantom behavior logs, undocumented expeditions, but Schmidt expected it would come at some point.

"Was he even rescued?" Lee asked.

"Captured. Akhlut was captured in 1985." Schmidt stopped. "Listen, if this is headed where I think, I'll tell you what I know. I'll break my NDA. Go to the media if I have to. But first things first—we need another pot of coffee."

THE CAPTURE

M ark Schmidt sat on the deck of a salmon seiner one gray February morning in 1985. In the years since the debacle at Puget Sound, the company had had to become creative in how they found whales. There were successful collections from Icelandic and Arctic waters that brought the total number of orcas at the park to five. But Tom wanted more. Their population had to be sustained. Funding hunts across the globe wasn't cost-effective. Not when there were orcas in the Pacific. All he needed was to secure one more to get the breeding program up and running. With that in mind, he took a chance. He sought a capture permit from the National Marine Fisheries Service. The memories of the hunt in Puget had become a faded page in history. Tom soothed any lingering fears they had. Marineworld wouldn't capture one hundred orcas. The company only wanted one. A bull to breed. It was still a surprise when they issued the permit. One hadn't been issued in years. NOAA was leery but decided that taking one whale wouldn't impact the wild stock of orcas. The conditions required that capture occur "away from the coast, during the off-season." These were reasonable to Tom, and rather than risk a public relations nightmare, he chartered a seiner instead of an unorganized fiasco of speed boats, planes, bombs, and cowboys. He replaced brute force with tact.

Mark was in charge of the five-man crew. They were experienced except for the two deckhands that stacked the corkline and lead line. The pair fumbled with the nets as the rest prepared. This wasn't their usual quarry. They jumped at the prospect of an orca hunt. It was new and exciting for them. A once-in-a-lifetime opportunity to work with Marineworld. The fat check and promise of a bonus for a successful hunt didn't hurt either. They charted a course northwest from San Diego towards Santa Catalina and San Clemente Island. It was rare, but during the winter months, orcas were spotted making the lengthy journey along the coast towards Antarctic waters. Schmidt's goal was to catch them during this leg of their annual migration. There was a risk that Marineworld could lose a nice chunk of money on this expedition. But it was nothing compared to what they'd lose if they chartered another expedition to the North Atlantic. Besides, the reward for success was worth it. Tom agreed to a local search instead of a journey up the coast when Mark convinced him it would be a successful journey without turning into a sideshow. The people of Washington had seen enough orcas poached from their waters. Even a covert mission might draw suspicious eyes. California provided a perfect foil.

The crew made their last checks on the equipment, lines, and gear before the boat got underway. A deckhand confirmed that the Puretic power block, a specialized mechanical winch used to haul in the nets, was in full working order. The skipper, a dark-haired man in a blue cable-knit sweater, shuffled across the deck towards Mark.

"Much bigger fish than tuna today, eh?" His cracked, yellowed teeth stood out against the haze. Mark wanted to correct him but knew better. It might be a long day; best not to start by calling out his stupidity on his own ship.

"Yeah. You sure your boys here are up to the challenge?"

"No doubt. Check will clear regardless, though," the skipper said. Mark forced a laugh and made his way aft, towards the stern. He needed to inspect the skiff he'd operate.

"Squared away with the bait?" Mark asked.

"Your nose work?" The skipper motioned towards two large containers lashed at the rear. The tops were covered with tarps to prevent bombardment by gulls and terns, but Mark could smell the fresh herring. Nine hundred pounds of it was packed into the tubs. While it wasn't their typical food source, Mark hoped the animals wouldn't pass up a free meal.

"Sometimes I wish it didn't." Mark looked over the skiff. It seemed in perfect order.

"And you're sure you can man one of these?" the skipper asked. Mark's demeanor gave his doubts away. He tried to hide his concern about running the skiff, but it showed. He had been around the water since he was a kid, piloted all types of crafts. This was no different. It was the responsibility of the catch that made him nervous. He'd seen the photos of the dead calves laid across the beach from the 1970 hunt. There was no way he'd put the chance of a mishap in the hands of one of the crew.

"Look, Skip, it's the most important part of this little fishing trip. I know your crew knows what they're doing, but I can handle this."

"Hey, it's your show. Your people cut the check. You can pilot the whole damn seiner if you'd like," the captain half-joked as he moved back to the wheelhouse. Mark rested on the skiff.

Once there was a confirmed sighting, the seiner raced ahead of the pod. When they were a suitable distance ahead of the animals, they'd dump the herring overboard as bait. As the orcas swam in for the food, Mark's skiff would be lowered into the water. He would pilot a large circle around the ship to lay out the purse seine as he went. When he completed his circular route to trap them, the crew could engage the power block to cinch up the net and prevent their escape. From there, he'd select a bull specimen of the right size and health and isolate it.

Finally, they'd tow the animal back to San Diego into the waiting arms of Marineworld staff. Cue the champagne. Mark lit a cigarette and took one last glance over the skiff before getting underway.

"All set and ready to head out," the skipper said.

"Anything on the radio?" Mark asked.

"Nothing yet—we'll head for Santa Catalina and see where it takes us. I'll raise the boys at K&M Landing once we get further out."

"It's best if you stay off the radio, Captain. We want a low profile. Listen, but don't raise them unless you absolutely have to."

"You got it. I'll dial in to a low frequency the charters use." With a shrug, the skipper engaged the engines and headed out of the harbor.

Now it became a waiting game. The crew stood on their toes for lookout. They searched the waters for spouts and spray as the whales' warm breath condensed in the cool air. It was tough to spot them from a distance in the rough waters, but the distinct whitish-gray saddle behind their dorsal fin was a dead giveaway at close range. Unfortunately, February was the midst of the migratory season for gray whales. Tens of thousands of them migrated from Alaska towards Baja to give birth. As they chopped onwards to Catalina, the sailors spotted their distinct V-shaped spout and cried out. From his post on the bow, Mark was nervous the entire trip would pan out to be a fruitless gray-watching expedition. The skipper hung his head out the window and snickered.

"You sure Marineworld doesn't want a gray? Doubt you'd have a tank big enough to hold a devilfish."

Mark ignored the captain. As the boat came to the large channel between the islands, the radio in the cabin squawked to life.

"This is Mary from the *Amethyst*. Just spotted a group of killer whales heading south along the east coast of San Clemente. Looks to be four of them."

124

"It may be your lucky day," the skipper said as he slowed the engines and turned starboard.

"This is as good a place as any to wait for them. Once we confirm the sighting, we can drop the bait and get to work."

"Better hop in the skiff, then." The captain radioed to his crew on deck to prepare them. It wouldn't be long now. A deckhand was the first to call out. Mary was spot-on in her observation. There were four orcas heading right for the ship. The crew unlashed the herring and sprinkled it over the side. It splashed into the sea, leaving a thick greasy sheen. Gulls held at bay by the tarp attacked the fresh food source. Mark sat in the skiff as a deckhand used a winch to lower it. He held the sides of the craft in anticipation of what came next. When Mark was half-lowered down the "ramp," the deckhand needed to unlatch the skiff to drop it into the ocean.

"You ready?" the man Mark's age asked.

Mark returned a half-hearted thumbs-up, and the deckhand un-latched the skiff. Its descent was slowed by the net attached to the back. It was more of a bumpy plunge than a free fall. The raft bobbed as the ship pulled away and the orcas advanced on the bait. They were close now, within a few hundred yards. He had to act fast to ensnare them. Mark pulled hard on the cord for the motor. Nothing. He yanked on the string again for good measure. Nothing. The engine didn't turn. Its refusal to cooperate made him furious. He ripped at the cord again. After he'd promised Tom he'd deliver, if he failed the expedition, he'd be a laughingstock. The primer! Mark reached around and felt for the primer bulb. He pumped it. This time when he ripped the cord, it coughed and sputtered to life. The engine released a cloud of black fumes into the air. Before he sped off, the crewman saluted Mark with tongue-in-cheek thumbs-up.

The skiff bucked as he surged through the waves. He made a wide arc in the opposite direction of the seiner. It was crucial he finish the circle before the orcas completed their meal. He pulled alongside them at a distance of a hundred yards before he turned hard starboard to finish setting the net. There was the tall dorsal fin of an adult male and the shorter, curved dorsal fin of a female. Near the female, one juvenile and one calf stuck close by. Mark didn't break eye contact with the pod as he made the return loop to the seiner. They sensed the danger they were in. As Mark made the turn, the male charged ahead towards the gap between the net and the seiner. The female stayed behind. She tried to get the attention of her offspring who churned up the waters around the free food. The pair continued to happily push it under and frolic in the fish. She nudged them from their meal and followed her mate with a sense of urgency. The entire pod headed directly towards Mark's skiff. It was going to be close. His heart beat wildly in his chest. They would crash straight through his skiff if it meant freedom. He ratcheted up the throttle and braced himself. Members of the crew feverishly waved their arms and beckoned him towards them. They hollered encouragement. The male was the first to rip past the skiff into the big blue beyond. Mark was in awe of its enormous size as it escaped the trap. Its dorsal fin was at least six feet high, and it left a massive wake as it passed. The dread of failure set in. There was a short distance to go, but the orcas moved too fast. The sea was too turbulent. Soon, the others would break out.

There was a splash from the seiner as a voice rose above the cheering crew. "C'mon! Over here! Over here!"

Mark couldn't believe what he saw. The deckhand flung herring towards the remaining animals as they approached the skiff. They dribbled out the barrel across the deck. He wildly grabbed at the fish and chucked it at the orcas.

"Right here!" The bait splashed feet from the animals. The female and the juvenile slid between the skiff and the seiner, so close they brushed against the vessels. Mark flattened himself in the skiff to stabilize it. Icy water dumped over the sides and licked at his boots. As it attempted to follow its family, there was a loud thud as a herring thumped the calf in the back. It swung around and gave Mark enough time to finish closing the net. Panicked, it cried out to the others who had escaped the noose. The pod whistled from the opposite side as they circled. Their clicks and pops were deafening. There was a competition between the noise of the orcas and the voracious cheer of the crew.

"Nice job, quarterback!" Mark said. The deckhand received pats on the back and high fives from the captain and his crewmates.

"Just trying to get paid!" He rubbed his thumb and index finger together in the universal sign for money. This caused a fresh cheer from the crew. The cries from the orcas grew louder. The clicks and pops transitioned into terrified squawks in harsh tones. They volleyed over the net. Mark didn't feel like celebrating. They cried out for their child, their sibling.

"Let's finish this," he said to the crew. One engaged the Puretic power block to tighten the net. Before he re-boarded the boat, Mark needed to take measurements of the calf and make a general assessment of its health. They were incredibly fortunate to have only captured the one. He preferred not to wrestle with the nightmare of separating it from the others. The cries continued. It was odd, how they respected the net. Such powerful creatures made docile by twisted strands of nylon. They inspected the boundaries of the netting between their cries as if it was an impenetrable brick wall. The calf resigned itself to its fate. It pressed tightly against the side of the net. Based on its size, Mark reckoned the young calf was a male, maybe a year old. It was already twelve feet long and appeared to be in good health. He had a good width, which meant he was eating well. His skin was clean and free from abrasions. No indications of bacterial infections or parasites. Undoubtedly, he required tests back at Marineworld, but all signs showed a pristine specimen.

They only needed to tow their trophy back to the bay. While Mark made his assessment, the mother remained tight against the calf. The checkerboard pattern of the net pressed into her skin. When she surfaced, she stared at Mark. Her eyes seared into his memory. They were wide. So wide he saw the whites of an orca's eyes for the first time. Only they weren't white, they were blood-red. Frantic. An animal pushed to the edge. She was pleading for help. Mark turned his back to break the gaze of the mother. A sharp screech hounded his eardrums. He waited, listening for the sound of an inhale paired with the churn of waters behind him as she dove. If he stayed with her a moment longer, maybe it would have turned out differently. He liked to think he would have commanded the crew to abandon their mission. Convince them the money wasn't worth it. Severing a family was unthinkable. The commotion on the deck died down considerably as they readied the ship for its home journey. Hunched over the rail, the quarterback spoke to him.

"Why are they still doing that?" he asked. The male and juvenile were bobbing, shrieking out as they breached the surface before they disappeared and reemerged with fresh high-pitched squawks. Mark didn't want to answer him. The man was used to catching fish. When you catch a fish, its parents don't linger by your net, crying out.

"Worked up from the excitement. I'm done here. Help me back up?"

The quarterback nodded. He wasn't satisfied with the response but made his way across the deck to lift him back into the boat. Mark couldn't bear to be with the orca any longer. With a massive groan, the winch pitched to the side.

"She's pulling!" Mark said. He shuddered as the circular netting deformed.

The mother tugged hard at it. It was an act of desperation. She wouldn't be able to chew through the lines. She'd tangle herself in panic. Ten tons of force to batter them and demolish the winch. "Drop the line!" he ordered as the crew obeyed his directions. The ship bounded under the waves with each tug.

Scuttling from the wheelhouse, the captain fought to keep his balance as he clutched a brass monstrosity. The antique gun was designed for a giant, not a man. He buckled over, trying to wield the weapon. It didn't belong on the boat. It belonged in a museum. He heaved the barrel of the rifle upwards and tried to set it on the side rail.

"Don't!" Mark roared. For a moment, the captain listened to him. He hesitated as he raised the gun from the railing and placed it at his shoulder. "Don't!" Mark turned towards the orcas and closed his eyes. In a second, a medieval round would end his life. He had zero faith in the contraption's accuracy, let alone the captain. With a dull chunk, the whaling gun exploded and flung him to the deck. The lance whistled past Mark's ear before it drove into the mother with a wet thud. A trail of blood sprang from above her eye where it had pierced the thick blubber. The mother groaned and released her grasp, backing away from the net. How would he rationalize this? He'd told Tom there wouldn't be cowboy antics. An orca with a harpoon sticking out of its face didn't scream "new way of doing things." This was precisely the type of shit he'd demanded not to get involved with. Worse yet, how would they put the damn thing out of its misery?

There was a sharp crack as the lance embedded in the orca detonated. Water mixed with blood and viscera spewed high into the air. Pink spray rained upon him. A cocktail of blood, blubber, and flesh. Chunks of the orca pelted him as he rose from the position. White noise sizzled in his eardrums. The captain regained his footing. He held his lifeless arm, but his lips peeled back in a satisfied sneer. The carcass floated on its side. The top half of her head was split back, creating a grotesque flap of muscle and fat over the yawning wound. Mark could still make out the blood-red eye, only no light flickered in it as it peered into the sky.

"Saved the prize!" The captain gestured while he held his shoulder. The calf resurfaced inside the net near where its mother had been. Her body floated lifelessly towards it. When it reached the net, the calf wheezed a slow, mournful call. It was near-human. It bumped against the carcass, causing the slick of blood to distort and twist. There was no prize. He was wrong. This was murder.

The other two whales surfaced for air. The large dorsal fin of the male remained at a distance from the body. He was out of reach of the gun that had taken his mate's life. Unlike the calf, both orcas outside the net remained silent. The juvenile investigated. It swam in a serpentine pattern to its dead mother as it drew back into range of the whaling cannon. Sweat beaded on Mark's back.

"Don't you fucking dare!"

The pale face of the captain contorted into a grimace. Both of his arms rested on the deck rail as the brass weapon lay at his feet. A loud slush severed the silence. It was the sound of waves breaking, but the weather had settled. With speed, the juvenile rammed the carcass. The force of the impact closed the wound. For a second, the mother was whole. Her body sunk lower. Another impact. Another sickening slurp as the gash was closed. A pink froth of blood spurted forth, and with each try, the body sank deeper beneath the surface. It wouldn't be long before the remains attracted interest from the scavengers of the seas. Gulls already circled. The presence of the other orcas kept them at bay. The male vacated his protected position to approach. He curled himself between the juvenile and the body. In vain, the animal heaved itself against its father. There was no longer time left to linger. He herded his only free offspring away. Away from the carcass, away from its sibling. The net danced outwards as the calf dove. It followed the sinking body of its mother. As she descended to her last resting place, it pushed outwards, yearning for a last moment of contact.

Mark maneuvered around the boat and waited for the winch. The deckhand stretched out to position the hook before it was lowered. He slipped on the oily, bait-soaked deck. His feet faltered under him. In a blink, he hit the ramp hard and pitched into the sea. After the crash, the cries of the gulls fell silent.

"Man overboard!" Mark barked at the top of his lungs. He prayed the fall hadn't knocked him unconscious. Drawn by Mark's screams, the crew made their way to the stern. One fumbled to grab a life ring before he pitched it overboard. Each second lasted a lifetime as they watched for him to resurface. It was an eternity, but he finally materialized with a gasp.

"Damn it, Danny!" the captain shouted from the deck.

"I'm fine!" Danny brushed aside the life ring and treaded water. Mark sighed in relief and reached out his hand.

"You sure you're okay?" Mark asked.

"I've been better," Danny rasped through clenched teeth. A winding click rocketed throughout the water. It reminded Mark of a heavy cellar door groaning as it opened. He took his eyes off Danny to search for the calf, for the other orcas. They were nowhere to be seen.

"Help me in, man."

Mark's attention jerked back to Danny, clutched to the skiff. A chorus of shouts arose from the deck. The calf emerged from the dark depths with its jaws wide, its white underbelly only visible right before it struck. The orca's jaws snapped shut across Danny's thigh. The blood drained from his face as a wobbly scream came from his lips.

"Help... me in!"

Mark grabbed Danny by his wrists. His leg was in the orca's mouth from his knee to his ankle. It threatened to pull him under. Danny trembled. "

He—"

This time his plea was cut off by his own agonizing scream. Mark felt the pressure from the bite increase. It clamped down, sawing through muscle and sinew. Ignited by the cry of their colleague, the crew hurled whatever objects weren't bolted to the deck at the animal. Pliers, hooks, and wrenches sailed through the air in the beast's direction. The pair lurched to the side. The skiff threatened to capsize if the calf pulled away further. Danny's eyes grew wide.

"Don't let me go!"

The orca tugged hard, causing spray to lash over the rim of the skiff. Mark would try to forget the screech Danny let out as the orca's teeth shredded his leg to ribbons of muscle. Blood dyed the sea as it oozed from the wound. There was no time. Without thinking, Mark released his hold on Danny's wrist and shifted out over the orca. He made a fist and plunged it into the animal's blowhole. It immediately released its prisoner. Mark rolled Danny over and hauled him into the boat. Deep gashes ran the length of his lower leg. White streaks of fat were visible. He'd bleed to death if something wasn't done fast. Mark leaned his full weight over the laceration. Bright red blood flowed through the cracks between his fingers. Pressure alone wouldn't stop the bleeding.

"You're gonna be okay, Danny," Mark repeated to himself. He removed his belt and cinched it around Danny's thigh. The calf wailed. There was no response. His mother was dead and his family was long gone, but he continued to call. Each chirp was more sorrowful than the last. Eerie and otherworldly tones drowned out Mark's words of comfort. "It's gonna be fine. You'll be okay. You'll be okay."

A DAY OFF

Lee was motionless as Schmidt recounted the story of Akhlut's capture. He had a million questions to ask but wasn't sure where to start. He was as entranced as the first time he'd heard Schmidt speak in the auditorium, albeit for different reasons.

"What happened to Danny?" Lee asked. Schmidt fought off a grin. He continued in a whisper.

"He didn't die. The quick-thinking captain—he radioed for the Coast Guard when he heard me shout 'man overboard.' Told them it was a boating accident."

"And that was it? How come no one's ever heard of this?"

"It was a different time. Hell, we didn't even have cell phones. The pod was long gone by the time the chopper arrived. I doubt they even knew what we were doing. They airlifted him to Scripps, in La Jolla."

"No way they kept silent."

"They weren't gonna at first. I stopped them from killing him right there in the net. Had to remind them of how much money they stood to make if they brought him back alive. I believe the captain's words were 'What's one whale?' Once we got word from the Coast Guard that Danny was stable, they changed their tune. Money's persuasive that way."

Lee didn't know if he should feel betrayed. The burden of the secret tormented his mentor. Schmidt's face grew younger in the early-morning hours. Recounting the tale had lifted a great weight from him, but it wasn't the end.

"Why didn't you say something?" Lee asked.

"I came up with my reasons to stay quiet. At first it was loyalty. I convinced myself it was just part of the business, I guess. That didn't last long. Then it was money. I was young, didn't think I'd get paid as well anywhere else. After a while I realized I was the only one who saw them as more than assets. If it wasn't for me to stick around and help them, who would?" Years of conflict unfolded as he spoke. He stopped. "You'll need to convince Tom to bring him in. Who knows what else he's been up to out there?"

"Any ideas?"

"Find data where his swimming's erratic. Not from around the pen. Tell him it might be a health issue."

"I could tell him it's for a check-up. We'd release him again after tests."

"Good idea. But he won't want to bring him back unless he thinks it's serious. He'll ask you to collect samples without taking him to the lab."

"We can offer to do that. Take blood samples and blowhole swabs, tell him it's septicemia. That we'll need to run a full course of antibiotics."

"That might work. Even if you fake it, you'd need to bring the samples back to the lab for analysis. Tom's not an idiot. Complete blood count or culture takes time to get results. That's another day of him roaming free. It'll take more convincing than you think." The men silently reflected on how to make it work. Neither's brain fired on all cylinders at the early hour of the morning. "Look, it's a good idea, but we don't have to settle on a plan tonight. I'm exhausted. I know you are too. Go home, get some sleep, and think on it."

"I'm sorry, Doc."

"What are you sorry for?"

"You had to deal with it for so long."

"Don't be sorry, we'll fix it. We can make it right."

A cloud of uncertainty fell over Lee as he walked out of Schmidt's bungalow. He'd sought the doctor for advice, not a revelation. It would have been easier if Schmidt had told him his suspicions were nonsense. If he'd kept his secret to himself. Let it be. Being the one to decide meant dealing with the outcomes. He'd never settled on a plan his entire life. Half the time he fell into situations that benefited him. This was different. People's lives were at stake. He couldn't sit back and do nothing. What if someone else got killed? Or if they got Akhlut back and Tom still swept it under the rug? He could skip bringing him in and go straight to the media. But that left the problem of leaving him in the ocean. Would there be legal trouble for sharing information with the media? There wasn't direct evidence that he'd killed Mike. If he couldn't prove that it was Akhlut's fault, he'd be free and Lee would be broke and jobless. That didn't leave him with the resources to pull the killer from the water.

Questions bombarded Lee even after he made it to bed. He hadn't checked his phone since he'd left work. The soft glow of the screen bathed his room in a blueish hue. Seven unread messages. Mostly from Chad, but there was one from Stacy. He saved the best for last and scrolled through the messages from the intern first. The first was a picture at a bar with Amanda and Stacy. It was adorned with 'Where you at?!' overlaid at the bottom. The name of the bar and messages that deteriorated into gibberish followed. Confused, he opened the message from Stacy; it was much more clear. "Your friend is drunk. Ocean Beach tomorrow around ten. Hope you're there." Lee's thumb hovered over the reply button before he decided against it. He set his phone on the nightstand. If he didn't force himself to sleep, he wouldn't get up in the morning. As he rolled over, the electric whirr of a text caused his phone to dance. Another picture message. Chad passed out across a table while Amanda held two thumbs up. It read, "He probably won't make it." Lee typed back, "Probably not." After thinking, he added, "But I will." Satisfied, he hit Send and set an alarm for 9:00 a.m. Six hours of sleep was plenty. He laid his head back and waited.

His eyes closed for seconds before the sharp ring of the alarm jolted him awake. Any other day he'd hit the snooze button a few times before he got up, but today was different. Instead, there was a smiley face text from Stacy. That was a good sign. He started to text the intern instead. He needed to make sure he was awake. Midway through his sentence, he decided a call was better. On the fifth ring, a very groggy Chad answered.

"Hello...?"

Lee imitated an automated call. "Hello, you've booked a beach date with your coworkers today! If you need help to get your hungover ass out of bed, press one. If you need me to forcefully drag you from your home, press two."

"Damn it, Lee." He could hear the headache in Chad's voice as he spoke.

"Hey, man, get up. We're meeting Stacy and Amanda at Ocean Beach in an hour."

"You might be, I'm not."

"Why is that?"

"Because I am severely dehydrated, man."

"You mean hungover?"

"Yeah, that too."

"About that tracking data. I found something else out."

The voice on the line regained its familiar clarity.

"What'd you find?" Chad asked.

"I met with Schmidt. We'll talk in person."

"Sounds good. Think you can pick me up? I'm ninety-five percent sure I left my car at the bar last night."

"See you in a few."

He jumped out of bed to pull on a pair of jeans and made it to his bathroom before he realized a swimsuit was an excellent idea. His trunks were on a folded pile of clothes that sat on his dresser. He threw them on under his jeans and spent more time than he cared to admit picking out the perfect T-shirt. It was a quick ride to Chad's apartment off Muir Avenue and an even shorter trip to the beach. They didn't need to drive, they could walk, but something told him Chad wasn't up for the exercise. Despite his condition, the intern could offer insight on what to do next.

Lee barely noticed the warm, sun-soaked day as the single-bedroom beachfront apartments melted past him on his journey. Under normal circumstances, he could enjoy the pleasant breeze coming off the ocean while his car idled at each passing intersection. For living in San Diego, he never got to the waterfront as much as he wanted. Tourists dreamed of retirement and spending days at the beach. They pictured life there as a permanent vacation. For whatever reason, though the Pacific was minutes away, life blocked the simple luxury of a beach day. Even on the busiest days of the year, nothing beat lying on the warm sand and listening to the rhythmic crash of the waves on the shore. This could've been the perfect day off, a day to unwind and spend time with Stacy. Instead, he had to figure out a problem very few believed existed. He'd almost convinced himself, but his conscience wouldn't allow it.

When he reached Chad's weatherworn apartment on Muir Avenue, his coworker waited for him in the doorway. Dressed in his swim trunks and a tank top, he braced himself on the door frame with his head nestled into the crook of his elbow. He gave a lazy wave with his free arm as Lee pulled into the driveway.

"Did I miss an earthquake?"

"You're funny," Chad said. Daggers flew in Lee's direction from behind the thick frames of his sunglasses. "Come in for a minute."

Lee stepped inside, only to figure out why Chad stood in the doorway. The temperature in the tiny living room was the same as outside. The doorway was the best spot to catch the breeze that blew through the apartment. "I got pizza left over from last night. No idea what's on it, but it's yours if you want some." Lee inspected the extra-large pizza box on the coffee table. The contents looked ravaged by woodland creatures.

"I'm not hungry." Lee sat on the ragged sofa closest to the door.

"You missed out on one heck of a night, man." Chad plopped beside him and rummaged through the remains of the pizza. "What did Schmidt say about it? Coincidence, right?"

"He showed me files, stuff Marineworld buried, things he took when he was canned. It didn't ease my mind. I knew Akhlut had a mean streak, but I had no clue how far back it went."

"How far back was that?" Chad picked off toppings and ate them one by one.

"Since the start, since Mark captured him—"

"Captured? Wasn't he brought in for rehab?"

"That's the company line. Walsh signed off on it back in eighty-five." Chad stopped foraging. "There's a fisherman upstate with one leg because of it. When they got Akhlut in the net, he ended up with him. The way Mark described it, it wasn't pretty."

"You think he killed the maintenance guy?"

"I'm sure he had something to do with it."

"You gonna talk to Tom?"

"Yeah. I don't know what I'm going to tell him yet. I know we've got to bring him in. Maybe come up with a medical test we need to run."

"He's gonna be tough to convince. He'll know if that test is a bullshit excuse."

"I know."

"How do you make that work?"

The pair didn't speak as the breeze pulled through the house and swayed the blinds. It felt like they sat there quietly for the entire afternoon. Chad rested his hand on his temple. They were stuck in the same place as Lee and Schmidt hours ago. He spoke first. "Can it wait till tomorrow?" He paused. "We have this wonderful day to enjoy with two lovely ladies. After you talk to Tom, bring him in, things are going to get crazy. Can we have today before everything changes?"

He hated the thought of leaving him free. But right now, there wasn't much he could do. Chad was right, it would change. Things couldn't go back to how they were. He knew too much. He couldn't idly dismiss the accidents anymore. But that didn't mean he had to spend the whole day suffering with his thoughts.

"You're right."

"I'm right?"

"Yeah. When I go in tomorrow, I can get the tracking data and work on getting it sorted out. Let's have today."

"It's settled. Let's go, then!" Chad stood up, then instantly sat back down.

"I take it you need me to drive?"

"That would be excellent, man," Chad said. Lee shook his head. On the way out, Chad messaged the trainers.

"She says they're by the volleyball courts, near the dog beach." He drummed his fingers lightly on the windowsill of the car. "Not a bad little spot."

Minutes later, they were parked and combed the beach. It was busier than normal. A vibrant array of tents and umbrellas freckled the sand, surfers floated on their boards past the breakers, and anglers crowded the pier.

Today, all of San Diego had decided it was an excellent day to go out for a swim. Lee's eyes darted from umbrella to tent, looking for signs of Stacy and Amanda.

"They should be right near Lifeguard Tower Number 5," Chad said, his head buried in his phone. A familiar voice rang out to his left.

"Hey, Lee!"

In a fiery orange bikini, Stacy stood out from the crowd that blanketed the beach. They lay on towels beneath a large blue umbrella. Before he could respond, Chad answered the trainers.

"Well, you two survived last night just fine."

"Did someone hit you in the eye?" Amanda turned on her side to him. "Those are the most ridiculous sunglasses I've ever seen."

"It's sunny out," Chad fired back. "You didn't bring water, did you?" Amanda gestured to the cooler as Lee spread out his towel next to Stacy. It was the right decision to have one more normal day.

"So that's not a Marineworld wetsuit," Lee said. He looked away towards the surfers paddling out to catch the next set of waves, an obvious attempt to avoid looking directly at her. Stacy's lips flickered.

"Well, you know I usually wear it 24/7. Today it's at the cleaners. We can't all wear jeans to the beach."

"Swim trunks underneath."

"Even though you don't swim?"

"I don't, but I'm a good wader." Lee took off his jeans as he settled in. He made sure the shade of the umbrella covered his pale torso. Waves licked gently at the sand people frolicked in the surf.

"Let's make a deal. Let me lay out for a few more minutes, then I'll teach you to swim," Stacy offered as she rolled over on her stomach. Lee's fear of the water didn't register. Whatever it took for a few minutes alone with Stacy. If he looked like an idiot with his doggie paddle, so be it.

"I guess it's time I learned, huh?" He shut his eyes and listened to the waves crash, the hum of the surrounding crowd. Without intending to, he drifted off to sleep in the warm sun.

A cold nose rudely awakened him. It was accompanied by the monstrous noise of sniffing.

"I'm so sorry!" A man yanked the leash of his black Lab. The dog retreated to the side of his owner, satisfied with its investigation. Lee couldn't guess how long he'd slept, but judging by the sun overhead, it was just long enough to put him out of the shade of the umbrella. He rubbed his eyes and hunted for his group. The fierce rays stung his skin. Stacy and Amanda were nowhere to be found. Only Chad remained nearby, knocking back his third bottle of water.

"How long was I out?"

"Twenty minutes," Chad said.

Lee shook the sleep from his brain.

"Where are the girls?"

"They went to cool off. They'll be back in a minute."

Lee rested on his elbows and adjusted the umbrella to block out the sun. True to his word, he ignored the swirling cloud of questions regarding Akhlut and Marineworld. His upcoming swimming lesson from Stacy was on his mind. It was a half-truth, that he couldn't swim. He knew how to stay above the surface, but depths more than a backyard pool were a struggle. That was why he told people he couldn't swim. It was easier. Easier than admitting he'd spent his entire life around the water and still swam like a toddler struggling not to drown. Maybe Stacy knew a hidden technique that could erase two decades of futility.

"What's going on there?" Chad asked. A swollen mass chattered at the shore excitedly. Lee squinted hard towards where they pointed. Something in the water caught their eye.

"Probably harbor porpoises past the breakers." Tourists freaked at the sight of a dorsal fin. Hollywood had conditioned them to think it was a great white coming to gobble them up. In the real world, they never swam at the surface with their dorsal fin exposed. They came up from below. A swimmer would be gone before they had a chance to scream "shark." Luckily, humans weren't on their menu.

A high-pitched throttle sliced through the air as a four-wheeler kicked up sand during its approach to the crowd. That was odd. Lifeguards trained to spot the differences between species of marine life. They didn't chase false alarms like the tourists.

"Something's up." Lee tried to find the source of the commotion. He couldn't see anything. There was an electronic whirl as a lifeguard launched a drone from Lifeguard Tower Number 5. The entire beach was drawn towards the waterline. Lee waved to the man that operated the drone.

"Seal scare a tourist?"

"Something like that. We got an unconfirmed sighting of a killer whale coming in close to the shore from the north. We're just trying to confirm it. See if we need to close the beach until it passes."

Lee staggered back towards Chad. The "bowl of spaghetti" tracking data hadn't lied. Akhlut passed by the mouth of San Diego Bay often. He cursed himself for putting it to the back of his mind.

"It's him, I know it's him."

"He'll pass by. It's fine."

"But what if he doesn't?" Lee asked.

The men hurried to join the ever-growing crowd. Swimmers exited the surf, beckoned by beach staff and lifeguards. It was orderly. No panic yet. Still, each one peeped over their shoulder before they assembled on the beach. They wanted to see the whale for themselves. Everyone except Lee.

"There it is!" a woman gasped. The spray from the breaching animal dribbled to the ocean. People fumbled to find their phones for photos and videos.

"Do you see them?"

"There they are!" Chad waved at the trainers, calling them to come in. With all the commotion, there was no chance they'd hear him. Out further than the other beachgoers, they'd raced to the offshore buoy before the lifeguards signaled. But the trainers were excellent swimmers, and they caught up to the exodus of bathers swiftly. "They'll make it," Chad said. Lee's eyes hadn't left where the spray had landed. He waited for the orca's dorsal fin to resurface and prayed it wasn't the tall monstrosity.

"No way! Look! Look! Look!!" a child screeched as she dropped her ice cream to the sand. A black fin climbed skyward as it powered towards the last group of swimmers. Lee's face was washed in relief. It was smaller and rounded. The fin vanished as it came within one hundred feet of them. The trainers were too far from the shore. They wouldn't reach it before the orca caught them.

It reemerged and looped through the bathers in a winding motion. The fin weaved between them, cutting off their escape. When they realized it was an orca and not a shark, a wave of excited shouts came from the water. They weren't the bone-rattling screams of people being eaten. No, they were tinged with wonder. It was a magical event, something they'd tell their grandchildren about. The two trainers fell motionless in the orca's path.

"No! No! What are you doing?! C'mon!" Lee furiously waved them towards the beach. Effortlessly, the fin glided through the patch of swimmers and churned towards the trainers. It bowed to the shoreline in a waving motion. Fear coursed through his veins as it rolled. The pectoral fin slipped below the waves to reveal a sharp dorsal fin as tall as a man. It was Akhlut. Plenty of people shouted. Lee's calls were drowned out. He stood helpless on the shore. Useless. He couldn't reach them before Akhlut. Amanda slapped the water with an open hand.

"Why the hell is she doing that?" Chad asked. His mouth hung open.

"She wants him to come to her." Lee didn't believe it.

"Why? Why would she want that?" It was a question he didn't have the answer for. Then again, she didn't know what he did. If she did, he guaranteed she wouldn't be slapping the water.

Akhlut dipped beneath the waves. Any second now he'd rip one of them below the surface, never to return. Amanda swiveled to face the shore. Akhlut surfaced behind her with a spray. She was jerked forward as he speedily pushed her towards the beach. Her radiant smile was unmissable. No trace of fear as Akhlut propelled her forward with arms outstretched. The maneuver was well known to those who made a trip to the orca stadium. Stacy trailed behind in the wake. The onlookers clapped and cheered. They didn't have to pay an entrance fee to enjoy the spectacle. With a final forceful shove, Amanda glided into the shallows and strolled onto the soft sand. The transition was elegant. A hush spread through the crowd. Hundreds of eyes were on her as she wrung the water from her ponytail. Once she realized she was in front of an audience, her smile never faded from her lips. It widened until it was ear to ear. She swept her arm in a wide arc and took a bow.

The air reverberated with applause. Amanda waved back towards Akhlut with a flip of her wrist. He flung his tail flukes forward to send a splash towards shore. His show completed, he swam west. As his fin dipped beneath the horizon, the crowd pressed in around them. Everyone tried to get closer to Amanda.

"Do you see her?" Lee's voice cracked as he turned to Chad.

"Yeah, I see her, she's crazy." Chad grinned as a girl tugged on Amanda's hand impatiently.

"No, Stacy." Lee escaped the swarm towards the water. Panicked, he searched the waterline. Attacks happened right on the shore. They slid right onto the beach to collect seals. It was the same way they slid onto the stages during performances. His heartbeat grew faster with each passing second, but he couldn't bring himself to back out of the ankle-deep water. No Stacy. No Akhlut. Why had he thought they'd be safe at the beach?

"Do you see him?" The touch on his sides surprised him. He fought his instincts to leap forward. Stacy's bright smile erased his fears. The ocean seemed to calm as she led him out of the surf. Lee awkwardly wrapped his arms around her in relief.

"You always hug people after a swim?" Stacy said before she noticed the lack of color in Lee's face. "What's wrong?"

"I'm fine, I'm just... glad you're okay." There was a different tone in his voice. It wasn't the usual worry.

"We've worked with him for years—better us than anyone else." Her confident smile faded.

"You're right." Lee shook his head in disbelief.

"Luckily, he didn't forget his signals yet," she said.

"Yeah, luckily—" Lee struggled to figure out a way to keep things normal for a while longer.

"Lee, relax. It's okay. We're both fine, no one got hurt." She led him back to the mob.

"I'm glad she's going to be the one on the news," Stacy said. Her smile returned as they stood on the outskirt of the ring.

"Are you a mermaid?" The little girl's voice sparkled with delight.

"Maybe just part." Amanda winked at the girl as she squealed with glee. She was a performer again. It had been a long time since she'd swum with an orca in San Diego. They watched her play up to the crowd together. She entertained them with all the facts she knew about orcas and lines she'd memorized from the Marineworld shows, happily answering the questions they had. It had been foolish to think they could enjoy one more day before everything changed. Change would come, whether he wanted it or not.

145

NOT THE MARINEWORLD OF THE 1970s

"What the fuck happened out there?!" Robert Rousch tensed, ready to slam whatever was in arms reach against his office wall. Schmidt and Tom sat inside their boss's range as he bellowed. "Christ. A helicopter to La Jolla? What did you sign off on?!" He pressed his finger into Tom's chest and gritted his teeth.

"Rob, I wasn't on the boat," Tom said. "Mark was, and from the way it soun—"

"I don't care. You signed off on the expedition. It's your job to stop this."

"Nothing could stop it. We're dealing with animal—"

"Nothing? Maybe start with not chartering a goddamn boat with Captain Ahab?"

Mark remained silent as the tirade slowed. Rob leaned back in his seat. "Maybe you should have let him kill it, Mark. We could chalk the whole thing up as a wash. Only have a kid with a flayed leg to show for it?"

"The kid's gonna be fine—" Tom started.

"Is my wallet going to be fine?" Rob dug through his desk before he pulled out a leather-bound checkbook. "Here!" He threw it at Tom. "Make the check out. The members of the crew too. You've done it already. Now you just need to fill it out."

146

"You know that's no—" Tom tried to speak again.

"Shut up! I gotta pay off this kid, the crew. And for what? One animal? For what it's going to cost, we could have got six. And what happens when a whale with its fucking skull split open washes up on the beach? Are you going to be the one shoveling it into a pickup before reporters find it? We're not the Marineworld of ten years ago, gentlemen. It's time we act like it."

"Listen, it's—"

"No, you listen. You'll be lucky to keep your job. You can bet your ass I'm bringing it before the board." Rob turned to Mark. "He's the smart one. Had the common sense to keep his damn mouth shut. Now go take a walk, I don't want to see you for the rest of the day." Tom resisted the urge to interrupt the boss once more and left with his tail tucked between his legs.

"Why are you still sitting here?" Rob asked.

"I just wanted to say—" Mark tried.

"You don't get a say either. Jesus. After I just paid you a compliment. You think you're safe? You can't even control a crew of fishermen. Go stick your head in the sand. Maybe you two can plan your next career move."

Mark minded orders and left with his head hung low. He should have tried to stick up for Tom. Aside from not going on the expedition, there was nothing that could have prevented it. Rob would cool off. He always did. They accounted for incidents during collection trips. But he didn't enjoy paying more than he could have. Mark walked to the medical pool where the young orca was quarantined. He draped his arms over the glass partition and whistled. The animal had been quiet since its arrival. The last noises he'd heard from it were wailing cries drowned out by the screams of Danny. His body involuntarily trembled as they echoed in his memory.

"Here, boy." Mark whistled again, but the orca paid him no attention.

He twisted like a ribbon in the water, delightfully indifferent to the man that called for him. At least he was active. Mark crept to the shallow ledge, closer to the animal, and let out a sharp whistle. Still nothing. He hoped the bomb lance hadn't impacted his hearing. If he'd endured all that to bring back a handicapped orca, his days at Marineworld were truly numbered. He smacked the water. The animal had to learn how to respond to the basic signal. The young orca stopped spiraling. Mark slapped again. It did the trick. The orca powered over and exploded from the water. Mark sprang backwards to dodge the animal.

"Whoa, easy there." He lowered his tone to speak with the animal. "How are you today? Are you ready to talk?" The orca popped its jaw but didn't make a tone. "Fine. You don't need to say anything yet." The scar around the animal's blowhole showed signs of healing. "I'm sorry about that. You were just scared." Schmidt scooped up a handful of water and dripped it over the orca's head. He didn't have fish handy for reinforcement. "You'll be okay. I promise." He lowered his hand to pat the orca's rostrum.

"Mark!" The orca fled to deeper water as Tom shouted. "What the hell are you doing?"

"I wanted to check on him. To apologize."

"Were you planning to apologize to me after it shredded your arm off, then?"

"Tom, it wasn't like tha—"

"Like what? You couldn't say one word back there? Now you're saying sorry to a whale you watched turn a leg into Swiss cheese? What's up with you, man?"

"You didn't hear it. The way he cried for his family. What we did—it's not right."

"No, you know what's not right? You sat there and didn't say a damn thing in my defense. You were the one on the boat, the one who fucked it up. It'll be your fault we have to hunt for jobs."

148

"Is that what this is for you? That guy won't be able to walk again."

"You're right. And you're out with the whale? You need to get your head on straight. This is business. He's going to live a life of luxury now. Hundreds of fans visiting him. Fed daily."

"You weren't—"

"I wasn't there. I don't care. It's a wild animal. You want to be upset about something, be upset over the people. That kid in the hospital bed. The captain who has to live with hiring him." Tom walked away from the poolside before shifting backwards. "Hey! At least the crew got a payday, huh? And you've got a new friend. Fuck him, and fuck you too!" By the time Mark picked the perfect vulgarity to respond with, he was gone.

Tom was right. He needed to stay focused on the human impacts. But that didn't mean he'd neglect his duties. The orca was his responsibility. He'd give him the best chance to have a happy life behind the glass. It was the oath he took for every animal under his care. He hadn't been on the boats that had collected the others. There was a reason Marineworld contracted captures out to other companies. When questions came up, there was the wall of plausible deniability. Kjetil, Kjell, Kassuq, Ollju, Shurik. Did they share similar bloody stories of separations from their pods? Family members mutilated and plucked apart in front of them? Mark didn't want to consider the idea. They were supposed to set the example for the industry. And they did. With veterinary care and training, the competition wasn't close. But when the collection was held under a microscope, the differences between Marineworld and a roadside circus melted away. They still charged a quarter to watch a dancing bear. It had to get better.

* * *

149

After two weeks of quarantine, they cleared the orca for interaction. With clearance came the official announcement to the public. Rob handled the press release. Plastered on the news, he announced the animal had been rescued after beaching on the Northern California coast.

"Our team worked tirelessly to save this orca. A local seiner helped bring him in once our team arrived. He's been in the expert care of Mark Schmidt and our veterinary team. It seems he's predisposed to beaching. We're looking at options to release him back to the wild, but at this time, we don't think he'd make it. While we wait, I think it'd be wonderful if we could give the little guy a name." In one five-minute segment, he disarmed the public. They ate it up.

Mark launched his remote at the TV when he saw the clip. It hit the wall beside it and splintered to pieces. Batteries and chunks of plastic were sent flying across his living room. Rob had ensured Mark wouldn't say a word about the capture. He didn't trust him to stick to the NDA, to leave what had happened on the boat alone. Not a soul had known who Schmidt was before Rob had mentioned him on TV. Now the city saw him as a hero. The first training session with the orca was scheduled for the next day. There would be media to cover the feel-good story. Mark wouldn't be able to acknowledge anything different.

He didn't sleep that night. When he arrived at the park in the morning, he could barely keep his eyes open. If one of his trainers showed up in that condition, he'd bar them from entering the pool. But he'd be in a very different deep end. Rob waited for him at the employee entrance. Clad in a pinstripe suit jacket, he puffed on a cigarette as he paced back and forth.

"You look like shit." He ground it to dust on the brick wall.

"Didn't sleep much last night."

"Freshen up before you meet with them."

"They're here?" Mark asked.

"Poolside." Rob straightened the sides of his jacket before he jammed a mint in his mouth. Mark hurried into the changing room that trainers used. He cupped the cool water from the sink in his hands, letting it trickle through the cracks before flinging it into his face. He repeated the progression twice more. Invigorated, he stared in the mirror. Rob was right. He looked like shit, but at least he was awake. It was a bad sign that reporters were there. They wouldn't film an empty enclosure. Rob should have waited for him to get there before they started. When Mark blinked, images of Danny's leg clicked through his brain like photos in a slideshow. The blood oozing from the open wounds. White chunks of fat and deep red strips of muscle.

"You fall in?" Rob asked from the doorway.

Mark dashed one more handful of water on his face before he blotted a crumpled ball of brown paper towel across his forehead. He tried not to blink as he headed back to his boss. Rob put his hand on Mark's shoulder as they worked their way to the orca stadium. "Relax. Tom's warming them up for you. But before you head in there, remember, it was a rescue." When Rob emphasized *rescue*, Mark choked back his breakfast. He grated his teeth.

"I can't say we tore him away from his family? Killed his mother?" Schmidt's response was unexpected. Rob took a step backward and raised his hand before he caught himself. Mark steadied himself for the tirade of expletives to replace it, only it never came. They were within earshot of the stadium; Rob whispered.

"What you need to understand—the only thing you need to understand—is the welfare of that animal is your responsibility. Who knows what might happen if you weren't around?"

Mark flinched as Rob gave him a firm pat on the shoulder. He escorted him into the stadium. A single reporter and her cameraman stood next to Tom. Marked sighed in relief. One reporter was easier to manage. Water cascaded over the glass to the filter system below as an orca glided near the window to send a fresh burst over the edge. Mark recognized the black notch in his eye patch. Kjetil.

"Doesn't that waste water?" the reporter asked. Tom rested his hands on his hips.

"Not at all. Our filters do an amazing job. But Mark here could tell you better than I can." Tom introduced her to him. She assured Mark they'd run through questions first before recording.

"You're the one behind the rescue of the little guy?" she asked. Mark cringed. He didn't know how much information Tom volunteered before he arrived.

"He's your man," Rob said. His breath stank of tobacco and peppermint. "When we got the call for a beaching, he worked with a local to crew rescue him."

"How did you all manage it?" she said. "That's not him there, is it?" the reporter asked.

"No. That's one of our other orcas. Kjetil. Our new friend is hiding in the back pool. He's a little shy. He's been quiet since we pulled him off that beach, but he's coming around," Mark said.

"Can we get him out here?" Rob asked.

"Of course, we'll make sure you get the perfect shot," Tom said. He hustled around the pen to talk to the trainers. One was on the stage working with Kjetil as others unlatched the gate to let the newcomer out. He rocketed from the back pool and pinned Kjetil against the glass. A fresh wave of water surged over the top towards the group. He swam over Kjetil and spiraled in the water.

"Wow! He's a playful thing," she said. "Too bad we weren't rolling for that. Do you think he'd do it again for the camera?" she asked. The aggression surprised Mark, but he was grateful it took her mind off the story of his rescue. The shy male hadn't been aggressive since his arrival. He hadn't had the chance to interact with the others.

"I think he would, but we'll split them up so you can get footage of only him," Mark said. The trainers didn't need to be told to separate them. They saw it too. They motioned Kjetil into the back pool. The orca fled from his attacker but was rammed in the abdomen. A spurt of water flew into the air as Kjetil was lifted. The thud of the impact reverberated through the stadium.

"That's normal?" the reporter asked. She didn't have a clear view of the strike, but the commotion drew her curiosity. The turning of heads to view the aftermath of a car crash.

"Of course it is." Rob looked at Mark for confirmation. Mark tried to hide his worry.

"Two young males. They roughhouse. Boys will be boys," Mark said. She was satisfied with the answer for the moment. "Rob tells me the station is running a contest to name our friend. What's leading at the moment?"

"Some Eskimo name. Adlartok, Amaruq. Jim, what was it?" she asked her cameraman.

"Akhlut," he responded as he hefted the camera on his shoulder. "You ready to roll?"

***When the news crew cleared out, Mark sprinted to the back pool. He was glad he hadn't had to say much for the interview. It would be a fluff piece to fill five minutes on the evening news. They'd rushed out as soon as they'd gotten the sound bite they needed. He still wasn't happy telling the world he helped save the orca, but he wasn't worried about that now.

"Call Kjetil over." He was barely older than the new calf. Minor injuries during development could create lifelong problems. A trainer blew his whistle and motioned to the slide-out. Within seconds, Kjetil skidded from the water onto the platform, his mouth opened in anticipation of the reward for a behavior well done. Mark grabbed a fish from the bucket that hung over the glass and tossed it in the orca's direction.

The throw was off target, but Kjetil snagged his prize regardless. "How's he moving? Has he been sluggish?" Mark asked.

"No. Nothing like that. We kept an eye on him. Probably got a nice bruise, though. That was a hell of a smack."

"Those look fresh." Mark pointed to the rake marks on the base of Kjetil's pectoral fins. They were made when an orca dragged its teeth across another's flesh. Usually, they were light scratches. These were deep gouges. The four gashes had only recently stopped bleeding.

"I don't know how we missed those. Must have happened before we separated them." Rake marks could be signs of rough play—it was hard for the animals to get away from each other in the enclosures—or an act of dominance. The new orca had a mean streak. A play for dominance this early after his arrival was unexpected.

"Let's keep those two separated for now. And Shurik. Don't put the new one with him for long. I don't want him to challenge him." Mark knew it wasn't likely, but the bull would make quick work of the newcomer if he tested him. He could get away with raking Kjetil, but that wouldn't fly with the dominant male. "You have to stay on top of this. They're stressed. Anxious. This is a whole new world for them. They'll strike out at each other if we don't give them time to adjust. Or worse, one of you," Mark said. The trainer nodded as he gave Kjetil another fish and rubbed his head.

Rob pushed them. He referred to Kjetil, Kjell, Kassuq, and the fresh male as the new batch. Marineworld sent its seasoned orcas to other parks around the country. Only Shurik remained from the old guard. Ollju established herself as the matriarch, but she was barely older than the others. With this new batch of orcas, Rob insisted on a change of training. He wanted them to perform the entire catalog of behaviors. It was for flexibility during shows. One could be swapped out for the next if it didn't respond. But it caused problems. Not every animal took to all behaviors. It was stressful for the animals and the trainers. Their frustration leaked into performances. Without positive reinforcement, they lost interest in flips, twirls, and splashes. Why put on a show without the reward? They gravitated to the full food buckets, knocking them out of trainers' hands.

If it was a failure as part of a paired sequence, they took out their aggression on each other. Rob laughed at it. "They'll learn quicker that way. A little nip could do them good." He wouldn't listen to Schmidt. His true focus wasn't on their training for shows. Captive breeding was the future of the industry. The writing was on the wall. What had been the golden era of plucking orcas from the ocean had passed. The capture of the young male was to be the last in US waters. Breeding to sustain the population was critical.

"Mean little bastard, isn't he? Want to thank me for saving your arm now?" Tom asked. He leaned against the ledge of the tank. "Sorry for going off on you the other day. Rob's a prick. I was pissed at him. I shouldn't have taken it out on you."

"It's fine. I'm not going to thank you, though. We've got to do something about their training." Tom rolled his eyes. He'd heard Schmidt talk like this, right before Rob had told him to kick rocks. What a waste of an apology. "Look, the breeding program. It's not going to work." He earned Tom's full attention.

"Why's that?" he asked.

"Look at them. They're beating the shit out of each other. You think one will carry to term if she gets rammed like that? They're hostile. Pissed to be here."

"Well, what's your idea?"

"Shake up the training. More enrichment. We don't force them to do every single behavior. Let them stick to the ones they're good at. We can build the shows around that. I'll profile the animals. Figure out which ones work well together and stick to it. No more of this 'Jack doesn't like Jill' bullshit that only certain trainers remember. We'll put it on paper." He picked his words carefully, made sure not to mention animals' health or happiness.

"Rob hasn't gone for it before. What's different this time?" Tom asked.

"His dreams of little calves are done if he doesn't buy into it. You'll do the talking."

"Why would I do that?"

"Because you want to get paid."

CHASING A GHOST

What had happened at Ocean Beach spread like wildfire. Cell phone footage and video from the lifeguard drone flooded social media. Activists and experts alike dissected it. They openly challenged the merits of reintroducing Akhlut. Marineworld's image was at stake. The triumph of the sixtieth-anniversary celebration threatened to turn sour. Tom wouldn't let it continue. When he'd been promoted to director of the CRI, they'd rewarded him with a package of Marineworld stock. The price had doubled when the CRI had opened. With the release of Nayak, it had risen again. Putting Akhlut back in the ocean had sent it careening into orbit. It was finally his payday, and a stupid orca wouldn't ruin it. He needed to control the bleeding. The stock would take a hit when they returned Akhlut, but it was nothing compared to if someone figured out what had happened to the diver.

There was an all-staff meeting the next morning. Tom called everyone involved and instructed them not to give interviews or say a word to the media. Press was to be handled through Marineworld channels. He spun the incident as a one-in-a-million occurrence. It wasn't far from the truth.

The employee turnout made it tough to escape and talk to the press. Trainers, maintenance divers, and employees crowded into the hall. Lee pushed his way to the head of the pack as Tom started his speech.

157

"First off, thank you for showing up so early. I know it's strange seeing this place without guests. By now, you've seen the video of the incident at Ocean Beach. Luckily, our staff members who were there were unharmed. They even arrived early this morning after the excitement. We did what we thought was best for Akhlut by releasing him. Unfortunately, his time with us has made it impossible for him to survive in the wild. That's not his fault. But it's our responsibility to bring him home before someone gets hurt."

The crowd took sips of coffee from Styrofoam cups as their director spoke. Lee squirmed. Edgar and Mike were dead. Akhlut was home. He needed to be returned to his prison before he claimed another victim. "Bringing him home won't be easy. His tag stopped transmitting. This doesn't mean we don't know where to look. We've reviewed the data and created a search grid that covers his highest-traveled areas. The crew of the *Blu Endeavor* have graciously volunteered to lead the search party. You know the fantastic work they do with white sharks. They have the expertise and equipment to bring Akhlut home safely and fast. As for our part, we've assigned staff to boats to aid with spotting him. Each one will be equipped with reinforcement aids from San Diego. Our trainers can appeal to the showman in him. The goal is to route him to the *Blu Endeavor*. We want to stress him as little as possible. We're not chasing him in speedboats. The captains have been briefed on where we're starting our search. Boat assignments have been emailed out. I'll answer questions before we get going. Otherwise, we start at nine. Let's bring our boy home."

Lee set his coffee on the floor. It was news to him that Akhlut's tracking tag had stopped transmitting. At least he had the physical copies of the tracking data in his office. Akhlut had to be returned, but this was overkill. He was trained to follow the *Shepherd* like Nayak. A team with a few trainers could get it done. There was no need to rope in the great white hunters and set loose an armada. Tom turned it into a performance. Lee opened his phone to check his email and frowned. He was assigned to the *Blu Endeavor*. Tom fielded questions from a group of employees.

"Tom!" Lee got his attention. A sideways scowl momentarily shattered his pleasant facade. Before he repeated himself, Stacy whispered in his ear.

"You think that's a good idea?" she asked.

"I don't get it," Lee said.

"Don't get what?"

"Why did we go through the trouble of training him before release? Does he have no faith in us?"

"He wants it filmed so the public can see an amazing rescue."

"He's an a—" Tom had made his way over to the pair.

"Stacy!" His trademark enthusiasm returned. "How's Amanda? I was surprised when she said she was ready to go today. She's tough."

"She wants to make sure he's safe. I don't think you could stop her."

"Right? Just incredible. Do you mind if I borrow Lee for a second?"

"Be my guest," Stacy said. She followed the crowd towards the docks.

"What's on your mind?" Tom asked.

"Why not put me on the *Shepherd*? He's conditioned to follow it."

"I wish it was that simple. There's a lot riding on this. If the tracking tag were working, the *Shepherd* would be perfect. It's not. This is our backup plan. Believe me, I wish your team could ride out there and grab him. We're still using the *Shepherd* with the fleet. But I need my Head Cetacean Behaviorist to be there when the *Blu Endeavor* tows him home. They have the best chance of finding him. You know him best. Can I count on you?"

"Yeah," Lee said. There was no use arguing. He walked away to contain his frustration. At least he didn't need to convince Tom that Akhlut had to be returned. The deluge of half-truths that spilled from him was relentless. They'd worked for months to get Akhlut to follow the *Shepherd.*If the reintroduction went south, a plan was in place to send the team out and collect him. Because they'd ended up on the news, the plan had gone out the window. Now they were sending a flotilla armed with a TV crew. Tom transformed into a promotional stunt. Despite their best efforts, Marineworld was still rooted in the entertainment business. This was great for business.

* * *

Lee surveyed the ocean from the deck of the exploration vessel, as it navigated the search grid. A former Alaskan crabber, the 126-foot *Blu Endeavor* dwarfed the boats clustered around the docks of the CRI. After its stint as a crab boat, a San Diego investor had purchased it and converted it into a yacht. Unsatisfied with his new pleasure craft, he'd added a hydraulic lift to move his forty-five-foot fishing boat between the deck and the water. Funded by Marineworld, the research group had purchased it at auction and renovated the lift into a flat platform. It stuck out as the most unique feature on the craft. Like the rest of the ship, it had undergone a metamorphosis from its previous life.

The biologists sought to expand the public's knowledge of shark biology and conservation. The lift was their ticket to instant publicity. Once lowered into the water, the team baited a great white shark to it. When the shark was in position, they raised the platform to take it out of the water. The team descended upon it to collect tissue and fluid samples and remove parasites when it reached the deck. In most cases, they attached tracking devices before releasing it. A capture event was must-see TV. The research team didn't work with mammals, so Lee's interactions with them were limited.

When Lee had first started, Mark had kindly described the crew as a bunch of stuntmen who were only interested in National Geographic specials. The way they shouted at each other made him inclined to agree with his mentor. There was an overwhelming hum of excitement in the air. To them, this was another adventure for publicity. They knew it wasn't just another capture job. He frowned at the lift platform above the water.

"How long is it?" Lee turned to a worker.

"Thirty feet. Big enough for a great white," he said confidently.

"You're gonna need an extra two feet," Lee said. The worker stared at him, astonished he questioned the vessel. The ship beneath him shook as it shuddered to life. Even though it was the lead ship, it was the last to leave the harbor. A colorful skiff led the fleet. He'd prefer Stacy wasn't on it, but nothing he could say would stop her.

The search grid ranged from South Coronado Island to San Diego Bay. A helicopter provided aerial support. The chopper was the most efficient way to cover the grid, but there were restrictions to the height it could fly. With the weather, it would be much better to slowly hover at lower altitudes, but NOAA guidelines required that they stay at least one thousand feet above the surface. Akhlut wasn't the only wildlife in the waters around the CRI, and there were stiff penalties for disturbing it. On the other hand, a quick fly-by would miss him. He could stay under for ten minutes at a time. Judging by the murky surf, the chopper was useless unless the fleet found him first.

The roof of the *Blu Endeavor*'s wheelhouse sat thirty feet above the water and provided the perfect perch for spotting. Men stationed on the corners were equipped with scopes and binoculars. They'd find Akhlut and be on solid ground before long. If the tracking tag had been functional, the search would have been over before it started. Lee headed to the wheelhouse roof as the CRI shrank into the distance. There was no special trick to spotting an orca. Daily whale watching tours had trouble locating any animals in rough seas, let alone a specific one. Picking out the iconic spout against choppy waves was impossible. Their biggest asset was patience. If they did a speedy survey of the entire grid, they'd come up empty-handed.

"Make sure you scan slowly." The orders came out of Lee's mouth unnaturally. A deckhand let out a grunt as he panned the lens. Lee tapped him on the shoulder. "May I?" He needed no excuse to pause his search. He yawned and stepped back from the scope. Lee doubled-checked it was on low magnification before he tracked across the horizon line. A sudden pop of color exploded across the waves. The lead skiff darted ahead. He switched the objective to a higher magnification and focused on the vessel. Stacy was out on the bow. She held the roof and pointed in the direction she wanted the craft to maneuver. Her hair blew backwards as the boat sliced into the waves. She was a mile away, but the determination on her face was visible. If he squinted, he could spot the freckles that dotted the bridge of her nose.

"Thought we were looking for a whale, not birds, mate," the crewman said, interrupting his search. Clearly caught, Lee stumbled with his response.

"I was just, uh, checking the focus."

"Right," the deckhand grumbled as he wedged Lee from the scope and renewed his hunt. He paused. "I'll scan slower."

* * *

From her spot on the bow, Stacy directed the skiff. Based on the data, they had a good shot at finding Akhlut near Sunset Cliffs or the entrance to Mission Bay. The large crab boat trolled behind at a steady pace. Elevated positions on the *Blu Endeavor* offered the best odds of spotting Akhlut, but the small boats were more agile. Covering more water meant they'd pick him up first. She had been paired with him for waterwork. It wasn't a random orca they were tracking; it was a former partner. Early in their career, trainers all got the same speech from management. The orcas needed to be treated as wild. Even the ones born in captivity. They were unpredictable beasts that did as they pleased. Schmidt had broken it down for them. They weren't dogs. They wouldn't answer to the positive reinforcement of treats endlessly. Trainers had to be hyper observant whenever they entered the orcas' domain. There could be signs, little tells, that an animal was off, but sometimes there wasn't anything at all. When you viewed them as dogs, trouble started. No matter how agreeable they appeared, accidents happened. Don't anthropomorphize them, he preached. If management felt a trainer was too comfortable with one, they'd be moved elsewhere in the park. Better to keep them safe with seals or dolphins. But Marineworld took advantage. Trainers learned not to ask questions; otherwise, they'd end up in the kiddie pool. This created a strange comradery between trainers. They spoke up only to each other, hid injuries, and played down close calls. They didn't want to be separated from the orcas they loved.

As trainers gained experience, individual orcas' personalities bloomed. Whales like Akhlut thrived on performances. It was their time to interact with someone, something, besides the walls of their enclosure. Their glazed-over eyes longed for stimulation. A way to grind out the monotony of the day. Trainers knew keeping the orcas locked in tanks was unethical. Even though it meant the end of their careers, it had been a relief when Marineworld had opened the CRI. Their partners had a fantastic space to retire. They were in the ocean, where they belonged. The company made things right after decades of the questionable choices. Enthusiasm for the project had only increased when the board had presented their plan for reintroduction.

Tom had talked an excellent game. He'd insisted orcas be evaluated on a case-by-case basis centered on the opinions of experts like Schmidt. When he'd been fired, the plan had unraveled. Without Schmidt, there wasn't a safety valve to keep Tom in check. It left

Lee as the expert to pass judgment. Tom twisted his words against him. Hammered to the wall that Akhlut was an optimal candidate for release. The board was more than happy to listen. To put their star back where he belonged was great PR. It would close a dark chapter in their history. Things couldn't be easy, though. Akhlut wouldn't be allowed a fairy-tale ending. His only hope was retirement. Stacy's heart sank at the thought of him confined again. But it was an order of magnitude above being stuffed in the shallow tanks of San Diego. He wasn't fit for reintroduction. She owed it to him to bring him back. It was better for a friend to guide Akhlut home instead of a boatload of strangers hired to hunt him.

Her radio hissed. "We might have something to your northeast. Glimpsed a spray off the coastline. Keep your eyes peeled." It was the captain of the *Blu Endeavor*. The crewman aboard her skiff let off the throttle.

"What about the chopper? Can they see him?" Stacy asked.

"No-go on the helicopter. Low fuel. Headed back to the CRI. Couldn't see a thing in this pea soup anyways."

The hard khoosh was unmistakable. It was enough for her to know it was him. Other trainers claimed they couldn't hear it, but whenever Akhlut surfaced, she swore she heard a tiny whistle on the end of his breath. She insisted it was from a healed cut behind his blowhole—a scar he'd picked up before his time at Marineworld.

"There he is!" She faced off the bow as the boat reengaged its engine. They needed to draw him towards the *Blu Endeavor*. Each boat was equipped with training aids: long poles with foam balls on the end, underwater speakers to emit tones, and even chunks of ice. All could be deployed to entice Akhlut. He'd shown a willingness to repeat learned behaviors. They hoped the tools still influenced him.

"Keep your distance, we don't want to spook him," Stacy instructed the skipper. "The last thing we need to do is lose him in this mess."

"How close do you want us?" he asked.

"A hundred yards. Close enough for him to hear the tone, but not so close he dives and runs."

He dutifully followed her orders and pulled within a football field of the orca. Stacy lowered the speaker as Akhlut coasted away from them. Connected to a laptop on board, it played the same tones used in Marineworld shows. They'd modified sounds from wild orca recordings to motivate the whales to perform a multitude of behaviors. There were audio cues for everything from being called out to the show pool to sliding onto a stage for medical treatment.

"Are they set on the *Endeavor*?" She rocked in the boat and tried to find the tone she wanted to use.

"They're good to go whenever you're ready, Stace. Think he'll respond?"

"One way to find out." She double-clicked the trackpad and instantly knew it was a mistake. Akhlut registered the electronic squeal as it traveled through the water. He dove beneath the waves with a sharp flick of his tail. It dredged up powerful memories he wanted nothing to do with.

"He's running!" she said. The boat motored forward to regain sight of the animal. Depending on how long he stayed submerged, it would be hopeless trying to locate him again.

"What did you play?"

"Callback tone used to bring them to the stage. Guess he doesn't care for them anymore."

"That's an understatement. Bullets move slower. Are there others you'd care to try?"

Stacy scrolled through the tones, calculating how he might respond. There had to be something to draw him. Something for him to investigate. "The target pole? Would he go for that?" the skipper asked. She ignored his questions. There was one thing that interested him. Yesterday at the beach had proved it. She grabbed the aluminum frame of the craft for stability and zipped her wetsuit.

"Stop the boat," she said.

"What? Why? We'll lose him."

"We've already lost him."

The color drained from the skipper's face.

"Don't!" He grabbed at her arm. With a perfect dive, she put space between herself and the boat. The chilled water reminded her of the stadium in San Diego, only there wasn't the sting of chlorine in her eyes, just the taste of salty surf. Waves made it difficult to tread water, but she stayed afloat.

"Here." The skipper extended his hand over the side to Stacy. "Come on, you'll drown before he even turns around!"

She ignored his pleas and sharply smacked the water.

"Not gonna hear that, c'mon!" he said. The skipper reached for the target pole to extend to her. If Akhlut surfaced, she'd be able to see him coming. If he lurked in the cloudy depths, she wouldn't know until he was on top of her. As a matter of preference, she didn't care to be surprised by a seventeen-thousand-pound beast. With a whistling whoosh, he surfaced in the distance. He'd traveled further than they'd expected but plodded steadily on a return route.

* * *

When she dove off the boat, a wave of helplessness washed over Lee.

"Your friend—she's mad, isn't she?"

He didn't listen to the crewman. He ran to the steep metal staircase. His only goal was to radio Stacy's boat and do it fast. His legs pumped as he tumbled down the near-vertical stairs and threw himself through the door.

166

"What the hell?" the captain protested. Lee pushed him aside and grabbed the radio.

"What's the frequency for the lead boat?" He turned dials and switches on the console. Eyes locked on him. With an exasperated sigh, the skipper spoke first.

"It was tuned before you started messing with it." He calmly took the radio from Lee and readjusted the dials before handing it back to him. "Here."

"Get her out now!" Lee's voice dripped in fear as it came over the speaker. He repeated his message to the lead boat again.

"What's wrong? She's drawing him back," the captain asked.

"It's not safe! Get her out!" He raised the boat, but the skipper didn't answer.

"She's worked with him before. She knows what she's doing." The captain's demeanor infuriated Lee. He didn't understand what Akhlut was capable of. Lee dropped the radio and rushed out to the deck of the former crab boat. "Check why he's so worked up," the captain said.

Lee slipped across the spray-soaked deck. Once he reached the rail, he could see the lead boat with Stacy again. She was a powerful swimmer, but she was too far out. Her skills were useless if Akhlut got close. She was in his domain now.

He flailed his arms, shouted, and jumped, to no avail. No matter what he tried, he couldn't catch their attention. Akhlut cruised lazily at the surface. He didn't deviate from his course towards her. The deck was chaos as scientists and crewmen prepared for the orca.

"What's the matter?" the crewman sent for Lee asked. "We've got him—it's fine." He didn't hear the man.

Lee stopped shouting. He should have told her how dangerous Akhlut was at Ocean Beach. It was his fault that she was in danger. He could return to the captain and tell him to put the ship in the path of Akhlut and Stacy, but by the time he made his argument, it'd be too late. Plus, Akhlut would just dive under the boat. A distraction might work, but tiny splashes at this distance wouldn't draw his attention. It had to be bigger, sustained.

Lee's knuckles burned as he gripped the railing. His legs had a different idea. The two halves of his body were locked at war. It would be like hitting concrete from this height, but that wasn't the worst that could happen. He took a deep breath.

"Hey!" The crewman's voice broke as Lee hurled himself over the rail.

He plummeted to the surf and pierced the waves as a spear. Fear enveloped him as he sank deeper below the waves. He pawed wildly at the sea in a blind attempt to find the surface. His lungs burned as his body told him to gasp for air. If he surrendered to the request, it was over. Blackness creeped into the corners of his brain when a wave of thunder cascaded through his chest. He snapped back to full alert. There was a fate far worse than drowning that waited for him. He kicked ferociously in the direction he imagined the sky to be. Away from the thunder that loomed. He waited for the next ping of echolocation. Instead, wind rushed over his face. He greedily sucked in air to put out the blazing fire in his lungs. Each gulp subdued the pain.

The crewman shouted at him. His words were inaudible over the noise of the boat and the swirling sea. The saltwater spray was blinding. He swapped scorched lungs for stinging in his eyes. Every wave carried a fresh surge of fear. He wasn't alone. There was a splash nearby. This was it. He shut his eyes in anticipation of the teeth. It would be fine. Stacy was safe. Hours passed as he waited for the impact. He barely heard the hollering from above. Cautiously, he cracked an eye open.

"Grab the damn ring!" The voice was clear now. The crewman stood on the ledge where Lee jumped. A long-threaded cord was lashed to the rail. The opposite end was tied to a white life ring that floated feet from him. He stretched his arm to reach it, but his head dunked beneath the waterline. It drifted further from his grasp. With every try, his head raised less. His muscles ached from the struggle. He made one last lunge at the ring.

The water exploded as Akhlut erupted in front of him. He seized the ring in his jaws and slammed back onto the surface. The force of the wake pushed Lee into the depths. Exhausted, he sank. As he descended, the whale toyed with the ring, driving it down before he flipped it onto his rostrum. Lee's mind drifted. Darkness seeped into his consciousness. An eerie sense of calm came over him. He was tired and desperately wanted to rest.

A jolt of pain ricocheted up his back. He couldn't figure out how he'd hit the bottom so soon. Akhlut was a few feet above. Lee groped behind him for the source of his pain. The roundness of a metal bar instead of sandy seafloor surprised him. A rumble of the ocean floor went unnoticed. He concentrated on the orca as the blackness fought for control.

The platform would deliver him straight to Akhlut's waiting maw. The bar dug deeper into his back as he moved toward his fate. Now untouched, the life ring rocked on the waves. As his world faded to black, Akhlut filtered towards him. The orca cocked his head inquisitively. Gently, he bumped the limp body with his rostrum. Frustrated by the lack of response, the whale bumped him with more force. Lee's body twisted over the railing and tangled among the bars. Delighted, Akhlut chirped and let out a stream of bubbles. He glided close again, bobbing his skull and letting out a long, high-pitched click. The platform came to a rest just above the waterline with a loud mechanical thud. Water tumbled from Lee's mouth as he draped over the rail. What started as happy squawks from Akhlut changed into lower agitated tones. There was a symphony of screams as the crew sprang into action. Lee sputtered and coughed up the saltwater.

Dazed, he sagged precariously close to the jaws of the orca.

"Grab him!"

Akhlut's thrashing held the crew at bay. The platform groaned and creaked with each shift. His mouth sprawled wide, the orca whipped his head and tail in alternating directions. Rows of razor-sharp conical teeth acted as a spiked barrier. His irregular movement made it tough to time a rescue.

"Get him off the bars!" Ducking under the animal's tail, the crewman who had thrown the life ring clambered to retrieve it. "Hey! Hey! Hey!" He hurled the ring over Akhlut. Like a massive golden retriever, the whale's body tracked it as it sailed past out of reach.

In a flash, another crewman grabbed Lee and dragged him towards the main deck. With his prize taken from him, Akhlut reared and snapped his teeth. To calm the orca, a someone threw a wet blanket over his head. The thrashing stopped as if by magic.

"Is he all right? Is he breathing?"

A group circled around Lee. His eyes rolled forward in his skull as he regained consciousness. A queasy feeling swept over him. They tipped him on his side when he vomited. He snapped awake. Panicked Lee slipped as he struggled to stand on the deck.

"Easy there, easy."

His movements slowed. His feet felt the solid surface of the deck.

"You're one crazy son of a bitch."

He focused on the familiar accent of the man with the scope. Lee swayed as his eyes adapted. The man tapped him on the leg.

"And I said she was mad!" He roared with laughter.

Thoughts of Stacy rushed to Lee, and he bolted upright. Wrong choice. His head wobbled on his neck like it could detach and roll into the sea.

"Whoa, whoa, whoa—easy, buddy." The voice echoed around him as he dropped unconscious back to the deck.

Lee came to as the *Blu Endeavor* docked at the CRI. He lay across a cot with thick wool blankets. His surroundings were unrecognizable, but a familiar freckled face sat next to him.

"How you feeling?" she asked. He was a pile of hot garbage, but he smiled.

"I'll make it," Lee responded. The crewman who'd thrown the life ring and the one with the scope stood at the door.

"You sure you're not gonna pass out on us again?"

"Yeah, I'm good," Lee said.

Satisfied with this answer, the crewman whispered to his partner. They exited the wheelhouse laughing.

"What did he say to him?" Stacy asked.

"Probably something about us being mad." He paused. "Are you all right?"

"Oh, I'm fine. I actually know what I'm doing."

"That wasn't why I was worried."

"Thank you," she said. "Those swimming lessons would've helped."

"Something always gets in the way."

"Well, that something is safely in a pen."

"He didn't cause trouble for the crew?" Lee asked.

"None. Just swam in circles. He'll settle down."

"It'd be nice to get away from the water."

"Oh, you're only saying that because you almost drowned. Quit being so dramatic." She brushed the hair from her face.

"I'm totally telling them I saved you," he said.

"Yeah, it's too bad you didn't need CPR. I'm sure one of those *Blu Endeavor* guys would have been more than happy to."

His heart fluttered. It threatened to burst through his rib cage. Maybe it was the oxygen deprivation, but she had to be flirting with him. He racked his brain for the perfect witty response. A one-liner to seal the deal. There was a bang on the glass.

"I'm not interrupting, am I? Some guy with an English accent told me you were in here." Chad casually strolled through the entryway.

"No," Lee said. It wasn't the closing line he hoped for.

"Can I steal him from you for a minute?" he asked sheepishly, pointing to Lee.

"Not a problem. I'm headed to the pens to check on our friend." Stacy got up from her seat. "See you later." She gave a playful wink before she left.

"I totally interrupted something, didn't I?"

"Yeah, you did," Lee said.

"And the wink, was that for me or you?" Chad asked.

"Me." Lee's face flushed red.

"Sorry. I just wanted to see how you were doing—" Chad stopped.

"And?" Lee asked.

"It's the tracking data. It's gone."

He froze. Without it, there was no evidence. He'd be left with only a hunch.

"What do you mean it's gone?" Lee asked.

"It's gone, man. I checked the Wildlife Systems database while you searched. There's nothing for the day the maintenance guy died."

"Nothing?"

"Not even a blip."

"Maybe the system was updating?"

"You should come see."

Lee got up from the cot. His body was fatigued. Muscles he hadn't known he had were sore. More than anything, he wanted to sleep. Instead, he followed Chad through the back halls of the building to his office. Word of his heroics had undoubtedly found the ears of his coworkers. He dreaded being stopped for questions. People checking if he was okay. Asking why he'd done it. Questions on top of questions. The pair paused before they reached the main atrium. Crew members of the *Blu Endeavor* stood near the reception desk and blocked the path to the staff offices. They were preoccupied with their chat and didn't notice the two approach.

"When do you think they'll put the film together?"

"A month. Tops. They'll want to push it out while it's still fresh in the news."

"Think I'll be on camera?"

"They'll focus on that guy. Crazy bastard."

Lee pushed Chad into the atrium ahead of him. He used him as a shield as they made their way forward. The two men stopped talking and leered at them.

"Mr. Hero!" one shouted. Lee gave a quick wave as he ducked into the office.

"You could've signed an autograph for the guy," Chad said. Lee pushed old paperwork aside. He longed for the days when he'd avoided visitors in the lighthouse. They seemed like decades ago. He accessed the Wildlife Systems database. Chad hovered over the back of his chair as he changed the filters to search for Akhlut's records. He typed the date Mike Fischer had died and watched the lines disappear. It was blank.

"What the hell?" Lee adjusted the time frame. It added lines to the map after each click. "Is it only for that day?" Lee wrinkled his face and studied the screen.

"It's gone," Chad said.

"It didn't just vanish. We both saw it." Lee flipped through the files on his desk. He printed a weekly hard copy for his records and put it on top of the newest folder. He searched the stack of files again and again.

"It's not here," Lee said.

"Yeah, we've established that."

"No. The hard copy isn't here either."

"Did you print it?" Chad asked.

Lee hadn't forgotten to print them out. Something else had happened. This was Tom sweeping things under the rug. He pressed nine on the phone next to his monitor to dial the outside line.

"Who you calling?"

"Wildlife Systems." Lee patiently waited for the operator to pick up. A cheerful voice answered. It wasn't someone he was familiar with. Lee introduced himself and described the missing data from the tag.

"Hmm." The Wildlife Systems operator pecked away at her keyboard. "The tag for that animal stopped transmitting. It's giving me the error code we typically get when the sensor's damaged."

"Is that the only day data is missing?" Lee asked.

"Let me check... huh... the week before, we received no data either." The pace of the clicks decreased. The rep scrutinized the records in more detail. "It's odd, but it looks like the tracking tag may have malfunctioned."

"Is there a way to recover it?" Lee asked.

"There wasn't data transmitted to recover, sir."

Her response sucked the air out of the office. Lee was drowning again.

"I looked at this data two days ago. It was there."

"I'm sorry. Our records don't show anything for that day."

Lee didn't know what to say. He fell silent as he tried to think of a way to fix it.

"Mr. Ingram, are you there? Can I help you with something else?"

"No, that's okay. Thank you for your help." Lee's voice rang hollow. He slumped in his chair and hung up the phone.

Chad hunched over the desk, his hands clasped together. "I saw it! You saw it!"

Lee wasn't ready to talk yet. He tried to figure how to make it work. Without the new data, there was only old evidence. Things closed out by Tom. Without that tracker, Schmidt wouldn't come forward. He'd be sued into oblivion for breaking his NDA. Especially with the number of files he'd borrowed. With only Ed's death on record, there was no pattern of negligence. Things had reverted to normal. There was zero accountability.

He paged over the folder on his desk and waited for it to magically manifest before him. When that didn't work, he went back to his computer and refreshed the page. He prayed for a miracle.

"That's it, then."

"What about the guy? The one Schmidt mentioned from the capture?" Chad asked.

"Marineworld paid him out big-time. There's no reason for him to talk." Lee didn't want to accept someone who'd been playing the game longer had beaten him.

"That OSHA guy? You can call him."

"And tell him what? That we saw data disappear? He'll call Wildlife Systems and get the same answer we did. I'll call him, but I don't know how much it'll do. There's not a chance he saw the data the day of." He tried to think. There had to be something he had missed. A piece of the puzzle he could discover.

"The Marlin Heritage sailboat!" Chad interjected.

"The what?" Lee was thoroughly confused.

"Few days ago, the Coast Guard towed in a Marlin Heritage sailboat near the central island."

"Some kid probably just got stuck out there." Lee didn't see the relevance.

"There was a police boat with it," Chad added.

"What day was it?"

Lee typed in the date Chad gave him. A white squiggle popped up around Central Coronado Island. Akhlut had been there the entire day.

"It shows he was there. Call."

Lee pulled up the data from the release of both Akhlut and Nayak. The map from the Coronados to San Diego was covered entirely in white. "You're telling me there hasn't been a single person who drowned near one of these lines during that time? They'll say it's a coincidence."

"It's not a coincidence. You know that. We won't know what they'll say until you call."

Lee stopped. He hadn't considered the weight of what he had just asked. Had drownings increased this season? Were there others? Should he try to cross-reference drowning cases with Akhlut's movements? Lee put his head in his hands and sighed. "There's no way to do this without looking crazy." He paused and let out another deep breath. "We can't prove—"

"It's not our job to prove it. They'll investigate. You may not believe it, but that title of yours has some power now. Use it," Chad said. Lee doubted a full-scale investigation. "Maybe they find nothing, but staying quiet doesn't help anyone."

Lee played out the scenarios but couldn't visualize the ending he wanted. He'd lost. Getting the story out wasn't the problem. Making sure those responsible were held accountable was. The data held the case together. Without it, all he had was the history of a violent prisoner. If he went to the media, Marineworld's army of lawyers would make him out to be the villain. Why was he bringing up this theory now? If he knew Akhlut was so dangerous, why had he allowed him to be released in the first place? He closed the screen on his laptop. The ceiling tiles stared at him. His mind was a muddled mess.

"Wanna grab some food?" Chad asked.

"No, I'm not even hungry." Lee's rumbling stomach betrayed his response. "I'll check in with Stacy."

"Good idea. She'll know what to do." Chad hopped off the desk and gave Lee a pat on the shoulder. "Let me know what she says."

What would he say to her? How would he explain it? By the time he walked to the pens, the crewmen from the *Blu Endeavor* were cleared out of the main hall. The CRI was deserted, its emptiness unsettling.

Each footstep echoed in the cavernous space. They moved Akhlut to an interior pen. He'd find her there. Lee navigated the same route he'd walked hundreds of times since they'd moved to the CRI. The walkways he traveled felt different. There was less awe in the intricate sculptures adorning the halls, less bounce in the catwalks that surrounded the sea pens. Stacy sat near the edge of one, her knees drawn up to her chest. He kept his distance from the water.

"A little close to the edge, don't you think?" Lee asked. Akhlut drifted in the center of the enclosure. His eyes stared right through them. Lee sat beside her.

"I wanted it to work so bad. For him to find his place. All those hours with him, preparing him for release. The lights are on. It should've worked," she said.

"There's nothing you could do. You didn't fail," Lee said.

"We all failed. We broke him. We thought we could fix it," she said. Lee thought of the secrets Schmidt had shared with him. How he'd tell her. It wasn't fair to add more weight to her burden. She paused as Akhlut dipped below the surface, his white underbelly exposed as he glided through the pen. Powerful and deliberate movements. Lee scooted closer to her.

"There's more to it," he said. "He wasn't rescued. He was—"

"Captured." Stacy cut him off. "Schmidt came to me the first day they assigned me to Akhlut. He told me his history. The capture. The incidents." She imitated Schmidt's voice and facial expressions. "It's not right for you to work with him and not know." She paused, returning to her regular tone. "That's why I can't stay here anymore. I want to see them in the wild. What he could have been."

"So I didn't need to jump?"

"Nope. I knew what I was doing. But I appreciated the gesture."

"Those incidents," Lee said, "we have"—he stopped—"had data he was near the pen when the diver drowned. Chad thinks there might be another one. I should have told you sooner. I'm sorry." He felt like a coward. It made sense not to go to the public without direct evidence, but to not tell Stacy was pure selfishness.

"You didn't want to be the one to ruin the magic of them for me. I get it."

"No, it's not okay. It's not protecting you to stay silent. I won't do it again."

"You wouldn't jump from the deck of a fishing trawler for me again?" she laughed.

"No, I won't keep anything from you. I promise."

"I'm glad you didn't have to kill yourself to figure that out." Akhlut returned to his post. This time he floated on his side, but his gaze remained transfixed on Lee and Stacy. "It doesn't surprise me, that he killed the diver. He's broken. This is his cell. But what do you mean *had* data?"

"It's gone. Missing from the online database. File's gone too."

"So, what are you going to do?" she asked.

"Retire," Lee said.

"Don't do that. You told me you were a good waiter. Maybe Coastal Basket's hiring?"

"Wader. With a *D*."

Lee's face turned a whimsical shade of red. It was the most color it had had since before the capture. She suppressed a giggle. He smiled because she was smiling and moved closer to her, closer to the pen. Their arms brushed against each other.

"Seriously, you'll tell someone, right?" she asked.

"Besides you? You're the most important person here," Lee said.

"I'm calling the OSHA rep in the morning, maybe the news." It was hard to stop smiling around her, even when she glared at him behind scrunched eyebrows.

"Look at you. You've already learned how to communicate better." Her voice turned serious. "I can help with whatever you need. I know it feels like a lot to give up," she said.

"How long you plan on sitting out here?" Lee asked.

She leaned her head against his. "I'm not sure. This is kind of nice." She took Lee's hand and held it in hers. They rested on the walkway until long after the last ferry departed the island.

BREEDING PROGRAM

Mark's plan had worked flawlessly for a decade. Tom helped convince Rob that the requested changes would lead to a successful pregnancy. They'd already seen their share of miscarriages and stillbirths from the females that had been shipped off to other parks. Mark guaranteed that not only would those numbers decrease, but they'd have a baby calf born right there at the park, alive and happy.

His list of demands for a successful breeding program was short. It started with changing the training so every orca wasn't required to learn all show behaviors. The reduced stress would lead to happier animals who would be more likely to breed. He asked for more detailed reporting on the orcas and written records of behavioral incidents. This would help with keeping track of their cycles as well as aggressive tendencies. Pairing less aggressive animals together for extended periods when a female was cycling would increase the odds of a pregnancy. His last request was increased enrichment opportunities. They needed things to keep the orcas engaged and occupied. Swimming in a concrete box filled with water didn't exactly set the mood.

Mark lied. He never wanted the breeding program to get off the ground. Akhlut was the last orca to be taken from the wild by Marineworld. That was a success. But to have one born into captivity?

That would be a travesty he wouldn't be able to live with. All of his requests were rooted in the welfare of the animals. He never wanted to figure out which orcas worked as breeding pairs. He wanted to keep them separated. Reducing stress would keep them from constantly ramming and raking each other. Keeping better records would give the trainers an idea of which ones had aggressive tendencies instead of an "eye test". More enrichment would keep them from gnawing the concrete off the sides of their tanks until they got their teeth drilled. All it took was a mention of how the improvements would be a beneficial to the breeding program.

"You want to use toys in their tanks?" Rob asked.

"Not toys, enrichment. To keep them from getting bored," Tom said.

"That sounds like toys to me. And some of this isn't going to work. Rocks, faux kelp, we'd have to keep clean. I'm not paying divers to go scrub them so they're not living in scum. They're going to bump into them when they investigate. You think the scrapes and tooth work are bad now? Wait till one eats a section of your plastic plants and gets an impaction. Plus, all that crap blocks the view of the tourists. No. But if buying hula hoops and an RC car will keep them happy enough to breed, we can do that." Mark knew that asking for permanent objects was a long shot. Everything Rob had said was true. They were hard to maintain, could lead to more injuries, and stopped guests from getting a perfect view of the orcas. In an ideal world, they'd be able to make it work. That wasn't why Mark had asked. It made the little things look reasonable in comparison. Ropes, barrels, balls—they all made their way into the pools as positive reinforcers. "And who's going to be putting all these new reports together? Do you want to make the trainers do it? I'd be surprised if any of those idiots could read, let alone write a report."

"Schmidt will. He's offered to make a log of them. Said he'd work on them at night so it didn't interfere with training," Tom said.

"If he wants to do it on his own time, that's fine. While he's here, he needs to be working with the animals. Whatever. As long as it produces results. I'm sick of wasting time. And, Tom, cut this divorced parents shit. Tell him to come in and explain his ideas next time. I'm glad he's finally on board."

Some parts of the con were simpler to keep up than others. The logs were the easiest. It took nothing to change the dates of their cycles. Schmidt tracked the veterinary records and had his trainers separate the males from the females during estrus. The problem was they were variable. None of them had a set cycle. If he wasn't careful, he'd miss one. The number of miscarriages and stillbirths dropped to zero. To Tom and their bosses, it looked like he was making progress towards the birth of that elusive calf. Only it never came—he kept up the charade for years. Management was frustrated, but they tolerated his excuses. Tom figured it out. Either Mark didn't know what he was doing, or he was actively sabotaging the program. Only one made sense.

The technology he pursued wasn't new. Artificial insemination had been around since the turn of the century. Livestock, horses, it was old news. Trialing it in orcas wasn't, but Tom needed a new approach.

"It's about time he thought of something new," Rob said. "I'm surprised you boys didn't think of this sooner. Is it going to require a bunch of new equipment?"

"Mark says the veterinary staff has almost everything they need. We'll need a new liquid nitrogen freezer. What we have won't cut it. Maybe some bags to collect the samples. Big bags," Tom said.

"And how does one go about collecting these samples?"

"That's the best part. They're trained to roll over for husbandry procedures already. It won't take much extra time to stimulate them."

"Not something we can put in the job description for our trainers, huh?" Rob laughed. "I think it's a great idea. We'll give it a shot. When can we start? Mark's directing the veterinary staff and trainers on this?"

"He's wrapped up with behaviors and show work. I'm going to take the lead on this one if it's all right with you?"

"I don't care who's running your experiment. I just want to see results. Long gestation periods, intermittent cycles, I'm done with the excuses."

"So am I."

"Well, good. Keep me updated on the progress, and let me know if you need anything else. Way to step up to the plate."

Tom wanted to keep Schmidt in the dark, but it was impossible to keep him there for long. He insisted on being present when the veterinary staff conducted their procedures and checked samples before tests were run. The best Tom could manage was getting the new equipment ordered and installed in the lab.

While looking over blood samples scheduled for estrogen-level analysis, Mark noticed its appearance right away. Next to the regular refrigeration equipment, there was an isothermal freezer. It looked like a stainless-steel garbage can with a hinged lid and digital display. They had a smaller countertop version they'd occasionally used for vials and blood bags, but this much larger. He immediately knew what the cryogenics unit was for. He lifted the lid, and a cloud of fog bellowed out to block his view of the storage chamber. If he grabbed the handle for the storage rack barehanded, it would peel his skin off. He reached for the insulated gloves nearby.

"It's empty," Tom said as he entered the lab.

"You knew about this?"

"Sorry I didn't tell you. It was Rob's idea. I knew you'd be pissed."

Mark hid his anger well. They'd worked behind his back. It was fair—he was in the lab to mislabel blood samples so they didn't show Ollju was in estrus.

"It'll be more work than the natural way," he said.

"I know, but the natural way isn't working. Where's the payoff?" Tom asked.

Mark wasn't going to pick a fight. It was one more thing he'd have to battle covertly. "You're right. Let's give it a try. You going to be the one to work out the samples?" He laughed as he closed the lid.

"Isn't that we have trainers for?"

The first samples were collected over the following weeks from Akhlut, Kjetil, and Shurik. Once they were on their back for medical tests, trainers stimulated their genital area by hand to arouse them. When the orcas figured out they were being stimulated in an erotic way, it was off to the races for sample collection. Adding artificial insemination to the breeding program greatly increased the odds of securing a viable pregnancy. When it was fully running, they wouldn't have to worry about managing aggressive orcas or determining which ones paired well together. It would only take a short procedure during other husbandry practices. While it wasn't particularly comfortable for the females, twenty minutes of work could catch the company up on a decade of unsuccessful attempts. Based on Mark's assessments, management identified that it would be best to use samples collected from Kjetil to impregnate Kjell. If her pregnancy was a success, the others would be rotated into the breeding program. It would be too difficult to manage three pregnancies at one time. Rob wanted Akhlut to sire their offspring. He'd grown during his time in captivity and was already over twenty feet long, an impressive lineage to pass on.

Schmidt saw it as another challenge. He'd have to make sure the samples weren't viable. The only problem was the veterinary staff would check them before they were used. It wasn't as simple as unplugging the cryogenics unit and letting the vials spoil either. They'd want to verify the sperm was healthy and motile before dedicating their time to artificial insemination. Besides, if he did that, the world's loudest alarm would blare until a member of staff came to check what the issue was. He'd have to tamper with the samples after the health check, but before the procedure. It was a small window. One that could be easily missed, especially if Tom continued to run things behind his back. Cutting it that close was risky.

Before they scheduled the AI of Kjell, he needed to test various additives to the samples to find one that would make them appear viable while having zero chance of a successful pregnancy. While reviewing blood tests, he went to lift the lid of the cryogenics freezer. Strange. It wouldn't budge. They never kept the countertop unit locked. If Tom had made sure the storage unit was locked, that meant he was suspicious. He could be hiding all sorts of things from Mark.

"Did we put anything on the schedule for the AI program yet?" he asked the vet who was inspecting X-rays of Kassuq's teeth at a light table.

"Kjell is scheduled for tomorrow morning. I tried to tell Tom her estrogen levels are low, that she probably isn't in estrus, but he insisted that we have enough sperm samples to try anyways."

"That we do. I wanted to check the samples. Do you have the key for the storage?"

"No. You'll have to ask him for it."

"That's fine. We'll check them in the morning before the procedure." Tom was definitely on to him. The locked storage unit and the decision to schedule the procedure without notifying him told him all he needed to know.

When the next morning came, Mark was ready. A syringe filled with hydrochloric acid sat capped in his pocket. It was all he would need to kill the sperm before it was transferred to the tube for the AI procedure. He arrived early in case the team tried to carry it out before the time they'd told him. Trust was in short supply. He didn't put anything past Tom.

"Glad you could make it this morning." Tom smiled as he met him at the entrance to the lab. The vet and two trainers followed as part of his entourage.

"Not a chance I'd miss it. Ready to make a baby orca?" Schmidt asked.

"Of course. I'll hang with Sherry here while she gets the equipment and sample ready. Could you head poolside with Pete and Erica?" Schmidt couldn't argue. There wasn't a word he could say to get his hands on the sample. He stuffed his hand into his pocket and felt the syringe. It was useless. He retreated to the medical pool with the trainers and helped prepare Kjell for the operation.

The AI procedure went off without complications. It was almost too easy. Mark told himself there was a low success rate. Something would go wrong in the sixteen months it took before a baby would be born. But he couldn't count on it. There would be others. More attempts. He had to make sure they all failed. Back in his office, he stared at the wasted syringe as it lay on his desk. If he wanted to disrupt the breeding program, he needed to plan better. He couldn't be caught off guard and slap a plan together at the last minute.

Mark called the company that made the cryogenics unit. "Hi, this is Dr. Mark Schmidt with Marineworld. We ordered a storage freezer from you all a while back and I had a quick question."

"Is everything okay with the unit? Is it functioning normally?"

"Oh, yes, the unit is fine. It works perfect. The damnedest thing, though. Our vet lost the key to the lock on it. It's unlocked now, thank God, but we'd like a replacement to secure our samples."

"No problem. We can have one mailed out to you tomorrow. Unless you want to drive up to Sunnyvale and pick it up yourself?"

"Oh, no, it's not that urgent. Sending it through the mail would be fine."

"We have a Tom Walsh on file here with the order. Do you want me to send it addressed to him?"

"Well, Tom's the guy who lost the key. I'd hate to send it to him and see him lose it again before I can make a copy. Would you be able to send it to me instead?"

"Of course. You'd be surprised at how often this happens. Tell you what, I'll send you two so you won't even have to make a copy."

"That would great. Thank you."

Mark twirled the syringe on the desk. He waited for anything to go wrong with the pregnancy. It never did. For sixteen months, he contemplated ways to cause a miscarriage. They would all put Kjell at risk as well. He couldn't bear the thought of causing her death. Not to mention they would be suspicious. He had other orcas to protect. Scheduling her for hundreds of X-rays would let management know what his true intentions were.

Ivar was born on July 19, 1995. A healthy baby boy that was eight feet long and weighed three hundred pounds. He was the first orca born through artificial insemination at Marineworld. Mark saw it as his fault. He didn't think quick enough. And the pairing of Kjetil and Kjell? That was taken directly from his reports. The company celebrated. Tom was awarded a promotion. To Mark, it was his biggest failure. On the day of Ivar's birth, he reached into his pocket and felt the tiny silver key. It wasn't useless. He wouldn't let it happen again.

WHISTLEBLOWER

When Lee awoke at four o'clock, sunlight beamed in through the windows that lined the stairs of the lighthouse. He was alone. Sore muscles from the day before burned worse. Movement without a wheeze proved to be a chore. Images from the capture danced in his head. The frothing of the sea, the darkness that creeped to encircle him. There were flashes of dazzling white too. White eyespots, white underbelly, white teeth. An opus in black and white fueled a headache to rival the throbbing pain in his chest. He instinctively searched for his phone. He'd call Stacy and make sure not to miss the day's last ferry. One night in the lighthouse was enough. Only fifteen percent battery. It figured. He was just glad he'd remembered to stash it in his locker before the trip on the *Blu Endeavor*. There was something else. A missed call from earlier in the morning. No doubt it was Tom, congratulating him on a mission completed. Nevertheless, he keyed into his voicemail to hear the recording. For whatever reason, it was the only service that went through from the lighthouse.

"Hi, Mr. Ingram, this is Kim with Wildlife Systems. Hope all is well. I wanted to reach out to you regarding the tracking data. My apologies for not looking at this, but I'm still new to the system. I had one of our technical engineers look at it this morning. The data was deleted on your end by an administrator. Sometimes it happens on accident.

Fortunately, we restore backups through the cloud. Call me and we can discuss restoring it. And again, my apologies for saying it wasn't there! Please let me know if you need anything else." Lee hung up. This was it. He had it.

There was a sharp clack as the latch to the lighthouse unbolted.

"Sixteen hours of sleep was enough?" Stacy wore a Marineworld-branded dress from the gift shop.

"They have it!" Lee clung to phone.

"Who has what?" she asked as she sat on the couch beside him.

"The tracking data. Wildlife Systems still has it."

"That's great! You call the OSHA rep?"

"Doing that now." Lee fumbled with his phone. "I keep forgetting, no service."

"It can wait a few minutes."

"What? Why?"

"Because you haven't eaten for a day." She dumped a sandwich wrapped in white paper into his hands. "Roast beef from the dining center. If you don't like it"—he devoured it. It was the greatest cafeteria food he'd ever tasted. The lettuce was crisp, the tomatoes were juicy, and the meat was seasoned to perfection. Rye buns held it together. A pickle was tucked away somewhere in there too. There was a moment, as mustard dribbled down his chin, where he considered telling her he loved her. He dismissed it as the ravings of a starved man and became mortified by how slobbish he undoubtedly looked—"I can get you something else."

Lee wiped his mouth and thanked her for the food. "I wanted to ask you about last night."

He paused. A call to OSHA signaled the end of his career at Marineworld. He was ready for it. Until Chad had told him to use the power of it, he hadn't realized how much his title bothered him. He barely knew a thing about cetacean behavior. He was trained to write reports on interactions in their enclosures during the day; to manage what Schmidt put in place. His experience with orcas wasn't a lie, but they were captives, different from their wild counterparts. If he continued to cash Marineworld checks, it was a lie. Stacy had told him about her plan to join OAR the night before. The way she talked about it, saving the orcas of the northwest was a noble cause. It was a chance for redemption. Searching for the courage to invite himself kept him up during the night. He pushed ahead with his question.

"When you leave for Washington, do you need someone to help carry your bags?" It didn't come out how he'd planned. Instead, it came off as wanting to push her out of town. Confusion soaked the air while Stacy processed it.

"I can carry my own bags, Lee." She waited long enough to make him worry. "But they rotate researchers pretty often up there. I'm sure Ellen could find room for you."

* * *

When the day of the Lee's testimony came a few months later, it was ordinary. There was no sudden darkening of the sky, no foreboding strikes of lightning. Another brilliant Southern Californian day unafflicted by the people that flocked to the courthouse. Stacy drove Lee. They waited together in a side chamber until it was time for him to testify. He shuffled his feet back on forth on the well-worn carpet as he waited his turn. Countless witnesses before him carved a groove, and he carried on the tradition.

"Relax, you'll do fine." She laid her hand over his and gave it a tight squeeze. "They'll ask you questions, you'll answer, then you can go home and pack."

"Unless the trial drags out—then I'll be back. That's not fair to you. You've put off going long enough."

"You're right. I could go without you. It'd be easier." She squeezed his hand again.

"Funny," he said.

"Relax, Mr. Former Head Cetacean Behaviorist, I'm not going anywhere."

Inside the courtroom, the proceedings were underway. The judge cleared his throat from the bench.

"Let's go on record. This hearing is convened in the case of the Secretary of Labor versus Marineworld of San Diego, LLC before Judge Larry Prescott of the OSHA Review Commission. Let me just say this: there is no issue before me today whether Marineworld was responsible for the death of Mike Fischer. While there may be future proceedings regarding that matter, the issue today solely involves the OSHA investigation and potential destruction of evidence. It should also be noted the alleged violation occurred at Marineworld's facility on Coronado Island; however, based on the existing land-lease rights, and the company functioning as an extension of the San Diego park, it falls under the jurisdiction of this court. So, with that out of the way, let's begin."

It was the early afternoon before Lee testified. Even though he was the first witness, the court had to present background, preliminary matters, and opening statements. When the court clerk came for him, Stacy wished him luck.

The wood-paneled courtroom was smaller than he'd envisioned. Packed with legal counsel, there was little room left in the gallery for observers. It was for the best. Media coverage had subsided into occasional updates on the nightly news. From the start of the legal case, Marineworld had distanced itself from Tom. He had immediately been relieved of his duties as director. They needed to prove he'd acted alone, but that wouldn't be settled in a day. After they swore Lee in, the representative for the Secretary of Labor exchanged greetings with him. Then the long string of questions for examination began.

"As you know, I'm going to ask you some questions about this case. We'll start with an easy one. You've worked at Marineworld for the past four years, correct?" She was calmer than Lee.

"Not exactly. My first year with the company, I was an intern."

"And before you left Marineworld, what was your most recent job title?"

"H-H-Head Cetacean Behaviorist." Lee stumbled over the words. Tom sat in the gallery across from him with his hands tightly folded. The only thing that dialed back his intensity was the absence of bleached shark jaws backing him.

"You're gonna have to speak up, son," the judge said. Lee centered himself. When he opened his eyes, he spotted Stacy in the back of the gallery. She flashed him a quick thumbs-up.

"I worked as the Head Cetacean Behaviorist."

"And before you became the Head Cetacean Behaviorist, you worked as Dr. Mark Schmidt's assistant after interning?"

"That's correct."

"And, I'm sorry, cetaceans—that means you worked with the killer whales at Marineworld?"

"That's correct."

She continued her line of questioning to establish Lee's background. He answered questions that ranged from his predecessor to orca training to release procedures. By the time she asked how the animals were tracked, Lee had read the entire employee manual cover to cover. Then backwards again.

"These tracking tags you attach to the whales—they relay information continuously to an electronic network?"

"No. They only transmit when the animals breach at the surface."

"And using this breaching data, you've established a record of individual orca positions over time?"

"Yes, that information is kept on file digitally through Wildlife Systems."

"Did Wildlife Systems have location data for Akhlut on the date the incident occurred with Mr. Fischer?"

"It did."

The representative referenced a copy of the tracking data submitted to the judge. It was admitted without objection.

"This data showed Akhlut was present near Mr. Fischer during the time of his death?"

"Yes, it did."

"And these tags, they're accurate?"

"Typically within a few yards. The longer or the more often the animal breaches, the better the data."

"Part of your job is to review this data?"

"Yes."

"And after you reviewed this data, at some point it was removed from the system?"

"It was."

"How many people at Marineworld can remove that data?"

"There are a few directors, and myself."

"Would Mr. Walsh have the ability to delete that data?"

"Yes. He had access to the administrative login."

"I don't have any further questions for Mr. Ingram."

Compared to the wait to testify, the speed at which it was over was astounding. As a counselor, she knew her job well. She'd shown the evidence and left nothing to dispute. The cross-examination didn't last long. One or two more witnesses and they'd finish by dinnertime. The judge spoke to Lee before he dismissed him.

"Mr. Ingram, I will instruct you not to discuss your testimony with any person who may be called later as a witness in this case. Thank you for your time." Like that, he was done for the day. Lee stepped from the bench and walked the long aisle out of the courtroom. Stacy pursued him out the heavy doors as he exited.

"You did great up there!"

"Really? It felt awkward." The pair chatted as the court clerk led a red-haired girl in an ill-fitting pantsuit into the courtroom. He knew it had to be Kim from Wildlife Systems. She guaranteed Tom's fate in the civil case. He wished he could see the look on his face when the verdict came, but he'd settle for listening to it on the news. Besides, there was the criminal trial. He'd be asked to return, along with Schmidt, Danny, and others. That was when the proper punishment would be doled out. The wait was worth it.

"Want to celebrate at Coastal Basket?" Stacy offered.

"I can't say no to tourists and oysters," he said.

LIFE AT THE OAR

Tom was found guilty of destruction of evidence. His defense tried to argue that there was no legal proceeding taking place at the time he'd deleted the data. The judge countered with the fact that an OSHA investigation constituted a legal proceeding by a government entity. He reasoned that when Tom deleted the data, he showed a "consciousness of guilt." It didn't matter what his motivation was. He tried to keep potentially unfavorable evidence, the fact that Akhlut was near the A6 pen when Mike died, from being found. The charge was only a misdemeanor. Tom earned a six-month stay in jail and a fine of $1,000 for his efforts. It could barely be considered a minor victory, and it proved to be their only win.

After the ruling, separate criminal proceedings began. Marineworld successfully argued that Tom had acted of his own accord. After that, things went downhill fast. The charge in the criminal trial was involuntary manslaughter. In order to secure the conviction, it needed to be established that Tom's action, the forced release of Akhlut, had directly led to the death of Mike Fischer.

The prosecution's case was weak from the start. It was broken down into three main parts: establishing Akhlut's violent history, proving Tom applied pressure to release Akhlut and deliberately withheld information that would have stopped his reintroduction, and inferring that, due to the lack of mechanical failure in Mike's dive gear, an additional outside factor had to be involved in his death.

Establishing Akhlut's violent history wasn't an issue. Testimony from Lee, Schmidt, and Danny, along with the presentation of behavior incident reports, ensured that. There was no doubt the orca was violent. While unfortunate, the disappearance of a sailboater near the Coronados couldn't be linked to Akhlut. No body washed ashore with orca bite marks. Ed's death, while gruesome, was the only one that could be directly linked to Akhlut, and he hadn't been held under to drown. In fact, only one behavioral incident showed Akhlut swimming over a trainer and dunking him. The defense reasoned that this hardly showed a history of trying to drown people.

Things really started to unravel when the prosecution tried to show that Tom applied pressure to force the release of Akhlut. Tom didn't personally demand the gate to be lifted the day Akhlut was released. He never threatened staff that they would be fired if they didn't go through with it. The board had made a complete assessment with every known record available for review. No information was deliberately hidden while they conducted their assessment. They signed off and approved of it. Even Lee contributed to the development of the reintroduction plan. Tom's defense argued that under those circumstances, half the staff of Marineworld would need to be put on trial.

The prosecution even tried to factor in the financial gains Tom stood to receive by increasing the company's stock value, but his attorney saw it coming from a mile away. He contended that it was irrelevant. Any employee, especially a vested one like Tom, wanted to see his company do well. At the time of Akhlut's reintroduction, all signs pointed to him being an ideal candidate. The one fatality the animal was associated with was a result of trainer error and the Danny's injuries occurred when Akhlut was a juvenile. Tom had no reason to believe that Akhlut shouldn't be released and that it wasn't in the best interest of the orca's welfare to do so.

Directly linking Akhlut to the death proved impossible. The circumstantial evidence wasn't strong enough. The leaps to connect the dots were too great. There hadn't been a scratch on Mike's body, no massive trauma like with Danny's injury or Ed's death. He'd drowned. The official coroner's report agreed when it listed the cause of death as drowning. Nothing was mentioned about "injuries consistent with an animal attack." White lines on a computer screen only meant that Akhlut had been in the area when it had happened. The judge noted that the context was intriguing given that Mike was an experienced diver well under the recreational dive limit. He even ordered the veterinary staff to pump Akhlut's stomach and search for a dive fin or human remains. Nothing. Mike could have become anxious during his solo dive and overexerted himself investigating the gate or struggled with an abnormal current. There were plenty of logical inferences that could cause him to lose track of his air that didn't involve Akhlut. The prosecution simply couldn't establish any link beyond reasonable doubt. And since Akhlut couldn't be put on the stand, the trial was over. If he wasn't the killer, then Tom was not guilty. The day the gavel fell, Lee returned with Stacy for Washington.

Lee's work with OAR kept him busy. Well, it was Stacy's work. The team studied orca communications and echolocation. Stacy applied the research towards her master's thesis. There was so much more to understand, to study, to learn. Work in the Pacific Northwest was a different experience. The dampness permeated everything. Equipment was constantly wet, coated by a fine mist that wrapped the inlets. It was a far cry from the sunny afternoons of San Diego. Lush vibrant green pine forests replaced concrete and palm trees. There was something freeing about the work. He was no longer confined to schedules dictated by the board at the CRI. Yet, despite it all, the company had given him opportunities he couldn't wish for in his wildest dreams. But his employment at Marineworld was a lifetime ago. The futuristic CRI for a tiny cottage that overlooked a foggy inlet of Puget Sound was a good trade.

Lee had prepared himself for the downgrade in living conditions, but it wasn't as awful as he'd expected. The cottage had three bedrooms, a common room, a kitchen, and a tiny office. As lead of OAR, Ellen Hayes claimed the master bedroom as her permanent residence. It was the only nonutilitarian room that hinted at a personality. Colorful paintings of marine life that she'd painted herself hung from the walls. They used the other bedrooms for the rotating cast of researchers who worked on their projects. Each was furnished with two sets of bunk beds, a bureau for clothes, and not much else. If one more dresser was added to the bedrooms, the floor space shrank to zero. They'd expected Stacy, but Ellen had made a special accommodation for Lee. It wasn't often that a behaviorist from Marineworld switched teams.

"I don't play favorites," Ellen noted. "A few of these researchers have worked here for years."

"And most of them have a strong opinion on our former employer," Lee interjected.

"Now they might not say it, but don't be upset if their attitude has a vibe of piss off. At least at first," she said. Stacy moved into the common room, after she threw a duffle bag of her clothes on a bottom bunk.

"Lee's used to that vibe, aren't you?" She returned to the entryway to pick up the last of her bags.

"Too bad you didn't get a top bunk," he fired back.

"It's better than your options," she said as she slung her backpack over her shoulder.

"What are my options?" Lee asked.

"The research team arrives in a day or two. I wouldn't want you in one of their beds when they get here. You'd probably be most comfortable right there," Ellen said. "Right there" was an old brown cloth couch in the common room. As soon as Ellen mentioned it, he itched. Not only that, if a mouse took a step in the cottage, he'd hear it.

"Any others?" he asked.

"Well, you could always ask Stacy if she'd share—"

"Not a chance. It's a twin bed," Stacy said from behind the pine door of the bedroom. With sleeping arrangements decided, the pair settled into a routine. Gone were the days where they wrote standardized behavior reports or interacted with orcas. Those were replaced by observations and notes from a distance.

A typical day started before sunrise. Lee made the first pot of coffee for the team. And the second pot. And however many more were needed to put him in their good graces. There was a cozy nook off the kitchen where they'd sit and listen to calls recorded during the night, when they couldn't be on the water. It took time, but with practice, he could distinguish the different members of the resident orca population from each other. Together they'd catalog the recordings for reference and analysis.

"Try again," Stacy said. "Really listen." He'd take her headphones and tune in to the low melodic chirps.

"That's Tahlequah, I'm positive."

"How do you know?"

"'Cause the little coo thing, Star does. You can hear that as a response. They travel together, so it's gotta be Tahlequah."

"You sure?"

"No. I'm never sure. It's easier when you can see the damn things."

"You're getting better. One day you won't even have to look at the ID card." She took a sip of her coffee. It was mud. She discreetly swapped her mug for Lee's—he forever put half a pound of sugar in it—and stole the headphones back. The two worked with the audio samples until the sun came up while they waited for reports on orcas moving near the inlet. Whale watchers were scattered along the coast. Tours were big business. They'd wait for a transmission to confirm sightings before packing up their gear and heading to the nearest spot to wait. Sometimes days were nothing but work from land. Those were Lee's favorite. They could spot the orcas from the rocky cliffs above, track their movements, and collect information on their dive times. Having an aerial perch provided insight into family groups, swimming, and hunting patterns. While it was excellent data, it wasn't what Stacy researched. You couldn't get vocalization recordings from atop a cliff, at least not directly. The OAR installed a chain of hydrophones along the inlet. They were arranged for near surface recordings. While they provided good background data, they depended on the position of the orcas and marine conditions. Calls could be distorted or unclear. Not to mention hydrophones occasionally went offline or didn't transmit. To augment the data, they set up an auxiliary array of remote underwater recorders. These recorders rested on the seafloor and continuously collected sounds under low power. They were great for the long-term acquisition of information, but the equipment needed to be physically gathered to download the sound files.

Unfortunately for Lee, the best place to collect recordings was from the water. OAR maintained a research shed filled with every piece of kayaking and audio equipment they could ever need. When the team received word of orca movements, they'd load the gear up into a truck and set out. With each trip, he ventured closer to the sea. He'd made progress from his first expedition, when he'd retreated to avoid the surf and ended up on his backside. But Lee still remained landlocked. He'd push Stacy's kayak from the shore and stick behind to guard the truck.

"They're not going to eat you!" she'd say as she slipped into the inlet.

"I know, but why risk it?" He'd watch as she shook her head. She'd entice him with one more call from the water.

"I'd get better data if you were out here with me," she'd plead to the scientist in him. It did nothing to wipe the image of Ollju's rehearsals out of his mind. He pictured the massive whale breaching above his head before slamming on the kayak. Maybe it wouldn't be a mistimed breach but a flick of the tail. Minimal effort to put Lee in the icy waters. From there, the darkest and most creative portions of his imagination took over. It was unreasonable, and he knew it. Ollju was locked up with Akhlut far away in the Coronados.

He'd try to compose himself with the thinking of a rational man. These weren't Antarctic orcas, they were southern residents—they hunted salmon. The tail flick technique wasn't in their repertoire. They'd never seen an ice floe. No matter how reasonable his argument, Lee's heart stopped when they surfaced, even from his spot on the cliffs. The air charged with a nervous anticipation each time they drew a breath. He expected the tall fin of Akhlut to rise silently above the water from around a rocky bend. A freak storm could have decimated the CRI and released the animals. He didn't forget to check the National Weather Service. Better to be irrational and alive than sane and dead. The shore kept him safe. After a day of collecting data, the two retreated to the cottage to review the audio. They'd stay up until late in the evening as they listened to the recordings from the afternoon. Both of them cherished the seclusion, the slower pace, but the CRI pulled at him.

"Do you ever think of going back?" He waited until well after the other members of the research team had settled into their bunks before he asked. Hearing the question might ruin their opinion of the former Head Cetacean Behaviorist.

"Not really." There wasn't a reason for her to return. She made genuine progress on her thesis. That chapter of her life was complete. "I mean, the people, yes. The job, no. I'd love to see Amanda and Mark, but horrible Marineworld? No, I don't think of going back."

"The orcas?"

"I couldn't do it. They're being well taken care of. It's a million times better than in San Diego. And we got to be a part of it. To help them. Going back now, I don't know."

"You're afraid you'd want to stay?" Lee asked. The headphones she wore sat cockeyed on top of her head. A speaker covered only the ear opposite of Lee. Even after fieldwork, her hair lay perfect.

"Listen…" She moved closer to him on the bench and extended the unused headphone. There was a low hum coupled with an excited chirp on the end. It was one call Lee had memorized.

"Nayak." Memories from her release stuck with him. Stacy was right. Not everything about their time at the company had been horrible. Nayak's reintroduction was something beautiful he'd contributed to.

"She's happy, Lee. I'm happy." There was no pull for her anymore. He huddled close and listened to the sounds. Maybe if he gave it more time, the pull would disappear for him too. It wasn't much longer before Stacy was fast asleep next to him. Carefully, Lee removed the headset from her. He tried to stay as still as possible to make his move. Bit by bit, his hand inched to the laptop that rested on the table. Hours passed before he hovered over the keys. Stacy lay still, her golden-blond hair draped across her face. She was out cold. Lee typed at a snail's pace. Each keystroke was an atom bomb to his ears. The sharp click of the letters threatened to wake up the entire house. She remained unmoved. After each letter, he checked if she was asleep. It took longer than expected, but he finished the entire web address of Wildlife Systems. Lee watched the data in real time, a tiny white line that traced around the Coronados. It swirled tightly on itself in gyroscoping patterns. The design was akin to giving a toddler a crayon and a blank sheet of paper. Unblinking, his eyes locked on the screen, tracking the line round and round. Minutes ticked by before Lee felt the leaded heaviness of his eyelids. He didn't dare move his gaze from the screen, but they betrayed him. For a microsecond, he drifted off before he violently jerked awake. Stacy stirred against his chest.

"Lee?" she slurred with her eyes still closed.

"Yeah. You fell asleep listening to the recordings. I didn't want to wake you." He cautiously closed the laptop screen.

"What time is it?" she asked as she stretched.

"Two."

"Mhhmmm," she groaned, "only a couple of hours before we need to get back up." Stacy yawned as she stood. "I wanted to get out on the water tomorrow." She paused and shook her head. "Today."

Stacy staggered towards the bedroom. She braced herself on the wall and ran her hand through her hair.

"Aren't you going to bed?"

"Yeah, in a minute." Lee shrugged. He waited until she disappeared into the blackness of the hallway before he reopened the laptop. The familiar white line continued its random route. He promised himself to stay up for only another half an hour, tops, but he'd catch hell if Stacy found him passed out at the table again. Screw it. Lee slammed the computer shut and hobbled over to the old brown couch. It was too risky to follow Stacy. A room full of bleary-eyed, freshly woken researchers didn't bode well for camaraderie. He was too drained to pull the thick wool blanket from behind the couch. The white line burned inside his eyelids as he tried to fall asleep. It was circling, waiting, biding its time.

* * *

Unsurprisingly, the bright orange kayaks were unwieldy after a couple hours of sleep. They tipped forward as Lee removed them from the bed of the truck, threatening to topple him over with them.

"You gonna make it?" The concern in Stacy's voice was genuine. He'd gotten no rest the night before.

"Yeah, yeah, I'll be fine." The way it swayed as he wrestled it to the ground wasn't comforting.

"You know, you don't have to do this today."

"Seems as good a day as any." The smooth pebbles of the shore crunched as he dragged the kayaks to the water's edge. Above them, a few gulls orbited in the dull gray sky. They reminded him of San Diego.

"Really, Lee, you don't. I can check the equipment by myself."

"I told you I'd help"—he swung a bundle of supplies into the front of the kayak—"and that's what I'm going to do."

Stacy wouldn't ask if he was okay again. She preferred not to make him more nervous. When he'd practiced kayaking in a stream, he'd tipped himself twice before he'd gotten the hang of it. She slid into the lead kayak. There was barely a ripple beneath her as she positioned herself in the seat. Gently, she dipped her paddle into the water and pushed back from shore.

"We're going to head around to the sea stacks. I want to fix the hydrophone that's been acting up there first."

She didn't hear Lee leaving the beach. In the morning mist, she turned parallel to the coast and waited. He stood with his hands on the very back of the kayak. His legs were stretched so the breaking waves couldn't touch his feet as they dissolved into the rocky shore. There were excellent odds he'd push it into the surf without jumping in.

"That's not the best way to do it!" She couldn't help but tease him.

"I'm aware!" he shouted.

"The water's a little cold for a swim," she said. Lee pulled the kayak closer to land before he hopped into the seat. It rocked as he settled into position and his momentum carried him out into the cove. She held her breath as he lost his hold on his paddle and caught it seconds before it dropped behind him.

"Got it!" Lee held it over his head.

He hung on until the pitching of the kayak stopped. She led them out of the cove while he hung back, taking time with each stroke to peer into the depths. Only the tops of giant kelp dancing beneath him were visible. Divers back in California explored these underwater forests, but the thought of being intertwined in the massive vines made his pulse quicken. One more thing to worry about if he discovered himself in the water.

Lee followed the limestone outcrop and shouted ahead, "You know, Ollju loved to flip kayaks." He battled against the tide so he didn't drift further out. Stacy gave him plenty of guidance. If he kept the rocks on his left as they departed, and on his right as they returned, he wouldn't have an issue, even in the fog. "Remember? If it was empty, fine. But put a person in there and—" No response. She moved around a bend. Still, she should respond. Unless—

He stopped dipping his paddle and stiffened. At first, he could only hear water brushing against the outcrop as he swayed on the waves. "Stacy?"

Ever so faintly, a recognizable sound resonated in the distance. He wished it hadn't. He waited, listening. It repeated. This time closer. The familiar khoosh of air being expelled from a blowhole. It explained why she hadn't answered him. Panicked, he searched for the closest beach. It was no use. He was too far from the launch point, and there wasn't another spot to reach shore until after the stacks. His mind flashed to Akhlut. That feeling of helplessness with nothing but the void beneath him. He cozied his kayak up to the rock face. The rational half of his brain shuffled through facts. There wasn't one documented attack on a human by an orca in the wild. They ignored humans and continued to their destination.

Ollju, Akhlut, and the others were contained. He'd checked the tracking data that morning. It wasn't physically possible to travel from the Coronados to Washington in that time frame.

KHOOSH! It was much louder now. They would pass him shortly. He couldn't see them yet, but they were there. They were close. His breath quickened, bordering on hyperventilating. A primal urge enticed him to leap from the kayak and scale the cliff. Again, the sensible part of his brain kicked in. It reminded him it was a vertical wall of jagged limestone. Think, think, think. He tucked his elbows to his chest and tried to make himself shrink. Minutes passed with no sound from the orcas. His voice failed. Stacy would've yelled if there was danger. Cautiously, he dipped the blade of the paddle beneath the waterline. His imagination created an orca to emerge from below to seize it before it ripped him to a watery grave. He ignored it and paddled around the bend to Stacy. A wave of relief washed over him. She was tucked into a tiny inlet. She held a finger to her lips and summoned him with her other hand. Lee happily obliged and pulled alongside her. His heartbeat slowed. She was fine. Pointing beyond the kelp bed she directed his gaze. KHOOSH! He saw the first orca twenty yards out. The distinct black-and-white color scheme shattered the glassy surface. It was unexplainable. The fear that had held him for so long melted away. With each passing orca it grew smaller and smaller. Instead of irrational daydreams of attacks, he focused on the good. To share the orcas' world again was amazing, even if it was only for a moment. Still, he tried to forget how massive and powerful they were up close.

"Terrifyingly majestic," he deadpanned.

"Recognize them?" Her digital camera clicked as she captured photos of the animals. "I can get the ID card," she teased.

Lee didn't respond. He couldn't pick out the exact animals, but he was in awe of the family groupings. The females led the way, trailed closely by the younger adults and calves. Only a few bulls traveled with the group. They passed last. An involuntary chill trickled up Lee's spine. The females were large, but the males were bigger. Not a single collapsed dorsal fin in the bunch, only tall and mighty triangular black sails. None were the size of Akhlut. He sighed in relief.

"How you holding up?" she asked. The last of the pod moved around the bend. Sounds of their exhalations grew faint in the distance.

"That was incred—" There was an eruption of spout. He cowered as the mist rained upon them. A dreadful smell singed his nostrils. It was a rotting sea creature stuffed in a metal barrel and left in the midday sun. Putrid guts and decaying fish. He wiped the droplets from his face and looked for the straggling orca. He didn't have to search hard. It spy-hopped so close he could poke it with the paddle. An old scar in the white skin of her lower jaw was a dead giveaway.

"Nayak!" he exclaimed.

"Hi, girl!" Stacy waved but stopped herself. She might confuse her with hand signals. Nayak looked at the set of kayakers before her. Lee licked his lips before he realized his mistake. The taste was worse than the smell.

Nayak twisted like a flag in the wind. She raised her tail flukes high and threatened to slap the water. Lee put up his arms in anticipation of the incoming splash. He'd seen it thousands of times in the stadium. Nayak's flukes stopped before impact and dipped gracefully. There was no splash as she cruised off to catch up with the rest of her pod.

"Still think it was incredible?" Stacy asked as Nayak disappeared into the distance.

"I could've done without the spray," he responded while futilely attempting to wipe the droplets from his face.

"Ha! That's the best part!" She paddled out of the inlet. "Some people wait their entire lives to be sprayed."

"It's disgusting."

"They find that out too."

207

That night, he stopped dreaming of orcas that lurked in tranquil patches of sea waiting to devour him. The sight of Nayak free with her pod was magical. They couldn't have cared less about him. But as the weeks bled to months, the magnetism of the CRI increased. He needed to see him with his own eyes. To know Akhlut was confined to his pen. Lee knew it was absurd. The dreams stopped, but he checked the Wildlife Systems database regularly to soothe his anxiety. When he ventured into the ocean to conduct research, he was intensely aware he was in their world. There was that same urge to flee he'd felt during his first meeting poolside with Ed. That fear never subsided.

AN OLD FRIEND

It was over a year before Lee found himself on the ferry to the CRI. Stacy had offered to go with him, but he'd politely declined. Deep down, he knew she didn't want to return. He'd chosen not to force the issue. This was something he had to do on his own. The ferry was heavily loaded with tourists in brightly colored shirts. He did his best to blend into the crowd. After the events of the capture, he had become a local celebrity. He pulled his baseball cap to his sunglasses and trusted his disguise worked well enough to avoid detection.

"First time going to the CRI?" The man across from Lee wore a bright pastel shirt identical to the one Lee had chosen for camouflage.

"Uh, yeah," Lee responded. Even behind his mirrored sunglasses, he avoided eye contact.

"You're gonna love it! Me and the family got season passes," he said.

"Yeah?"

"It's amazing what they do for these animals. A real shame what happened with the big one." He searched for the name.

"Akhlut," Lee said.

"Yeah, Akhlut! It's a shame, but better in here than out there. At least they tried."

"Yeah." Put off by Lee's curt responses, the man struck up a conversation with the group beside him. Lee walked the path to the CRI countless times before, but it was foreign now. He traipsed up the

209

same route to the main entrance as the visitors. This was no longer his home. It was familiar, yet remarkably alien. He wondered if it was a mistake to return. He could catch the next ferry and hop a flight back. No, he'd come this far to see it through.

The lobby stood untouched from the day he'd left it. When he passed the door to the offices Lee instinctively reached for the key card that hung around his neck, only it wasn't there. Instead, he walked towards the western underwater viewing area and moved under the central atrium. The display was as gorgeous as ever. He traced his hand across a limestone column, feeling the embedded shells, and counted the skeletons above him. The southern right whale continued its never-ending dive in the center. Orcas flanked the whale on either side, modeled in a slow, but steady climb to the surface. Dolphins and porpoises escorted the orcas. Light from above washed over the bones as it always had. He lingered for a long while, watching the artificial waves cast shadows over the bones. One thing he'd survive without was the echoes of the digital displays that piped in from the main entrance. The message to the visitors remained unchanged. Lee repeated the lines from memory as he descended the steps.

The underwater viewing space housed a towering window out into the sea pens. The glass was rounded like a flying saucer, the convex shape magnified the oceanscape. There were tiered theater-style seats equipped with headphones that connected to hydrophones spread across the island. If the orcas weren't within viewing distance, guests listened to their songs. Some stayed the entire day and neglected to visit other portions of the CRI. When they'd constructed it, they'd taken care to keep the netting surrounding the pens out of the tourists' sight lines. It provided the illusion that the animals swam free. If the visibility was exceptionally good, you'd make out the faint cross-hatched outline of the nylon ropes if you squinted.

Lee took a front-row seat in the theater. He slipped on the

headphones and waited. The air-conditioning units blasted him with a frigid breeze as he scanned the pen for orcas. Their calls greeted him. Familiar squeaks and whines like old metal gates that needed to be oiled. He smiled. He knew the voice. From beneath the blue depths of the viewing window, Ollju swam up towards the surface and nearly touched the glass.

"Hello, girl," he said as she breached. There were more sounds now. They were faint and further away. Lee clicked the volume on the armrest, but it did nothing; it was turned up to the maximum. He cupped his hands to the headphones tightly, trying to amplify and isolate the sounds. The songs were hauntingly comforting. Low stressed bass tones rhythmically pulsed. Gradually he made sense of it. The calls weren't from orcas inside the pen. They were coming from the waters beyond. He was listening to the notes of southern residents. A shrill call dropped off to a lower frequency. The chatter from the southern residents abruptly stopped. It was like a missile whistling back to Earth. His heart crawled into his mouth. He got up and walked to the viewing window. He took his cap off and pressed his face against the frosty glass. First, he gazed towards where he'd last seen Ollju. Only vast empty blue. There was a black silhouette to his left. Faint, but at once instantly recognizable. A tall dorsal fin with a healed notch. A new tracking tag was placed beneath it.

Akhlut surveyed the expanse of sea before him. If he didn't hear his call, Lee would have assumed the orca was dead. He expected relief. The sight of him imprisoned was why he'd made the journey. He needed to confirm his fears were imaginary specters. The beast was jailed. Lee was safe. Instead, there was a growing sense of dread in the pit of his stomach. He was torn between listening to the calls and continuing his watch. Ollju appeared from below and swam to where Akhlut was stationed. This time she carried a silvery fish in her jaws. She traveled along the black mesh only to stop and spit it through the netting. The cycle repeated itself. Each time Ollju returned with a fish, she sailed to the boundary before spitting it out of the pen. This continued until the feeder station stopped releasing food.

Lee stepped back from the glass. Akhlut snapped to life, swiveling to face him. The massive orca paused before fanning his flukes. With a ping of sound more detailed than an X-ray, he probed the viewing area. In a microsecond he dissected the entire auditorium and its contents. It was the magic of echolocation. He not only saw the tourists, he saw through them. Lee tensed. Had he recognized him as well? Even in the air-conditioned room, little beads of sweat bubbled on his neck. He knew the glass was strong. It was designed to withstand an astronomical amount of force.

He winced as Akhlut elegantly stopped and turned in front of the glass. There was a gasp from the people seated in the theater. The orca was perpendicular to the glass, lined up perfectly with Lee. He rolled over and stared. His eye burned right through Lee. With another ping of echolocation, Akhlut watched the rapid beating of his heart. Lee stared back in appreciation of the barrier between them. During their last meeting, he hadn't had the luxury. He desperately wondered what he was thinking. Was he excited to see an old friend? Or was Lee the one that got away? Akhlut rotated to orient his body cheek-to-face with Lee. The orca opened his mouth to reveal rows of deadly, brilliantly white teeth. A sickening display of knives. He nodded his mammoth head and dove from view.

It took over a minute for Lee's heartbeat to return to normal before he registered the Arctic blast from the air conditioner hitting the hot sweat on his brow. He wished he had taken Stacy up on her offer to come with.

"*Boo!*" A shout from behind sent him hard into the glass. He turned to a friendly face. "I didn't know we were getting a visit from a celebrity today!" Amanda chirped. Lee shushed her and donned his baseball cap.

"Geez. Do they teach trainers to do that?" he asked.

"Do what?"

"Never mind. Is there somewhere we can go to talk?" The eyes of the tourists were firmly fixed on him. Lee tugged on his hat and turned his back to them. Amanda's cheerful demeanor morphed into one of concern.

"Yeah, follow me," she instructed. Amanda led him far away from curious ears. Lee was trespassing in a place he didn't belong. He maintained a digital relationship with his former colleagues, but he had been traded to a different team. They exchanged data and research without personal interaction. It established a bridge between the sides, but the field of research and the entertainment industry were still worlds apart.

Amanda was one of the few trainers left at the CRI. When the company had transitioned from shows and waterwork, they'd become obsolete. That had always been the plan. She stayed on specifically for animal husbandry procedures. Someone had to assist with the routine blood tests, tissue samples, and blowhole swabs. She worked closely with the vets so operations and treatments were carried out smoothly. Under a new agreement with Marineworld's board of directors, she forwarded information from lab work to OAR. This sharing of data was unprecedented. It wouldn't have happened under Tom's direction. Lee needed to speak to his replacement.

"Is Schmidt in?" he asked. After criminal charges had been filed against Tom, it hadn't taken the board long to reach out to Schmidt. They had been played and they knew it. It was only natural for them to contact him. Another step in correcting the wrongs of their past.

At first, he was too proud to take on the role. They'd made their bed and had to lie in it. But the academic life wasn't for him. He enjoyed lecturing at the university but yearned for the opportunity to work with the orcas again. For every brilliant young mind he encountered, there were forty more who breathed through their mouths. A week passed before he called Marineworld back. He agreed to be instated as the director of the CRI under a strict set of conditions. These terms included the sharing of data with research groups and universities. The company wanted to put the black eye Tom had given them in the rearview and caved to Schmidt's demands.

Amanda led Lee to the director's office. He wasn't there. The office had changed under its new owner. Absent from the wall behind the desk were the menacing jaws. In their place, Lee recognized the Marineworld 25th Anniversary poster from Schmidt's bungalow. Bookshelves swollen with scientific textbooks, journals, and issues of *National Geographic* replaced the spartan walls. Business substituted with academia. Amanda picked up her radio.

"Anyone seen Schmidt around?"

"Last saw him out by the lighthouse," a voice chimed back.

"You don't need an escort, do you?" she asked.

"I think I'll survive on my own," he said. In their emails, he hadn't mentioned he'd taken up residence in the lighthouse.

With a quick goodbye, Lee started his trek over the island. Walking across the sunbaked outcrops of the Coronados was like riding a bike. He remembered the familiar boulders and cobbles as they crunched underfoot. If he hadn't left for Puget Sound, the hike would still be part of his daily routine.

For a split second, he nearly yelled "sir!" to the sunburnt man with a long white ponytail. By now he knew better.

"Mark!" He waved with one arm. The doctor didn't respond at first. Behind the dark tint of his glasses, Lee barely registered the confused look on Schmidt's face. His disguise must have been more convincing than he'd thought. He took off his cap and tried again, waving it over his head. "Mark!" That did the trick. Schmidt waved back before he went into the lighthouse. Lee scrambled the remaining distance to his former hideaway. A light covering of sand brushed onto the stone floor as he entered.

"You could've knocked!" Schmidt greeted him with a firm handshake. Despite his age, the squeeze turned his fingers to dust.

"Why? You're in my office!" Lee said as he slapped his mentor on the back. He wasn't lying. Unlike Tom's old office, Schmidt hadn't updated the lighthouse. Chad's "#1 Intern" photo remained vigilant from its place of honor above the couch in the entryway.

"He made me promise I'd keep it the same before he left." Schmidt noticed him staring at the picture.

"I'm staying with him while I'm back in town," Lee said.

"That's good. Has he suckered you into one of his boat tours? He makes a pass of the island most days. Waves to the tourists like an idiot."

"No, not yet. He still has time to convince me," Lee said. After Lee and Stacy had left the CRI, Chad hadn't stuck around much longer. Bored with computers, he'd created a land and sea tour business. Camping and guided hikes through the Anza-Borrego Desert State Park or Cuyamaca Rancho made up the land half. A sailing trip along Akhlut's recapture route that ended at the Coronados made up the sea half. He was booked through the end of the year.

"Things in Washington treating you okay?" Schmidt hadn't expected Lee. They'd spoken on the phone two days prior, with no mention of the visit.

"Things are good. Slogging away at the acoustics study," Lee said.

"Stacy got you in the kayaks?" Schmidt asked.

"It took persuasion." He paused. "Occasionally see Nayak."

215

"Nayak in the kayak, eh? I was convinced you wouldn't get wet again, let alone study them from the water." He plunked on the couch.

Lee hadn't made the trip from Washington for a friendly chat. There was an uneasiness in Lee's voice. Schmidt had to know why he'd come to visit. Even when they'd spoken on the phone, it was there. And in the pauses between words, there was a galaxy in the time that separated his thoughts. His mind wasn't in the moment. "You're still staying up till sunrise checking the tracking data?"

"Stacy told you?" Lee looked down, dejected.

"She didn't need to. We keep a little bit better track of logins now. You understand why." He paused. "At least *our* prisoner is still secured."

"I know, I only check twice a day now." He knew Schmidt talked to Stacy regularly. She probably told him how she'd woke up on more than one occasion to find him enshrined in the pale glow of the computer screen. He wished his joke had landed and his mentor half-believed him.

"That's progress." Schmidt nodded. "Did you pay him a visit yet?"

"I did. That's part of the reason I wanted to find you," Lee said. He'd put one fear to rest but created another. He took his time to explain Akhlut's behavior—how he communicated with the wild ones, how Ollju brought them fish from the feeders. "Mark, have you seen this?"

Schmidt's eyebrows rose. They recorded background chatter from groups of orcas as they crossed through the territory. Transients often passed near the islands, they cataloged offshore pods coming nearby, and on exceedingly rare occasions, residents visited from the northwest.

"We haven't noticed consistent visits. They come and go and that's it. Maybe once or twice I've seen them in the waters outside the pens. We get recordings from the hydrophones. You have copies of those." As part of his demands to Marineworld, Schmidt had made the vocalizations available online. They were free to members of the public.

At the OAR, the files were priceless treasures. Before the agreement, they'd had very few recordings of anything besides residents. The expanded library of songs allowed the team to make fresh discoveries on the intricacies of orca dialects. The variance between transients and residents was old news. Now, with the similarities between calls, it was possible to figure who the animal's closest relative was. Whole family groups could be deciphered on calls alone. Information on tone and duration helped researchers decide if they were hunting, resting or socializing. Lee was planning to help Stacy dig into the tapes when he returned.

"They're giving them food," Schmidt said. "Interesting for sure. But we've documented food sharing. It's not unusual."

"Mark, you've got an Antarctic orca delivering fish to residents while a transient looks on. This mixing of ecotypes, it isn't normal."

"That part—that part is unusual. The feeder boxes won't deliver enough to support the wild ones. We don't stock them for that."

"I'm aware."

"Hmm." Schmidt tilted his head back. For the life of him, he couldn't come up with a reasonable explanation for the behavior. If the orcas were in the same pod, it was logical. The splitting of a meal between family members was commonplace. If they were from the same region, it might make sense. But this. This was odd. There wasn't unlimited herring.

"Your southern residents—they're salmon eaters. Endangered because they can't get enough prey. They're notoriously picky. Hell, they find Chinook by echolocating their air bladders. So why in the world would they travel here for a light snack? That's a lot of wasted energy."

"What if it's a visit?" It was too obvious. He'd missed something so simple. Then again, Schmidt hadn't figured it out either. The speed of Lee's voice picked up. "Can you pull up today's audio?"

217

"It's a livestream. The day's data gets compressed and saved at the end of the night."

"Open it up. Maybe they're still here."

Lee waited as Schmidt pulled up the stream. If his hunch was correct, he wasn't the only former employee to make the journey from Washington. A sharp shriek came over the speakers, the pitch twisted and reverberated before going silent. It reminded him a finicky radio.

"There's your bo—"

"Shh—" He cut Schmidt off and leaned towards the speaker. He barely heard them, but he waited. Stacy could recognize members of the southern resident population by fragments of a call. It was uncanny. Lee didn't need to be that good. He only listened for one. There were at least three of them. Blended together, it was white noise. The orcas competed for control of the conversation. Then he recognized it. A sequence of clicks that built and morphed into a high-pitched squeak. The exact call from Nayak's release. There was no mistaking it.

"That's it. That's her! She's here!"

Schmidt smirked. "You're not the only one visiting old friends. We could go to the auditorium and look?"

"No. I could barely see beyond the net. They might be gone by the time we get there. Just listen." The two men sat and listened. The strident staccato of Akhlut cut off the others. When it was quiet, there was the low tuning whine of Nayak. Their calls were interspersed with excited squeaks from the partners Nayak had brought and the occasional chirp from Ollju. The sounds could be mistaken for a joyous reunion. But there was something new.

"Did you catch that?" Lee asked. Schmidt shushed his former intern. It was an original call. It wasn't resident, transient, or Antarctic. The note reminded him of an awful accent. A child that imitated a foreign film. Pitches undulated and cracked. It sounded as if they had run the calls through a digital filter.

"She's translating." There was a sparkle in Schmidt's eyes.

"This is being saved?" Lee asked for confirmation. Schmidt nodded. He suppressed the urge to high-five him. Stacy would be ecstatic. He couldn't wait to share it with her. Suddenly the sounds trailed off. The southern residents were departing Californian waters.

"I'm an idiot for not realizing it. They were in a tank together for twenty years. Of course they treat each other like family," Lee said.

"Yeah, and if you stuck me in the gulag for most of my life, I'd learn a little Russian," Schmidt said.

"God only knows what they're saying."

"Well, that's for you and Stacy to figure out." The laughter in Schmidt's voice faded. "But I have my ideas."

"Oh yeah? What's that?" Lee asked.

"Screw this place, screw these people."

SHENZHEN

The newly constructed stadium reeked of cheapness. It was a poor reproduction. Weekend do-it-yourselfers had recreated the San Diego park from grainy photos alone. Plastic seats bowed under the slightest weight, promotional posters peeled back from their placements, and a strong breeze scuffed the finishes. It was a surprise the tanks held water. That wasn't important. It was a world away from toiling behind the bars of San Diego Central Jail. He was a free man with a second chance. He'd accomplished what he needed. A tinge of guilt gnawed at him for having to uproot his wife and daughter. But there was no changing that now. Living in a foreign country would be fantastic for them. His baby would adjust to the new schools and way of life. She'd hardly remember California. It was perfect. There wasn't a chance in hell the industry would rehire him stateside. Not after what he'd done. While his sentence had finished, a Chinese holding firm had reached out to him. They planned to develop a series of parks in China, Hong Kong, Macau, and Taiwan. He was familiar with the company. Years ago, they'd contacted Marineworld, but management had flat out refused to cooperate or supply staff for training. They were dead set on being the trailblazers that marched forward with progress. Creating a sanctuary on one side of the world while developing aquatic prisons on the other didn't mesh well. Idiots.

His contact had assured him the infrastructure was in place in

Shenzhen—the San Diego park, updated for a new century. They were liars, but he got used to it. The park in Shenzhen was only one piece of the operation. A Russian group held newly caught orcas in Srednyaya Bay before they were transferred. Conditions in Srednyaya weren't ideal, but they got them to Shenzhen alive. He didn't work with the Russians directly. It kept the distance between his old title and current occupation. The less he knew about how they ended up in the tanks, the better. Instead, he acted as a consultant for the orca program at the park. Before Marineworld had ousted him, he'd copied every single manual and procedural book. As a show of good faith, he'd even sent over a technical outline of stadium operations before signing his contract. Sure, he'd omitted key portions from it, but they'd never figured it out. Withholding information provided another layer of job security. They emailed him a revised contract worth half a million yuan more than their initial offer. With a translator, he could open a park wherever they damn well pleased. This time it was Shenzhen.

Things were different in Shenzhen. Marineworld's board of directors didn't have their priorities in the right place. China was the wild west of the industry, and the firm gave him free rein. It was a shame he hadn't defected sooner. Being at the stadium was a welcome respite, no matter how sorry it was. The apartment the company had supplied him with was a shoebox. But he couldn't complain, it was better than a prison cell. An upgraded apartment would be easy enough to find when his family came. It would be another month before they made their flight to join him. She kept finding reasons to prolong her stay in San Diego. It was a sleepy seaside town compared to Shenzhen. Here, every corner of the city was under construction. The streets vibrated with activity no matter the time of day or night. Tom couldn't blame her for staying longer. She'd worked hard to keep the house in order while he'd had his vacation at Terminal Island. If it took her a month to come around, so be it. But the damn translator they'd given him—he mistranslated sentences on purpose. Not that Tom needed him for day-to-day living—there were enough English speakers for him to get by. When he used him to explain Schmidt's behavior techniques to the trainers, though, it was like doing brain surgery with a hammer.

"Show them. Show them how to do it." His supervisor skipped the translator and spoke to him in English. Tom wanted to knock his teeth out. When he wasn't yelling, frustrated Cantonese was his second option. The man spoke perfect English but only used it when he wanted to yell at him. "What do we pay you for?"

"It's not that easy, Jiang. Your guys won't listen. Look at these food buckets. They're not even half-full. Do they even bother to measure it out in the morning?"

"They'll get their food when they perform." He paused. "What's my guys? I thought we were a team? Show them. Show them how to do it." An orca circled the pool. It waited for a command. A trainer cautiously tapped the surface. The tiniest of ripples flowed from each blow. They were nearly undetectable. One trainer from Marineworld was what he needed. He'd watched them do it a thousand times. These people couldn't follow instructions. If he had convinced one trainer to come with him, this job would be light work. Whatever. He'd do it himself. Tom marched over to the trainer and bowled him to the ground.

"Look! It's not a fucking egg." Tom pounded on the water. It proved an adequate stand-in for Jiang's face. Or that smug translator. Water splashed onto his suit. "Like this. See?"

The orca followed the water droplets to his hand before he could hammer the surface again and sank her teeth into it. Tom screamed as they cleaved his bones. Thick drops of blood followed the orca back into the water. Jiang's shouts were no longer in English. He pulled the trainer backwards into the seating area.

The orca burst from the pool. There was no time to scream as Tom was pulled into the water. For the second time, the orca let go of her new toy. Tom struggled on his back. His tattered arm did little to keep him afloat, and a one-armed backstroke wasn't good enough to power him back to the ledge. Water gagged his mouth and stifled his shouts for help. She breached over him and pushed him below. He sucked in saltwater instead of air. Tom couldn't manage a single blow against the animal. Instead, he tore at its eye with his fingernails. Agitated, it dug its teeth into the flesh of his thigh. He wanted to kick at the creature with his free leg. It didn't move.

Jiang and the trainer stood at the pool. White patches. Two. No, four of them. They danced around like ghosts. Each grabbed one of Tom's legs and shackled him in place. Slowly, deliberately, they pulled in opposite directions. It was a calculated force. Neither tugged enough to dismember his limbs. His carcass went limp as the orcas split him vertically. Intestines and organs spilled into the pool. With care, an executioner plucked his liver from the mass. It offered a chunk to its partner, which was gladly shared.

"Fish whatever's left out. He never showed up for work today." There was no hesitation in Jiang's voice. Foreigners were notoriously unreliable. His wife would try to find him. They'd ignore calls and emails. Maybe she'd get the US consulate involved. There was nothing they would find. The firm would never cut her a check. They had bigger concerns. They needed to find another consultant to develop their parks. It wouldn't be Tom. His time in the marine mammal industry was finished.

Afterword

The first time I saw a killer whale was behind the glass of a tank. Anyone who has seen one in person can attest to how magical it is. Their size, power, and elegance in the water are unmatched. An almost mystical creature that holds you spellbound. During that first visit, I spent hours observing them and had to be dragged away at the end of the day. When I left, the entire outline for my book needed to be changed.

There was so much more to their story, both in the wild and captivity, than I'd ever dreamed of. My research led me to intriguing real-life heroes and villains, tragic tales of captures and reintroductions, and shockingly few triumphs. It doesn't take long to be enveloped into the world of orcas.

I debated long and hard over whether to include information about the current status of orca conservation and captivity. After all, this book was meant to be a "quick summer read." But it would be a disservice to these remarkable animals if I didn't. The debate regarding animals in captivity is one that has been argued by others far more articulate than me. Without zoos and aquariums, there would be far fewer wildlife biologists making positive impacts for species around the world. When managed properly, they can be an extremely powerful tool, but all animals have the right not to be exploited or abused by humans. The current state of orcas in captivity is entirely inadequate, and major advancements need to be made in order to compassionately care for these animals as they live the reminder of their lives.

While fictitious, the Coronado Research Institute is grounded in real science. The technology referenced in this book isn't something out of reach. The construction of a sea sanctuary would be the most humane and ethical means of "retiring" captive-born orcas. Wild-caught orcas should be released back to their native waters if the situation allows. Efforts to build such a sanctuary are currently underway in Nova Scotia. It aspires to be an "authentic sanctuary" that does not engage in performances, breeding, or access to the whales for commercial purposes. The development is being handled by a nonprofit that vows never to put profit above the well-being of the animals. I wish them nothing but the best and hope to visit their realized dream.

As of 2021, there are at least sixty orcas held in captivity around the world. While the US has experienced a cultural shift in its views of whales in captivity, countries like China and Russia still capture animals from the wild for display. Over 120 have died in captivity since parks and aquariums started their captures. Wild populations, such as the southern residents, have also been decimated by environmental impacts. Traditional salmon resources have dried up due to the damming of rivers; what little food they can find is contaminated by pollutants carelessly dumped in our waterways. There has been a marked decrease in birth rates and survival rates of calves. And it doesn't stop at physical impacts. Grief-stricken mothers have been observed holding their dead children afloat for days. Intergenerational bonds still haven't recovered from events like the Penn Cove capture of 1970. But there is a hint of optimism: four new southern resident calves have survived since 2019.

It seems we are at the precipice of change. But it will take much more to keep things moving in the right direction. If I've sparked your interest in orcas, then I've accomplished my mission. There is always something new to learn and discover. May your first encounter be on the open water and not behind the glass of a tank.

MARINEWORLD ORCA ANIMAL PROFILES

AKHLUT (Orcinus Orca) I.D. #MWS-Oo-7138

Sex: Male

Age: 32 yrs. (est.)

DOB: 1984 (est.)

Length: 32 ft.

Weight: 17,050 lbs.

Category: 5

Identifying Characteristics

- Tall (6 ft.) straight dorsal fin
- Wearing and abrasions on tips of flukes
- Large head and "jowl" area
- Small scar near blowhole
- No teeth drilled

Secondary Reinforcers

- Whistle (bridge)
- Ice cubes and ice blocks
- Body tactile
- "Indestructible" ball
- Group attention

- Ropes
- Fish catch
- Kelp
- Audible stimulation
- Trainer attention
- Watching other orcas
- SCUBA
- Barrel in water
- Retrieval of objects
- Fire hose spray

Finds Averse

- Repetition during training with incorrect responses
- Prolonged separation without visual and/or physical access to other orcas
- Seagulls in slide-out area
- Major environment change (addition/removal of orcas)

Aggressive Tendencies

- Akhlut has demonstrated a tendency to become very vocal before shows. This behavior is especially apparent if he has been separated from other orcas for a prolonged period. He emits long, low vocals.
- Akhlut has opened his mouth toward trainers in the water with him. This behavior occurs when training sequences are predictable and not challenging.
- Can become possessive of objects in the pool.

Behavioral Incidents
Date and Description
2/85 - Mouthed leg
4/87 - Came out at guest (land)
7/90 - Blocked trainer
11/90 - Swam over/dunked
4/92 - Block trainer
6/93 - Mouth-open lunge w/contact
5/04 - Came out at trainer (no contact)
9/06 - Blocked trainer
7/15 - Trainer error

Summary

Akhlut is a wild-rescued sexually mature male. Atypical of male orcas, Akhlut has asserted himself as the dominant killer whale since his arrival at Marineworld San Diego. Be advised that due to Akhlut's size and prior history, it is strongly recommended that he be handled only by experienced trainers.

When handled properly, Akhlut is adaptable and graceful during waterwork, with an extensive catalog of behaviors. Akhlut discriminates against inexperienced trainers and tries to control his environment if not adequately challenged. He may avoid eye contact, dive to the bottom of the pool, play with food, or refuse food when offered. Akhlut can encourage other orcas in the environment to exhibit these behaviors and has displaced orcas who continue to work with trainers. He was involved in an incident in July 2015 that resulted in a fatality. This was due to trainer error on a "rocket hop" behavior, and Akhlut did not exhibit aggressive behavior after the incident occurred.

Akhlut may be hesitant to separate from other orcas or trainers working with him. On occasion he has shown possessive behavior (blocking) of trainers and orcas in his environment. When frustrated, from separation or repetition, Akhlut has exhibited aggressive behaviors, such as vocalizations, tensing up, knocking gates, and occasionally lunging his control trainer.

Akhlut is an excellent observational learner and seems to delight in learning new behaviors. Overall, he is very tactile animal that likes relationship-building interactions (orca-orca and trainer-orca). He is extremely alert and aware of his environment and enjoys visual/auditory stimulation.

NAYAK (Orcinus Orca) I.D.
#MWS-Oo-7707

Sex: Female
Age: 28 yrs. (est.)
DOB: 1988 (est.)
Length: 18 ft. 4 in.
Weight: 5,720 lbs.
Category: 2

Identifying Characteristics

- Large pectoral fins compared to body size
- Crescent-moon scar on chin
- Pockmarks along right side of body
- Some erosion and yellowing of lower teeth
- Dark spots on roof of mouth

Secondary Reinforcers

- Bucket splash
- Fish toss
- Visual stimulation
- Cart follow with fish toss
- Ropes

- Kelp
- SCUBA feed through gate
- Slide-out play
- Bubbles
- Ice blocks

Finds Averse

- Major environmental changes
- Tactile given by "strangers"
- Getting stuck on slide-outs

Aggressive Tendencies

- None observed to date

Behavioral Incidents
Date and Description
2/96 - Mouthed foot
8/07 - Pushed trainer

Summary
Nayak was brought to Marineworld after a successful rescue in 1994. She was discovered beached on the Northern California coast near Eureka and was successfully rehabilitated by Marineworld veterinarians. Due to skin lesions and stress during her stranding, it was determined that she required ongoing care and observation.

Due to the possibility of reintroduction to her pod, Nayak has not been trained in show behaviors. When working with other orcas, it is important that Nayak be separated in order to prevent the learning of unwanted show behaviors. Since arriving at San Diego, Nayak has exhibited signs of dental issues. This should be monitored as the drilling of teeth may prevent reintroduction.

Nayak is reliable in all husbandry procedures, including X-rays, dental maintenance, measurements, ultrasounds, and blood/urine samples. From January through August 2007, blood samples showed elevated progesterone levels, indicating possible pregnancy. During those months, many behavior changes were noted in Nayak. She displayed some aggressive behaviors, including hosing, fluke splashing, and moving her head (mouth closed) towards trainers. These behaviors were isolated incidents that occurred during routine husbandry procedures. In September, her progesterone levels returned to normal along with her behavior. For more detail on this time frame, see the Behavior Logs.

Tactile reinforcement (fin rubs, body rubdowns) should be avoided with Nayak as to discourage interaction with humans as much as possible.

Overall, Nayak is a very good-natured, energetic animal who responds well to reinforcement and is extremely dependable.

KJETIL (Orcinus Orca) I.D. #MWS-Oo-0118

Sex: Male
 Age: 33 yrs. (est.)
 DOB: 1983 (est.)
 Length: 19 ft. 4 in.
 Weight: 8,140 lbs.
 Category: 3

Identifying Characteristics

- Squared pectoral flippers
- Dorsal fin collapsed to right
- Dental work completed on lower right (LR) – 1 and 2
- Noticeable saddle patch
- Large eye patches
- Notch of black in left eye patch

Secondary Reinforcers

- Whistle (bridge)
- Individual ice cubes
- Brush tactile/play
- Hoop and disk

- Gelatin
- Tire roller
- Balls
- Barrels
- Variable feed
- Play at glass
- Retrieval of objects

Finds Averse

- Being displaced by more dominant orcas
- Being separated from Kjell, especially when she is cycling

Aggressive Tendencies

- When separated from Kjell, may refuse to let trainer exit the pool. While not exhibiting aggression towards the trainer (mouth open), still refused callback tones and slaps in preventing exit from pool. Show behaviors should always be performed with Kjell in order to prevent incident.

Behavioral Incidents
Date and Description
4/92 - Blocked trainer
5/92 - Blocked trainer
7/95 - Mouthed hand
8/99 - Bumped hip
8/07 - Blocked trainer

Summary
Kjetil is a wild-caught sexually mature male who was brought to

Marineworld in conjunction with Kjell. Kjetil fathered Ivar (born 7/19/95). To date he has developed a large catalog of husbandry and show behaviors. He is a quick and motivated observational learner. During times of low activity, he will often knock his melon against the gates between pools.

Kjetil has a very strong bond with Kjell and performs best when the two are paired together. He has assumed a subdominant role among the orcas at Marineworld San Diego. Kjetil will occasionally leave control before the end of sessions to return to Kjell, so it is important to keep training sessions unpredictable.

Kjetil is an extremely dependable show animal, particularly when it comes to waterwork. He can consistently perform the lead role in shows and participate in single-, double-, and triple-whale waterwork. When he first arrived at Marineworld, Kjetil had issues with letting his control trainer leave the pool. This only occurred when Kjell was not present in the pool. As such, it is important that the two are paired together during shows.

After the birth of Ivar, Kjetil mouthed at a trainer's hand while he was touching the calf's tail fluke. Kjetil has continued to exhibit protective behavior over Ivar. Overall, Kjetil is calm and consistent with his behaviors. Although he can be difficult to control if Kjell is not present, he can be depended on to perform when other orcas refuse. However, we will continue to be diligent in all water interactions with Kjetil, as he is a protective breeding male.

KJELL (Orcinus Orca) I.D.
#MWS-Oo-4215

Sex: Female
Age: 33 yrs. (est.)
DOB: 1983 (est.)
Length: 17 ft. 3 in.
Weight: 4,650 lbs.
Category: 3

Identifying Characteristics

- Downward-curving tips to pectoral flippers
- Noticeable saddle patch with rake mark scarring
- Dental work completed on upper right (UR) – 9 and 10
- UR11 missing part of tooth
- Dorsal fin bend to the right (partial collapse)

Secondary Reinforcers

- Whistle (bridge)
- Individual ice cubes
- Brush tactile/play
- Hoop and disk
- Gelatin

- Tire roller
- Balls
- Ice block
- Barrels
- Ropes
- Variable feed
- Fire hose spray
- Play at glass
- Retrieval of objects

Finds Averse

- Being displaced by more dominant orcas
- Being separated from Kjetil, especially when cycling
- Husbandry practices

Aggressive Tendencies

- When separated from Kjetil, may refuse to let trainer exit the pool. While not exhibiting aggression towards the trainer (mouth open), still refused callback tones and slaps in preventing exit from pool. Show behaviors should always be performed with Kjetil in order to prevent incident.

Behavioral Incidents
Date and Description
5/92 - Blocked trainer
7/95 - Pushed trainer
12/02 - Blocked trainer

Summary

Kjell is a wild-caught sexually mature female who was brought to Marineworld in conjunction with Kjetil. Kjell gave birth to Ivar on 7/19/95. Along with her partner, Kjetil, she has developed a large catalog of husbandry and show behaviors. She has adapted well to performing major roles in shows.

Kjell has a very strong bond with Kjetil and performs best when the two are paired together. Without visual contact with Kjetil during shows, she may become disinterested. She has learned the majority of her behaviors quickly through independent learning.

Kjell is a dependable show animal both with waterwork and drywork. She can perform the lead role in shows and participate in single-, double-, and triple-whale waterwork. Along with Kjetil, she previously had issues with letting her control trainer leave the pool. This only occurred when Kjetil was not present in the pool. As such, it is important that the two are paired together during shows.

Separations can be a challenge for Kjell, particularly after aversive events (displacement, bloodwork, etc.). Kjell must be worked with confidence and reinforced regularly in order to gain her trust with separations.

She has displayed strong parenting skills with Ivar. She consistently nursed him as a calf immediately after birth. Kjell took time swimming with the calf, keeping him away from potentially harmful pool structures like gates and the glass until Ivar established better motor skills.

Overall, Kjell is a good-natured and energetic orca. Like Kjetil, she can be counted on to perform when other animals won't. We will continue to monitor her protective behaviors in regard to Ivar.

IVAR (Orcinus Orca) I.D. #MWS-Oo-3303

Sex: Male
  Age: 21 yrs.
  DOB: 7/19/95
  Length: 20 ft. 6 in.
  Weight: 8,220 lbs.
  Category: 3

Identifying Characteristics

- Dorsal fin leans to the left
- Large eye patches
- White mark behind blowhole
- Black dots on tip of tongue

Secondary Reinforcers

- Whistle (bridge)
- Ice
- Brush tactile/play
- Hoop and disk
- Gelatin
- Tire roller
- Balls
- Single ice cube

- Tactile play
- Remote control car follow
- Fire hose
- Trainer at glass
- Ball with fish
- Cart follows

Finds Averse

- None observed to date

Aggressive Tendencies

- None observed to date

Behavioral Incidents
Date and Description
3/00 - Swam over/dunked trainer

Summary
Ivar was born on July 19, 1995, to Kjell and sired by Kjetil. He is the first calf carried to term by Kjell. He learned many behaviors quickly through observational and independent learning.

Ivar has progressed and massively improved his waterwork. He can perform spy hops, rocket hops, fast swim rides, and stand-ons. That said, he is an environmentally sensitive orca. His control can be poor if there are changes in his environment, such as being separated from Kjetil and Kjell. He has also been slower to acclimate to new stimuli, such as CRI equipment tested in the pools. When Ivar has access to other females, particularly Ollju, he will often refuse control.

Overall, Ivar is a high-energy and playful orca. He is talented and can be a reliable show animal if his social environment is stable, but strong control is required to keep him behaviorally on target. As Ivar reaches maturity it is important to monitor all situations with him.

OLLJU (Orcinus Orca) I.D. #MWS-Oo-0943

Sex: Female
Age: 37 yrs.
DOB: 1979 (est.)
Length: 26 ft. 2 in.
Weight: 12,330 lbs.
Category: 4

Identifying Characteristics

- Notches missing on dorsal fin
- Soft yellow coloring (belly, eye patches, saddle)
- Dorsal "cape" with narrow border
- LL1 missing portion of tooth
- Scar across left eye patch

Secondary Reinforcers

- Fire hose
- Ice
- Bucket splash
- Cart follow
- Ice block

- RC boat
- Single ice cube
- Watching divers through gates
- Visual stimulation
- Ice pour
- Ice and water pour
- SCUBA through gate

Finds Averse

- Major environmental change

Aggressive Tendencies

- Ollju may attempt swim-overs if there has been recent stress on the social structure. Indicators of stress include gate ramming and vocalizations. Incidents are more likely to occur if she has been displaced recently by another orca in a challenge for dominance.
- When foreign objects (floating) are introduced to the environment, Ollju may create waves. It is important to control situations where new stimuli are introduced.

Behavioral Incidents
Date and Description
5/90 - Swam over/dunked trainer
9/93 - Mouthed waist
6/00 - Swam over/dunked trainer
2/04 - Blocked trainer

Summary
Ollju is a wild-caught sexually mature female who was brought to

Marineworld in 1979. As the oldest female orca at Marineworld, she has established herself as the dominant female in the social structure. She demonstrates submissive behavior towards Akhlut but has been aggressive towards smaller females (Nayak, Kjell, and Kassuq) and Ivar during his adolescence.

Ollju is highly adaptable when it comes to waterwork and has a large catalog of show behaviors learned. She does not like to work with more than a single trainer at a time and may ignore instructions during times when additional trainers are present in the water. To prevent this, Ollju should be separated when portions of a show require more than one trainer in the water.

Ollju has a tendency to "tip" new toys or objects placed into her environment. She will swim fast at the toy/object, then dive with a flick of her tail fluke. Because of her size, this can produce a large wave/wake in the pool. This behavior was most noticeable during the kayak portion of the Open Ocean show. Instead of the desired breach, Ollju broke from control and tipped the kayak when a trainer was in it. She did not exhibit aggression and immediately came back to control. With confident and consistent training, Ollju has not recently exhibited this behavior; however, trainers should be vigilant for any stressors that could indicate a return to this behavior.

KASSUQ (Orcinus Orca) I.D. #MWS-Oo-2116

Sex: Female
   Age: 35 yrs.
   DOB: 1981 (est.)
   Length: 18 ft. 9 in.
   Weight: 6,800 lbs.
   Category: 3

Identifying Characteristics

- Short pointed dorsal fin (bend to right)
- Closed saddle patch that extends past dorsal fin
- Teardrop eyepatch slanted downward towards the rear
- Black coloring extending into lower jaw beneath eyes
- Extensive wear and dental work completed on lower teeth

Secondary Reinforcers

- Barrel in water
- Ice cubes
- Gelatin
- Ice pour
- Scrub brush

- Hoop
- Retrieval of objects

Finds Averse

- Receiving large portions of base diet at a single time. They should be broken up into smaller portions throughout the day.
- Other orcas playing with preferred secondary reinforcers (hoop, barrel, boomer ball) in the same pool.

Aggressive Tendencies

- Due to dental work, may become aggressive after being exposed to new secondary reinforcers. It is important to trial new secondary reinforcers while Kassuq is separated from other orcas.
- Can become possessive of foreign objects.

Behavioral Incidents
Date and Description
7/83 - Swam over/dunked trainer
2/88 - Blocked trainer from retrieving target pole
2/92 - Blocked trainer
4/95 - Bumped hand

Summary
Kassuq is a wild-caught mature female who was brought to Marineworld in 1979. Kassuq was one of the first killer whales in a controlled environment to become pregnant. Kassuq unsuccessfully carried calves (sired by Shurik) to full term on three separate occasions.

Kassuq has a modest repertoire of show behaviors and can be difficult to work with. She will stubbornly ignore instructions and avoids interactions that involve textural stimulus of her mouth. She enjoys performing breaches and rocket hop interactions. However, trainers must be cautious to avoid placing downward pressure on her lower jaw. Kassuq will break control from a trainer and disengage if this happens. Because of this, we have decided to reduce the number of trainers allowed to perform rocket hops and eliminate the use of stand-ons.

Despite the challenges she has faced, she remains a calm and good-natured orca. While none have been recorded to date, due to the potential for aggressive behaviors, Kassuq should only be handled by senior trainers.

Made in the USA
Monee, IL
07 July 2021

73147709R00152